First published 2014 by
Welham Books

Author's website
www.welhambooks.com

ISBN 978-1-50090-251-3

Also available as a Kindle ebook
ISBN 978-1-84396-319-6

A CIP catalogue record for this
book is available from the British Library.

Pre-press production
www.ebookversions.com

THOMAS

A FIRST WORLD WAR STORY
OF COMPASSION AND COURAGE THAT
CROSSES THE CLASS DIVIDE

Mike Welham

WELHAM BOOKS

1

A death and a chance encounter would transform the life of Thomas Pierce, who had been born into a life of poverty. But right now, the sun was lowering on the horizon, signalling the end of another day. He was striding out to make the journey home, having endured long hours of hard labour. In truth it was not the hard work that bothered him, but more that it was the never-ending toil of drudgery, day after day, with no visible prospect of improving his lot. Many just accepted the situation, but Thomas was not like that. He expected a fair day's pay for a good day's work, however many landowners just exploited people through fear. Following the death of his mother, Thomas had been raised, from an early age, by his father who had no idea of what to do; that had been a hardship of a different type. His father worked on the land and was not well paid, but between the two of them, they were able to survive; that is, until his father took to drink. The demands on their income moved from providing food to supporting the local ale-house. The more pressing problem was that his father was behind in the rent: Sir Harry Calthrope, both employer and owner of the cottage where they lived, was fast running out of patience, of which he had very little in the first place.

Thomas had in some ways been very lucky. At school, his teacher Miss Acton had feelings for Thomas's father and had tried to enter his life through Thomas. But by the time he left school, she had realised that it was a lost cause and gave up; at least Thomas had gained a better education than most. Now a strapping good-looking, fair-haired and blue-eyed young man, Thomas pondered, as he walked, the prospects of having any sort of a meal that evening. Fortunately one of the farm-worker's wives had provided him with a meal at midday and he had made the most of it. The woman had smiled as she watched him take his fill; this gave him some comfort for the remainder of the day.

As he approached the tied cottage, one of six cottages set in a row, he noticed people gathered at the front door. His walking pace picked up until he reached the path leading to the front door. A neighbour walked down it to meet him.

'What's going on, Mr Sayer?' asked Thomas.

'Thomas, you have to be strong. There has been an accident; we brought your father home. He got caught up in some farm machinery. He's in a very bad way. We don't think he will last the night. As far as we can tell, there's no money in the house for the doctor so he has not been called,' said Sayer.

Thomas felt no great love for his father nor, in particular, for his drinking habit that had squandered what little money they had. Now, when they really needed it, there was none.

'Thank you for bringing him home, Mr Sayer.'

Sayer moved to one side, allowing Thomas to enter. At the door to his father's bedroom, he looked in and saw locals doing what they could to tend the broken mess that had once been the man who was his father. A local woman, who usually attended births, was bandaging wounds that immediately soaked the cloth being used, staining them red. Thomas knew that the battle for life was lost. It was confirmed when the woman looked up at him and shook her head. His father had died.

'He's gone, Thomas,' said the woman.

Thomas nodded. 'Thank you for what you did.' He then looked at the others in the tiny room. 'Thank you all.'

Everybody left the room and went downstairs.

'We will tell the vicar,' said Sayer.

'I've no money for a funeral,' said Thomas.

'He will be buried, but it will be a pauper's burial,' said Sayer.

People began to leave. There was little they could do. Sayer's wife told Thomas to come to their cottage for a meal; things could be sorted out in the morning.

He was grateful and accepted the offer. It was difficult for him as he could not find any kind words for the man, his father, lying dead two cottages away. The food was a welcome respite and he tucked into his second meal of the day.

Sayer attempted to explain what had happened:

'The machine needed repairs but the master would not get it done.' "A waste of money,"' he had stated. 'It still works.' They had all known that it was just a matter of time - and who would be on the receiving end.

'Thank you, Mr Sayer, but talking about it does not help. The machine just killed him before the drink did.'

They all focused on eating.

When they had finished, Thomas thanked them and walked back to his cottage. A million thoughts flashed through his head. How would he pay the rent on his meagre labourer's earnings? Would Calthrope allow him to stay on? Should he move away? Where would he go? All were questions that would in time be answered. He had to deal with the here and now.

In the cottage he lit the downstairs lamps. Staring at the

stairs, he reflected on the fact that his father was upstairs, not drunk this time but dead. He sat in what was the most comfortable chair and closed his eyes. When he opened them, it was approaching daylight. He stood and moved his cramped body, having slept in the chair. His first thought was to rush off to work, but he had been told that the vicar would arrange for the body to be collected. Sayer would explain his absence from work.

He made a cup of tea and ate the last piece of bread, which was hard work as it had become stale. The only solution was to dunk it in the tea and allow it to soak. He heard the horse and wagon arrive, then two men came to the front door. He recognised both of them from the village.

'Morning, Thomas,' said one. 'We have come for your father.'

'He's upstairs,' he said, leading the way.

The two men pulled the blankets round the body and used them to lift it. Manoeuvring to the door and onto the landing, one man went down first, holding the legs. The more powerful of the two carried the torso. They began the descent. Thomas followed. Outside, they carried the body to the wagon and placed it on the back.

'You had better come with us,' said one.

Thomas collected his jacket and cap and climbed up into the wagon. With the two men up front, they began the journey to the village. Thomas was lost in the world of the countryside as they passed it by; in the village he vaguely noticed people looking. When the wagon reached the graveyard adjoining the church, the vicar was waiting.

'Good morning, Thomas,' said the Vicar. 'We are sorry for your loss. The passing of a family member is always tragic.'

'Thank you, sir,' replied Thomas.

He nodded. 'We have found him a small place in the

graveyard.'

The two men lifted the body from the wagon and carried it to a quiet corner set aside for those who were unable to pay. Thomas noted that somebody had already dug the grave. When they reached it, the body was laid down. One of the men jumped down into the grave. The two men then manhandled the body into the bottom where it was straightened out as best as possible; then, with help, the man in the grave scrambled out. The vicar said a few words before indicating to the grave-digger to fill the hole. A lifetime was ended in a matter of minutes. The vicar wished Thomas well for the future and departed. The two men returned to the wagon to continue their working day. Thomas stood for some time, watching the grave-digger at work; then he left the place where two small mounds of earth were all that signified the location of his parents' final resting-place.

Passing through the village, a number of people expressed their sympathy. None offered anything constructive. The long walk home was not unpleasant and he was thankful that it was not raining. Reaching the row of cottages, he headed for the one he called home. Once inside, he made a drink then set about removing the remainder of his father's bedding. He took it outside into the back garden. Others grew vegetables, but only wild grass grew in theirs. He put it in a pile clear of the building. He made several journeys, collecting clothes that were fit for no other purpose than burning. The fire was doing his clean-up and he stood poking it with a stick, moving items to the strongest flames. The mattress, which had been soaked with blood, almost smothered the flames; but he kept the fire going until the flames took control. He had finished clearing the items from within the cottage and was checking the small front garden for any unwanted items that would burn.

There was no mistaking the noise of a horse at the gallop. He stopped what he was doing and looked up. He needed no introduction to the rider, Sir Henry Calthrope. The horse was brought to an abrupt stop close by the garden gate. Foam ringed its mouth and its eyes bulged, the whites standing out. It had been ridden hard, and it breathed heavily.

'Pierce, why were you not at work today?' shouted Calthrope.

'With due respect, sir, I had to bury my father. He died last night. I was told that Mr Sayer was going to speak to the estate manager.'

'He did, but that does not answer my question as to why you were not at work. Burying your father was not an excuse. You work for me and you do your burying in your own time, not in mine.'

'Sir, the burying had to be done when the vicar was available.'

'You don't work for the vicar; you work for me and you do as I say.'

'Yes, sir; sorry, sir.'

'Your father was a drunk and idle worker. I don't know why I put up with him for so long. I have a good man to replace him.'

'Right, sir.'

'You will be out of the cottage in two days. Anything that is left will become my property.'

'Sir, I was hoping to be able to stay in the cottage.'

'I obviously didn't make myself clear. You will be out of the cottage and off my land within two days. You are no longer in my employment. The offspring of an idle drunk is of no use to me.'

'I don't drink, sir, and I work hard.'

'Off in two days: or you will suffer the consequences.'

Calthrope, a smirk on his face, pulled the reins to turn the horse, and with a good kick caused the horse to jump forward and gallop away as fast as it had arrived.

Thomas stood looking at the departing Calthrope. His worst fears were now realised. No home and no job. Prospective employers wanted references and it was clear that none were going to be forthcoming here. He was initially unaware of the gathering neighbours, who had seen and heard everything. The Sayers would feed him, but could offer little else. Everybody was afraid of Calthrope and knew that helping Thomas could result in their being thrown out of their homes themselves.

The next two days were spent in limbo. Word had reached the village and some of his furniture was sold; other less attractive items were given away. He then opened the door and told people to take what they wanted. Those with little money brought gifts of food: he would not starve, for a few days at least. One visitor arrived who Thomas had never seen before; he stated that he was eternally grateful for the help he had received from Thomas's father when he had been in a desperate situation. He considered that, having heard the news, he needed to repay the debt. Too late to repay Thomas's father, he could help his son. He produced, from within a blanket, a neat double-barrel shotgun, much favoured by poachers. There were cartridges with it. Thomas was a skilled poacher; it was those skills that had kept him and his father alive whilst the ale-house benefited from the family income. Thomas was overjoyed and handled the weapon with its unique carving on the woodwork as if it were a beautiful woman; not that he had experience in that quarter, but he had heard talk. The man gave him a note that explained that the gun was Thomas's legitimate property. He left, wishing Thomas well for the future.

Thomas was up early, it still being dark outside. He ate and drank in the midst of the virtually empty cottage. He had one bag containing his worldly possessions. He had never owned much anyway; so there was no great loss. There was also his new acquisition, his gun. But his most prized possession was a faded photograph of his mother: she had died many years ago, but he still had memories of her. Perhaps if she had survived, things might have been different. Her legacy had been to ensure that he attained some learning; as a result, he could both read and write. He had said his farewells to the neighbours the previous night and so all he had to do was to walk out of the door and away.

It was dawn as he departed what had been a home of sorts and headed towards the village, away from Calthrope's estate. In the village, people were up and emerging to go about their business; they paid little mind to him as he walked straight through. Once clear of the village, he stayed on the road which did not see a lot of traffic. Perhaps the most prolific were the horse-drawn farm wagons and he was able to hitch a ride with one going in his direction. That direction was not planned, but he had an uncanny gift of knowing where he was at any given time. A series of lifts had taken him round the lanes and he was again close to Calthrope's sprawling estate. When he was dropped off, he could see the large forest that marked the boundary of Calthrope's land and the next land-owner's estate. He had no knowledge of Lord Charles Overbury, but he had heard that he was a good and fair man. In those days that was hard to believe. So he had a choice: turn right and enter the enemy's lair or turn left and explore new pastures. He opted for the new and turned left.

2

Thomas had entered the extreme boundary of Overbury's estate, walking along a road devoid of any habitation and thereby avoiding any chance encounter. It was a new area for him and he was aware that, apart from estate workers, there would be poachers who would consider the place as their domain. Contact with either could bring conflict and that was the last thing he wanted at present.

The forest he entered was dense and had not been coppiced for years. He moved with care around the impressive variety of trees and eventually reached a track that had not been regularly used for a long time. His keen eye spotted the imprints of horses' hooves: that was a warning to be careful. He crossed the track and moved further into the forest. When the land dropped down he discovered the river at the bottom. He was now on guard and moved cautiously to examine a stretch along the riverbank. He was searching for traces of poaching or gamekeeper activity and was pleased to discover neither. Moving back into the denser forest, he followed the line of the river and was searching for a place to rest.

He discovered a long-disused small stone building, covered with creepers and surrounded by trees, and approached it with care. He pushed open the well-worn door with some effort and entered. It comprised a single room with only one window opening. It was devoid of anything apart from what looked like an old steel oven. The earthen floor was not very even, but the slated roof looked watertight. He opened the door of the oven, to discover that it was empty but was a sealed unit. It was very evident that the building had not been used for a long time and so it provided him with an ideal base until he decided on a plan of action. He had pondered what to do with his bag as it contained food, which of course would be attractive to mice and rats as well as larger scavengers. The oven provided the answer and he managed to fit the bag into it and to shut the door. His precious gun stayed with him, not that he planned to use it. The noise would give his presence away.

Later, he removed the bag from the oven and, sitting outside, he checked through the contents. He had a pot for boiling water and had to decide whether to light a small fire. Smoke would hang about in the trees and anybody close by with a keen nose would smell it. He concluded that with the need to boil water and cook some meat, it was a chance he would have to take. Putting everything back in the oven apart from the water pot, he departed, carrying the gun, to the river. Locating an ideal spot, he filled the pot, then taking care he left the river. A good field-craftsman would soon see that somebody had been in the area; this remained in his mind. Back at the building, he collected dry wood and decided that the fire would be best controlled inside. With a skill learnt over many years, he soon had a fire burning hot without much smoke and the pot of water on the boil. He prepared a piece of rabbit for cooking that had been exchanged for an item of furniture, and as well as baked a potato in the hot embers. Although he was busy, he kept an ear open for any sound that was not normal in the forest.

His life settled into a routine. He would forage for

wood, collect water, set traps, catch fish, wash in the river and make the building a little more comfortable. One morning he was in the forest gathering wood when he heard the sound of a horse at the gallop. Being close to the track, he moved so that he could observe the rider but remain unseen. The sound of hooves striking the ground got louder, then at full gallop he saw a large brown horse pass along the track. It was riderless. For a moment Thomas contemplated the situation. Had the horse thrown the rider, or had the rider dismounted and the horse taken flight for some reason? Whatever the circumstance, there was somebody else now in the forest.

Thomas left the bundle of wood as he began to walk along the track, keeping to the edge. There was no sound or anything out of the ordinary so he kept walking with occasional stops to listen. He had travelled some distance when he saw what looked like a body lying at the side of the track. He moved closer, looking about for any other person; as he approached he could see that it was a woman and he ran the last few steps. The woman lay unconscious and Thomas assumed that she had been thrown from the horse. He did not recognise her but realised that she was a lady, possibly the daughter of a local land owner. He was in the forest of Lord Overbury; so it was probably his daughter.

Thomas was on his knees and speaking to her but there was no reply. He checked as best he could that there was no blood. Her arms and legs seemed, from what he could see, to be undamaged. The dilemma he faced was whether to lift and carry her along the track, which he assumed would lead to the big house. Or he could leave her and go for help; but he decided that if she came to and was alone, she might panic. If he carried her, they would be making progress to safety, albeit slowly. He chose the latter option, rightly or wrongly. With as much care as possible, he lifted her to rest in his arms across his chest. He began to walk. He had no idea how far he would have to go. He hoped that when the horse returned to its stable without its rider, the alarm would be raised and help would be forthcoming.

At Winslade Hall a stable boy met the horse as it arrived without Lady Clarissa. Having secured the horse, he raised the alarm. Devline, the estate manager, notified Lord Overbury and they all met at the stables. A search was hastily planned and the first searchers saddled up to depart along known routes taken by Lady Clarissa. Two of the searchers reached the track and began to follow it. When they met Thomas carrying Clarissa, they approached with caution.

'I found her along the track. Her horse had thrown her. She needs help,' said Thomas.

One man told the other to go and get help. He needed no bidding.

The other man dismounted and came over to look at her.

'Should we continue?' said Thomas, who was just about done in.

'Can you continue?' asked the man.

'I will try.'

Thomas began to walk. The man followed behind, leading his horse.

They heard hunting horns which were being used for communication. But it was still some time before help arrived. Men dismounted and took Clarissa from Thomas. They gently laid her down and covered her with coats. Shortly after, a horse-drawn wagon arrived. There was protracted activity in turning it round in the narrow track. Once it was ready, they lifted the lady onto the wagon and began the journey back to Winslade Hall.

During this time, Thomas sat on the floor, recovering from the ordeal of the rescue; he had had no help from the other man. As the wagon moved off, the man who had been with Thomas told him to follow, as he would be questioned at the Hall. He stood and trailed behind the wagon, followed by the man.

It was late afternoon by the time the injured lady arrived home. She was carried into the Hall whilst Thomas was taken to a stable and locked in. The doctor had already been summoned and by the time he arrived, Clarissa had regained consciousness. He did an examination and found nothing serious, just some bruising caused by the fall. She had been very lucky. He reported his findings to Lord Overbury, with the comment that whoever had found her had taken great care to carry her the correct way: this had saved her from possible physical damage. Whilst members of the family went up to Clarissa's room to visit her, Lord Overbury went to the stables.

'Ah Manson, where did you find her?'

'On the track, your Lordship,' said Manson, the man who had met Thomas.

'Well, it seems that you did a good job carrying her,' said Overbury.

'Well done.'

'Thank you, sir,' said Manson.

Overbury left the stables and went to see his daughter.

He entered the room and saw that she was awake. 'How are you feeling?'

'I am well; I just had a bump.'

'Good; Manson did well to find and carry you the way he did,' said a smiling Overbury.

'Papa, it was not Manson who carried me. I have never seen the young man who carried me before.'

Overbury looked at his daughter. 'There was no other

person. It was Manson.'

'Papa, it was not Manson. I came to whilst being carried and it was not Manson.'

'All right; you rest and we will discuss it later.'

Overbury was confused. He went back downstairs and walked through to the stable yard. He saw one of the grooms.

'You were on the search with Manson when you found her ladyship?'

'Yes, sir, I was.'

'So Manson carried her ladyship whilst you came for help?'

'No, sir, a young stranger was carrying her ladyship when we found them; he had walked some distance.'

'Where is the young man now?'

'Mr Manson locked him in one of the old stables.'

'Show me.'

The groom led the way to the stable. The door was slightly open. They could hear a voice. Overbury entered followed by the groom. They saw Manson standing over a man who he had clearly beaten with a stick.

'What is going on? Who is this?' demanded Overbury.

'A vagabond I found near her ladyship. I was questioning him,' replied a smug Manson.

Overbury turned to the groom, 'Go and get help.'

The groom was gone in a flash and returned equally quickly with help; Devline joined them moments later. They all crammed in the stable looking at Manson and the young man still on the floor.

'I arrived to discover Manson beating this man who he claims was a vagabond. Manson also told me that he carried her ladyship along the track. In fact her ladyship states that it was the young man and not Manson, which is also confirmed by a groom.'

'Devline, please take Manson to your office. I shall join you as soon as I have spoken to the young man.'

Devline ordered Manson to the office and was escorted by some of the staff. His head hung low, Manson walked away.

'Can you stand?' asked Overbury.

'Yes, sir,' said Thomas, slowly standing.

'Did you find my daughter and carry her to safety?'

'I found a lady who had been thrown by a horse and I helped her. I met the man you call Manson when I was carrying your daughter along the track,' he said.

'Come with me.'

Overbury left the stable and walked through the stable yard to the Hall; just inside was an office. It was the estate office and in it were Devline and Manson. Neither were communicating. Overbury directed Thomas to a corner, then joined Devline.

'Manson, I trusted you. I do not know why you lied. You do not claim to know the stranger. He carried my daughter towards safety and you did not help. When you got here you locked him up and you did not tell either Devline or myself. You then took it upon yourself to beat him. What do you have to say for yourself?'

'I was acting in the best interest of the estate. He is a vagabond and probably a poacher; I wanted to find out who and what he is.'

'That is not how we do things here. This is the second time I have spoken to you about this type of behaviour. Unless Devline has anything to say in your favour you are dismissed from service at Winslade Hall. Devline, do you have anything to say?'

'I have nothing to say on behalf of Manson, sir.'

'Manson, you will collect your personal belongings and leave the estate immediately. Devline, can you oversee

Manson's departure?'

'Yes, sir.'

They walked to the door.

'One further thing: if I find you engaging with anybody from the estate, or with the stranger who you assaulted, then I shall take the matter up with the police and the courts. Do I make myself clear?'

'Yes, sir,' said Manson.

Overbury had sat down behind the desk. He looked at Thomas. 'Come here.'

Thomas moved over by the chair in front of the desk.

'Sit down,' said Overbury, indicating the chair.

'I would prefer to stand if you don't mind, sir,' said Thomas,

'As you please. What is your name and where do you live?'

'My name is Thomas Pierce. I lived with my father in a cottage on Sir Calthrope's estate. My father was killed in a farming accident a few days ago and I was ordered out of the cottage. I had no money so I had to leave. He also terminated my employment and told me never to return to the estate. I found myself in a forest and have had to survive until I could decide what to do. I was gathering wood for a fire when I heard the galloping horse with no rider. I found the lady and carried her until I met your men. They brought her and me back here to the Hall.'

'Did you poach on my land?'

'If you own the forest where the track is, then yes, sir, I have caught fish and rabbit to eat.'

'What are your plans?'

'I will move on and seek work. I do not have a trade, but I can work in forests and I can read and write; not perfect, but I can get by, sir.'

'Who taught you to read and write?'

'I had to go to school. My ma made me. I learnt what I could until my father made me go to work. He needed the money for the ale-house.'

The door opened and Devline entered.

'Manson is being escorted from the estate as we speak, sir.'

'Thank you, Devline. This is Thomas, who has been very honest with me. Can you take him to cook and arrange for him to be fed and found a bed for the night? I will review the situation in the morning. Good evening, gentlemen.' Overbury left the office.

The following morning, Thomas was brought before Lord Overbury.

'Thomas,' said Overbury, who had mistakenly adopted his first name and not his family name. 'I am impressed by the fact that you went to the aid of my daughter and actually came back to Winslade Hall when I am sure you could have escaped into the forest. I am sorry that a member of staff mistreated you, but that matter has been resolved. What I propose is to give you a chance, on the understanding that you work for the estate. You will help the gamekeepers. Part of that proposal is that you live in the gamekeeper's cottage under the eye of Mr Moore and his wife. I have spoken to both of them and they are very keen on the idea. You will be paid as an under-keeper, and will do as Moore tells you. Do you have anything to say?'

'No, sir; I mean yes, sir, I would like the job. Thank you, sir.'

'Devline, do you have anything to add?'

'No, sir, I think you have covered everything.'

'Good. You can take your belongings over to the gamekeeper's cottage and make a start.'

'Thank you, sir, but my belongings are in the forest; I left them when I carried your daughter.'

'Right, go and collect them, then report to Devline who will direct you to the gamekeeper's cottage.'

'Thank you, sir.'

Thomas ran as if he were on fire and the wind could put it out. He followed the driveway to the point where he crossed a vast lawned area and located the track. Entering the forest, he slowed down slightly and savoured what was to be part of his working environment. Yesterday seemed like a nightmare from which he had now just woken up. He reached a point where he diverted off the track and into the forest. There was the bundle of wood he had gathered, which he now ignored. He moved with great care past the trees until he reached the building. The door was as he had left it. Even so, he cautiously opened it, allowing the daylight to flood in. It was empty. He went in and opened the oven. His bag was inside and he took it out. The gun was still on the beam above his head. When he had retrieved it, he broke it by natural instinct and checked that it was not loaded.

Outside, he closed the door and headed towards the track. His bag was slung over his right shoulder and he carried the gun in his left hand. On the track he was able to make quicker progress. It was now getting quite warm, although the sun had not yet penetrated the trees that were on either side. It was quiet: even the birds were not singing. That was until he heard a sound. It was off to his left and in the forest. He did not know what it was, but it was certainly out of place. He took two cartridges from his pocket and loaded them, closing the gun. There was another noise, as if somebody had stood on a branch, causing it to break. Then out of the forest came a person.

He recognised him immediately as being Manson. He looked like a wild man. Thomas moved the gun to hold it with both hands and eyed him up. He was not going to get caught out again. Manson did not move, but just stared at Thomas who had now walked past him. Thomas continued at a fast pace, looking back. Manson still stood looking at him. When Thomas had moved a fair way along the track, he looked back but could not see anybody. He knew he could move faster on the track than anybody could move through the forest. When he reached the end of the forest, he broke the gun and removed the cartridges. The gun was safe.

He walked up the driveway and was almost at the Hall when a female voice called out, 'I say, is that you?'

Thomas continued walking. No female with a well-spoken voice was ever going to call out to him.

'I say, I am speaking to you; yes, you.'

Out of sheer interest, Thomas looked around to see who was calling out. Standing by a large oak tree was the woman he had saved, Lady Clarissa. She was about the same age as him and had stunning features, which had not gone unnoticed the day before. She stood with the refined posture that went with her class. In fact she was, in his eyes, perfection itself. She was looking at him and it was obvious now that it was to him that she was speaking. He dragged the cap from his head and bowed in an awkward manner.

'My lady, I'm Thomas Pierce, gamekeeper.'

'Yes, I know who you are. Thank you for saving me yesterday. Had you not been there, I would have been in a frightful mess.'

'It was my duty, my lady.' Thomas was unsure what more to do or say.

'Well, thank you anyway,' she said, smiling at him. She then began to walk towards the Hall.

Thomas ran round the driveway to the estate office.

Devline was waiting for him. As Thomas entered the office, he looked at the gun.

'Whose is that?' he asked, nodding at the gun.

'Mine, sir. It was gifted to me after my father died. I have a note to that effect, sir.'

He found the note in his bag and handed it to Devline. Having read it, he handed it back.

'I need you to keep it safe, do you understand?'

'Oh yes, sir.'

'Right, let's get you to the keeper's cottage.'

When they arrived, Moore was out at work, but Mrs Moore was home.

'Welcome to our cottage,' she said, as both of them entered.

'Mrs Moore, this is Thomas Pierce who is to stay with you. If he causes you any trouble you are to tell me immediately.'

'I am sure we will get on just fine, Mr Devline.'

'Now, Thomas,' said Mrs Moore. 'Mr Moore is down by the river. He said for you to go down as soon as you could. If you go down the driveway to the bridge and go left this side along the river, you will find him. First, I will show you where you will stay. Follow me.'

At the top of the stairs she walked along to a door at the end of a passage. She opened it and they all entered.

'Mrs Moore, I have never stayed in a room like this. Thank you.'

He left his scant belongings and followed her downstairs.

'You call me Marge and I shall call you Thomas, all right?' said Mrs Moore.

Thomas departed, leaving Devline and Mrs Moore talking. This was his first proper job and he was with people who seemed kind. That was a good start.

3

Thomas walked along the footpath beside the river and spotted Mr Moore standing in the shadows beside a large tree. When he was level with him, Thomas stopped and looked straight ahead.

'Good morning, Mr Moore, I'm Thomas Pierce.'

Moore broke cover and walked down to join him.

'Morning, lad. So you have a keen eye. That's good. Welcome to Winslade Hall.'

'Thank you, sir.'

'No doubt you have been to the cottage and met Mrs Moore?'

'Yes, sir.'

'Well, you call me Bert and I will call you Thomas.'

'Yes, sir, I mean Bert.'

Moore gave a whistle and a collie bounded from the forest to join them.

'Her name is Patch, owing to the white patch around her left eye.'

Thomas relaxed and introduced himself to an excited dog. At a quiet command, Patch darted to stand beside Moore.

'She's a lovely dog. You have trained her well, Bert,' said Thomas.

‘I hope I can train you just as well,’ said Moore, grinning.

Thomas was also grinning. Those first few moments would set the scene for the future.

‘We will walk the path and check the riverbank for any activity,’ said Moore, leading the way alongside the river.

They checked numerous places and the further along they walked, the closer the forest got to the river until they were walking through the trees. Moore suddenly turned away from the river and walked through the forest and up an incline. Then, in an open area, he pushed the bracken back to reveal rabbit holes which had been set with traps. They found two large bucks and a doe. Moore watched as Thomas removed the wire from around their necks and placed the rabbits in one bag and the snares in another. They found two more does. Poachers had been busy. They would no doubt be back once it got dark to collect their bounty. Of course they would not be happy to find both snares and their contents gone.

Moore took two of the rabbits from the bag and put them in a sack. He hung the sack on the branch of a tree.

‘They are for us; we will collect them on the way back.’

Moore continued to search through the forest until they came out of it and had a view of Winslade Hall.

‘Right, Thomas, have you met Mrs Brown, the best cook the Hall has ever had? Her daughter Rosie is not far behind her in that quarter.’

‘I’ve met Mrs Brown,’ said Thomas. ‘But not Rosie.’

They entered the Hall through the kitchen door to a place that was large and a hive of activity.

‘Hello, Mrs Brown.’

‘Hello, Mr Moore,’ said Mrs Brown. She looked at Thomas. ‘I hear you have joined us, Thomas.’

'Yes, Mrs Brown, this is my new gamekeeper,' replied Moore on Thomas's behalf.

Thomas's attention was diverted as he looked at the young woman standing by the cooking range. Even in her work clothes she looked a picture. Her long, curly, copper-coloured hair was pulled back and there was a hint of freckles over her nose. Her eyes sparkled as she smiled at Thomas. Aware that he was staring, he looked away.

Mrs Brown became aware that all activity in the kitchen had stopped as the girls stood open-mouthed at the sight of the handsome new gamekeeper, and the footmen eyed up the competition that had just arrived.

'All right, stop staring and get on with what you are supposed to be doing,' said Brown.

'When you bring food to the kitchen you are entitled to join us at the evening meal. Will you be joining us this evening?' asked Mrs Brown.

Before Thomas could answer, Moore interrupted.

'Mrs Moore will be expecting Thomas to join ourselves this evening. There will be many more opportunities.'

'You are quite right; so, Thomas, you will join us another night.'

'Yes, thank you, Mrs Brown.'

With the rabbits delivered they left the Hall.

'Thomas, take us to the two rabbits we left on the tree,' said Moore.

Thomas led the way across the well-kept lawn and headed for the forest. He entered the trees and began to walk straight towards the sack. He untied it and looked at Moore.

'Thomas, I have to tell you, I have never seen anybody do that: get to the exact spot, first time. It took me years before I could do it. Well done.'

'Beginner's luck,' said Thomas.

‘No lad, that takes skill. Now take us to the cottage.’

Thomas needed no directions, he just knew which way to go. He could never explain how that came about; it just did. They came out at the driveway that led to the neat line of cottages.

Entering the cottage, both men removed their boots and top-coats, leaving them in the small porch.

Mrs Moore was waiting for them.

‘Right, Thomas, I have set up the bath in the scullery and have hot water ready. I have washed your clothes and they are waiting for you. So you go and do that, whilst I get the meal ready.’

Mr Moore just grinned, saying nothing.

Once he was ready, Thomas joined them at the table, with a clean body and clean clothes. It was a powerful end to a powerful day.

The meal was good and plentiful. They both asked Thomas questions about his past and he answered without elaborating too much. He stayed with the basic facts and said as much as he considered sufficient. Mrs Moore began to describe the young women on the estate and in the nearby village. Thomas concluded that on one hand, she was a mine of information and on the other, a wily matchmaker. Still, he was learning more about the estate and its people every minute. Mr Moore then described the Overbury family and their social traits. Lady Clarissa had a mind of her own and was the most grounded and down-to-earth of the females. Lord Overbury was very fair but could be very hard if the circumstances demanded it. His wife her ladyship doted on her daughters, particularly the two younger ones who complied with her idea of a “refined young lady”. Oliver Overbury was a chip off the old block and was moulding himself on his father. By the end of the meal, Thomas had a pretty good picture of the Hall and those who were involved in its affairs.

A routine was soon established. He followed Mr Moore throughout the day and did as was asked. He carried his own shotgun rather than one provided by the estate. He took the fresh kills to the kitchen where Mrs Brown looked after him, clearly with the future of her daughter Rosie in mind. There was always a drink and piece of cake provided. He would generally eat with the Moores, but would often join the staff at the Hall at their evening meal.

One day Thomas arrived early at the kitchen. The housekeeper Martha Smith, who had served the family since she first went into service, entered the kitchen and spotted him.

'Thomas, can I have a word?' She turned about and walked to her office.

Thomas stood up and followed her, wondering what he had done wrong. Perhaps he should not have been in the kitchen, but he was keeping out of the way of the kitchen staff. He entered the sacred domain of Miss Smith.

'Thomas, I am advised that you can read and write.'

'Yes, Miss Smith.'

'His Lordship has decided that I should take you under my wing and develop your reading and writing. He is of the opinion that the world is changing and that staff with such skills will be of value in the long term. I shall be more than pleased to undertake the task. How do you feel about it?'

Thomas was almost lost for words.

'I love reading and writing and would be pleased to be better at it.' He wrung his cap in his hands. 'Yes, Miss Smith, it would be very good.' Then, almost as an afterthought, 'I would have to ask Mr Moore first; after all, he tells me what to do.'

Smith smiled. 'Thomas, it was Mr Moore, when speaking with his Lordship, who proposed the idea.'

'He did?' said a surprised Thomas.

'Yes. His Lordship also wants you to be instructed in the etiquette of the dining-room. So I will sort out suitable times and will let you know.'

'Thank you, Miss Smith.'

Thomas returned to the kitchen, but said nothing about his meeting with Miss Smith. He stayed for the evening meal that day and was in the process of leaving when, on passing the pantry, he heard Mrs Brown and Rosie in conversation. It struck him that whilst he could hear them, he did not understand what they were saying. He left, deep in thought about what he had heard.

The following day he was getting ready to look for poaching activity in the forest. He checked his trusted shotgun and packed the food and drink Mrs Moore had prepared for him in a bag which he slung over his shoulder. He would not be back till late. Mr Moore was in the process of going to check on the wildfowl-rearing pens.

'Bert, last night at the Hall I heard Mrs Brown speaking with Rosie, but did not understand a word.'

'They would be speaking German. Mrs Brown was married to a man from Germany many years ago, and lived for some time in Germany. She was called Braun then but, as he died when Rosie was small, Mrs Braun returned to England. She changed their names to Brown but she continued to teach Rosie to speak German. Now and again, when nobody is about, they will speak it.'

'German?' said a surprised Thomas.

'Yes, German,' said Bert.

Both men departed in different directions.

Rosie, seemingly not having made much progress in attracting Thomas, decided she needed to be bolder in her approach. She had just taken a basket of food to the stables for the grooms and endured their lurid comments when she spotted Thomas.

'Thomas, I have a special favour to ask.'

Thomas found Rosie very attractive as well as very forward. It was said that she was a product of the changing world. He was not sure about that and now wondered what she was going to propose.

'What would that be?' he asked.

'I want you to teach me how to poach.' she said.

That caught Thomas completely off-guard.

'Why do you want to learn about poaching? It is a male thing; not for young women like you.'

'I want to learn and I want you to teach me.'

'There is never time,' said Thomas, pleased that he had thought of an excuse.

'Yes, there is. When I have my day off, I can accompany you. See: it's easy.'

'Mr Moore would not like it, nor would his Lordship.'

'They need not know. It would be our secret.'

Thomas could not see a way out and so changed the topic.

'I heard you and your mother speaking German. Do you know a lot of German?'

'My mother was married to a German. She came back after he died, when I was young. She continued to teach me to speak the language and we speak it sometimes so that I do not forget.'

'That's good,' said Thomas.

'Yes, it's like your reading and writing lessons with Miss Smith,' said Rosie.

'How do you know about that? Does everybody know?'

'No, just me. I am really proud of what you do.'

Thomas was a bit flustered. He could handle the rest of the female staff, but Rosie was different. He just looked at her, then he grinned.

She smiled. ‘I will teach you to speak German and you will teach me how to poach. Are we agreed?’

‘All right,’ said Thomas, ‘But tell no one.’

She leaned forward and kissed him on the cheek, before rushing off back to the kitchen.

Thomas did not know what made him look up, but he did. Standing at a window was Lady Clarissa. He realised that she had seen him with Rosie and had observed the impish kiss. He put his head down and walked away.

When Rosie had a day off she managed to sneak away and meet Thomas in the forest. She followed him and watched what he did. He explained what he was doing and why. She was a natural and soon mastered the art of placing snares, trapping fish and identifying where poachers had been. It was tickling trout that she liked most. She would lie alongside Thomas on the riverbank and he would point out a trout that was swimming upstream. It would come to the bank to find a place to rest, before continuing its journey. She would slip her hand in the water and pass her hand, fingers turned up, to begin tickling with her forefinger, gradually running her hand along the fish's belly further toward the head until it was under the gills. Then with a quick grasp, she would pull the fish out of the water and throw it onto the bank.

Whilst on these forays, she taught Thomas to speak German. He picked up the language quickly, surprising himself.

Thomas was at the extreme end of the forest, close to where he had found Lady Clarissa. He had left the cottage prepared to stay out all night to see what was happening, as he had discovered evidence of poachers. Once at the location, he checked the building where he had spent a number of nights after having escaped Calthrope's estate. It was empty and there was no sign that it had been used. He checked the riverbank and other locations for traps. Those he found he removed. It was clear that somebody was active in the area. He found a suitable hide and settled down. He slept: it was going to be a long night.

Darkness had taken over and all his senses were active. He listened for sounds that were not in the order of things. He was close to the river. Then there was a sound: something was moving about. Then it was quiet; then the sound came again, only closer. A shape loomed up in front of him, heading towards the river. It moved clear of the trees and was on the grassy area of the riverbank. The shape lay down. This was the time to capture a poacher, caught in the act. Just as he was about to move, there was another noise which stopped him. There was another shape heading towards the river. He now had two poachers. That presented a problem. One would not be a problem, but two in the darkness would be impossible. He watched until they had finished at the water's edge and departed the way they had come. It was a diagonal route, heading to Calthrope's estate.

Thomas explored the area during the night, but did not discover any other intruders. With daylight, he inspected the riverbank and could see where the body shapes had been. He moved in the direction that they had taken when departing. His gun was ready to use if the need arose. Eventually he came to the edge of the forest and could see the road that separated the two estates, as well as a slightly worn path that had been used a number of times which he followed to the road. On the other side he could see the trace of a path leading into Calthrope's estate. He headed back to the forest and walked up the tree-line. At the track he turned in and headed towards Winslade Hall.

He spotted the horse first. It was standing with no rider visible. He had been here before. Moving towards the animal, he spotted a second horse and then something on the ground close to the trees. He moved nearer. He saw that it was Lady Clarissa lying on her back with Calthrope straddled over her, holding her arms down. He was not sure what was happening, but it looked as if she was struggling and Calthrope was shouting at her to keep still. He could see that she was using every effort to struggle free and was shouting for him to get off. He let go of one arm and was trying to undo his breeches. With her free arm she was hitting him as hard as she could. For Thomas, his reaction was automatic. He ran over and struck Calthrope on the side of the head with his gun. The impact caused him to fall to one side, aided by Clarissa pushing him off and Thomas adding to the movement by using his booted foot to push the body away. He could see that Calthrope was dazed and knew that the situation could get nasty. Thomas pulled Clarissa up and guided her stumbling to her horse. He helped her to get up and onto the saddle and told her to go and get help. A heavy slap to the horse's rump caused it to gallop down the track, its hooves thumping the ground.

Thomas picked up his gun and pointed it at Calthrope.

Calthrope moved up onto his knees, holding his head. He turned to face Thomas.

'You are going to go to prison for a long, long time for attacking me. You should have died with your waster of a father,' he snarled.

Thomas moved clear of Calthrope and his horse and into the edge of the forest which was his domain, still pointing the gun. It was now a waiting game. Calthrope did not want to wait until Overbury's people arrived. He managed to stand and staggered over to his horse. It was an effort for him to mount the creature. Once in the saddle, he screamed at Thomas in the trees:

'You have not heard the last of this, you peasant. I am going to see you die.'

He turned his horse and made his way slowly towards his estate.

Thomas watched him go; once he was satisfied that he had really gone, he came out of the trees to begin to walk along the track. He heard the sound of galloping horses before he saw them. Devline was in the lead followed by four grooms. Thomas moved to one side, should they be on a charge to locate Calthrope. They stopped when they reached Thomas.

'Are you all right?' asked Devline.

'Yes, sir.'

'Good, hop up and I will give you a ride back.'

'If it's all the same, sir, I have two places to check so I would prefer to walk.'

'All right, come to my office as soon as you are back.'

It was two hours later when Thomas knocked on the door of Devline's office.

'Come in.'

Thomas entered.

'You have been a long time.'

'We have poachers down on the river and I wanted to check something before coming back, sir. I also thought I would not be welcomed back, having struck Sir Calthrope.'

Devline smiled, not something he did very often.

'Quite the opposite, Thomas, quite the opposite. I have instructions to take you to see his Lordship as soon as you return.'

They entered the Hall through the front door and waited whilst a footman went to announce their presence to his Lordship. When he returned, they were led into the large drawing-room.

The family was gathered there. He noted that Clarissa, who had changed out of her outdoor clothes, sat in a dress becoming her station; beside her sat her two sisters. Lord Overbury stood.

'Thomas, Lady Clarissa told us in great detail what happened - and how you came to the rescue once again.'

His lordship glanced at his wife as she gasped at the thought of her daughter at the hands of such a violent man.

'This family is indebted to you for your actions, not once but twice. We thank you,' said Overbury.

Thomas knew he had gone bright red at being the focus of such attention.

'I was only doing what was right and proper,' he responded.

'Calthrope had the audacity to telephone to say he was sending the police here. They have been and have interviewed Lady Clarissa; as we have decided not to press charges against Calthrope, the matter is dropped. In any event I do not want it discussed amongst the staff.'

Devline understood that the meeting was over and indicated to Thomas that they should leave. They both bowed their heads and turned to depart.

Clarissa followed them out and spoke to Thomas in the hallway.

'Thomas, I would like personally to thank you for saving me.'

'My duty, your ladyship,' said Thomas.

'I will never forget what you did.'

Thomas just smiled. The two men then continued to walk to the door. Lord Overbury caught up and joined them. At the front door, Overbury checked to see that nobody was listening.

'This will not deter my daughter from riding so I want you, Thomas, to accompany her from now on, to guard against such a situation arising again. I will speak with Moore as we are going to have to engage more gamekeepers anyway: it appears that we also have a growing problem with poachers. When not on escort duties, you will undertake gamekeeper duties, until we have more staff in place.'

'What will happen to me when the new staff are in place?'

'You will help, Mr Devline. You will be the assistant estates manager.'

Thomas looked at Devline, who nodded and smiled. He had smiled twice in one day! A situation that was unheard-of.

A groom delivered a message telling Thomas that Lady Clarissa would ride the following morning. There was no time given. He knew that she was often up early and out riding before the family was up. On that basis, he was at the stables early. Two horses were saddled and waiting. They did not have to wait long for Lady Clarissa to arrive. She was dressed in jodhpurs, riding boots, a white blouse and a small neat jacket. She led the way as they trotted down the drive, with Thomas a respectable distance behind. They turned along the riverside track heading in the opposite direction to Calthrope's estate.

She brought her horse to a walk. Thomas did the same. Then she stopped. Turning back to look at Thomas, she said, 'You are going to have to ride alongside me. I simply cannot talk to you if you are behind me.'

'My lady, it's right and proper for me to be behind.'

'Absolute nonsense; you will ride alongside. That is my instruction.'

Thomas knew it was wrong, but an instruction was an instruction; which, of course, he could not argue against.

'I hope you don't mind having to accompany me on my rides.'

'Not at all, my lady. It's a great pleasure.'

'Good. I hear you are going to work in the estates office. That will be excellent. You will have to travel round the estate and I shall be able to accompany you.' She turned to look at him. 'When we are away from the Hall and other people, you will call me Clarissa.'

Thomas's heart sank. All of these close encounters with a particularly beautiful woman of the ruling class, who he now had to call by her first name, were, in his mind, destined for disaster.

Clarissa stopped at a clearing alongside the river and dismounted.

'This is a good place to rest the horses,' she announced.

Whilst she walked over to the river, Thomas secured the horses.

She looked at the river.

'I can see fish.'

'They are trout moving along the river.'

'Thomas, I want you to teach me how to catch game and fish. I also want to learn how to shoot. Yes, teach me what a poacher would know and do.'

'I'm not sure that his Lordship and her Ladyship would be very impressed if I did that.'

'Nonsense. There is no harm in it and I would get to know more about what happens on the estate.' She turned and looked at Thomas. 'In fact, I insist.'

Thomas and Clarissa lay down on the bank of the river and watched the fish moving about.

'You see how they come to the edge to rest. That is when you can catch them,' said Thomas.

He waited, watching, then gave a demonstration: one trout was lifted out of the river on to the bank. Thomas leapt up to retrieve the fish and deposit it back into the water. Clarissa tried but had no luck. It was her first attempt but she was determined that she would learn how to do it.

On their way back to the Hall, Thomas began pointing out a multitude of things about the forest and the river. He told Clarissa how poachers operate and the sorts of places they will choose to poach. As they approached the drive, he dropped back and followed as they trotted up to the stables. The grooms took charge of the horses, leaving Clarissa to enter the house and Thomas to take up his gamekeeping duties.

With the changes in Thomas's duties, he was required to move into Winslade Hall. Also, a new young gamekeeper was hired who was to stay with the Moores. It was a sad day for Thomas when he packed his belongings and moved to the Hall. Mrs Moore said it was like losing a son and she cried. Mr Moore congratulated Thomas on progressing so well; he said that they would still work together, but not on a permanent basis. Arriving at the Hall with a suitcase he had been given, a bag and his shotgun, Martha Smith showed him to his new room. It was quite spacious and he had it all to himself. He left his belongings to sort out later and went down the rear servants' staircase to the kitchen area. Mrs Brown was busy directing her staff in the preparations for lunch and the evening meal. She had a warm smile for Thomas as he entered, as did Rosie. Staff who were not engaged in kitchen work were ordered out to get about their business, but Thomas was allowed to stay. In fact, he received a mug of tea and a slice of cake. Rosie did not take her eyes off him. Even when the other girls made fun of her, she did not take umbrage. They were just jealous.

'Do you need any rabbit, hare or trout, Mrs Brown?' asked Thomas.

'Oooh yes, that would be good,' she replied.

He stood. 'I'll see what I can do,' he said, walking to the door and putting on his cap. He winked at Rosie as he passed her and she radiated a warm smile in return.

He had agreed with Mr Moore that he would check for poachers in a quiet part of the forest. He made his way to the area and inspected it but found no sign of trespassers. He was able to catch four trout from the riverbank and then, when he checked some snares, he found caught in them three large rabbits. It was getting late when he got back to the Hall; he found Mrs Brown in the final stages of preparing dinner. The family were eating; as soon as they had finished, they themselves could eat. She was thrilled with the delivery of the results of his gamekeeping activities.

Thomas took the opportunity to go to his room to wash and change. He sorted out his limited wardrobe. What he did have, he looked after and kept clean. He kept his gamekeeping clothes separate and he hid the shotgun. He now needed to find a safe place to hide the cartridges. When the room was how he wanted it, he made his way downstairs. Most of the staff were seated and he slipped into a seat that always seemed to be left for him. On one side was Martha Smith, with Rosie sat on the other. It was an interesting situation because Smith treated him like her son, whilst Rosie grabbed his inner thigh at every opportunity. They all waited until Soames the butler entered and took his seat at the head of the table. He uttered a few words of thanks before they all tucked in.

Amidst the hubbub of cross-table conversations, a question was directed at Thomas from one of the footmen.

'Why do the masters call you Thomas, but the rest of us by our last names?'

'I don't know,' said Thomas. 'I have not really thought

about it.'

Soames, anticipating a debate at the table that he did not want, interjected:

'On the night that Thomas saved Lady Clarissa, his Lordship was given the name Thomas. Now, Thomas is also a surname: he assumed, in all the confusion, that Thomas was Thomas's surname and called him by that name, thinking it was correct. With all that was going on, nobody was going to raise the subject; so the name Thomas has stayed. That is the simple answer so there is no need to raise it again.'

Soames had spoken. There was a short silence as everybody absorbed the information and continued eating and talking. They had almost finished eating when a bell rang. They looked at the board where a series of bells were located. It was the parlour. The duty housemaid straightened her apron and hair and moved quickly upstairs to the appropriate room. She knocked on the door. A voice called to her to enter. Lady Clarissa was alone in the room.

The maid moved closer to her and curtsied. 'Yes, my lady?'

'Is Thomas downstairs?'

'Yes, my lady.'

'Can you tell him I shall ride in the morning, early.'

'Yes, my lady.'

In the kitchen, most of the staff had departed. It was an early start in the morning and they needed to rest. Thomas was still there, talking to Rosie. The maid passed the message on to Thomas and then sat down to await any other demands from upstairs.

Thomas also would have an early start so decided that bed was the next move. As he went to stand up, Rosie's hand moved up his inner thigh until it could go no further and she squeezed. Thomas stopped, then continued to move and took his leave from those left in the room. This was to be his first night in his new bed, but he somehow did miss the motherly, fussing attention of Mrs Moore.

Clarissa held the shotgun with the stock on her shoulder. She had found an old shooting-jacket that had a padded shoulder; the butt of the gun was against the pad. She was looking up into a tree where Thomas had identified a pigeon. She could see the bird and raised the barrel of the gun until it was pointing at it.

'Pull the butt hard into your shoulder and look over the barrel to point it at the bird. When you are ready, squeeze the trigger. Remember to hold the gun tight to take the recoil,' said Thomas, standing behind her and holding on to steady her.

She squeezed the trigger as instructed. The noise of the cartridge sending a spray of pellets skywards broke the silence. The bird lifted its wings, but dropped to the ground. Her first shot, her first kill. She wanted to turn round and kiss Thomas but he, anticipating the outcome, kept hold of her. It was not a situation that he disagreed with.

'Break the gun and remove the spent cartridges.'

She did as she was bid and the gun was safe.

'Thomas, that was great fun. Thank you so much. Can we do it again?'

During the morning she shot four pigeon and two rabbits. She discovered that the rabbits, when on the run, were the most difficult to get. It was Thomas's quiet instruction that guided her to handle the gun and do the business.

'I think we ought to be getting back, my lady,' said Thomas.

She was pleased with her outing and reluctantly agreed.

Clarissa stopped her horse at a place on the riverbank.

Thomas moved up alongside her.

'I want to see if there are any fish,' she declared.

Dismounting, she went to the edge of the river. Studying the river, she saw that the surface was rippling which made seeing fish almost impossible. Thomas had dismounted and joined her.

'You see how the water is disturbed by the flow and the breeze and restricts seeing under the surface. When it's like that it's almost impossible to see the fish.'

'You said it's almost impossible, but I bet you could find them.'

They both looked at the surface of the water. 'Not today,' said Thomas.

He began to walk back to the horses. She caught up. He was ready to help her mount when she leaned forward and kissed him on the lips. He pulled back.

'My lady, you must not do that,' said an embarrassed Thomas.

Clarissa laughed.

'Oh, you enjoyed it just as much as I did,' she added as she was hoisted up into the saddle.

Thomas was in a very difficult situation. The biggest taboo of the time was fraternisation between the classes. If his Lordship found out, it would be instant dismissal with no reference. He duly followed Clarissa back to the Hall.

Thomas also continued to cultivate Rosie's hunting skills whilst trying to avoid her advances. It had not escaped his notice that she spoke about the benefits of marriage. However, he had become very adept at avoiding the subject. Marriage was for the future and not for now.

The move to be integrated into Devline's empire had been seamless. He even had his own desk in the office. Thomas relished the job; he had truly found his niche. The only down side was that he had to escort Lady Clarissa on her riding ventures, which were frequent. It was not that he disliked the job, but he was being drawn across the social divide. It did help when he managed to persuade her to extend the rides to cover his duties on the estate. She still shot the shotgun and had evolved to the rifle. She was a brilliant shot and had bagged deer on a number of occasions. All the kills had to be credited to Thomas, to avoid anybody at the Hall finding out about it. She did not mind, as her reward was to flirt and kiss Thomas at every opportunity.

4

War clouds began to gather over Europe, creating a great deal of uncertainty about the future. Newspapers were full of articles about people and places nobody had heard of; in the case of some countries, people did not know where they were. Thomas had obtained an atlas and searched out these mysterious lands. They were, for the most part, a long way away from Winslade Hall; so why would the British Empire get involved? France and Russia were united in an alliance: they were two very large countries. He could not believe that they would be attacked. Germany was big, but not that big. Even combined with the Austro-Hungarian Empire, it would be a mammoth and dangerous task. They would have to fight on two or more fronts at the same time and that did not make sense.

At the kitchen table, the talk of war sounded like a big adventure to the younger male members of staff, who were keen to get into uniform. It would take them away from their humdrum subservient routines, keeping the Hall functioning. When Thomas delivered rabbit, venison, trout or game to the kitchen it was always welcome; but at the evening meal, the focus of conversation always reverted to war. Even when Soames forbade the topic, the younger male staff always returned to that of the pending war and the great adventure that lay ahead for them.

'We're going to join the army,' said a footman. 'What about you, Thomas? You'll be well skilled for the army, being a gamekeeper and all.'

'I have not given it much thought,' said Thomas. 'I don't think everybody will go at first. The army will go and then they may seek volunteers to help out. Anyway, how will the estate cope if we all go?'

'We are going,' said a second footman. 'It will be an adventure - and think about the uniform. All the girls like a uniform.'

Some of the girls sitting around the table looked at one another and giggled.

It was Martha Smith who interrupted the conversation. 'I am sure that when he is needed, Thomas will serve his country. No doubt he will be guided by his Lordship who is, as we all know, a colonel in the City of London Rifles. Meantime, Thomas will no doubt continue to help manage the estate as well as provide the kitchen with ample supplies of fresh meat and fish.'

'I just thought that Thomas would be one of the first to go,' said the first footman.

'It may not happen,' said Thomas, shrugging his shoulders.

'Oh, I do hope so,' said a footman.

It was a quiet morning at Winslade Hall. His Lordship had been in London, and had arrived home very late the previous evening. Clarissa decided not to ride that morning, as she wanted to know what her father had been told about the possibility of war. Her ladyship had breakfast in bed. Clarissa's two sisters were staying with an aunt in London. Her brother Oliver had been with his father and had not yet risen. Lord Overbury instructed the butler to gather all the staff together. Once that was done, he was to let him know.

It took about an hour to gather everybody and they all assembled outside the front door of the Hall.

Thomas stood aside from the staff, alongside Devline. He was wearing a new tweed suit. He had made a dramatic step in his advancement, and made every effort to fulfil the role and to look the part.

Lord Overbury came out of the front door, followed by Clarissa.

'Thank you for your patience. I know you have duties to perform and will be wanting to get on. I was in London yesterday and a very important decision was made. It has been officially announced and will be again shortly on the radio; but I can tell you, as of today, we are at war with Germany.'

As if on cue, Oliver exited the front door. He was dressed in an army uniform, with the rank of lieutenant.

His Lordship took advantage of Oliver's sudden appearance.

'You will see that one member of the family is already in uniform; no doubt, over the coming weeks and months, there will be others from the estate donning a uniform of some description. In the meantime, we will keep you informed as to developments as they become known to us. Thank you, Soames.'

The three members of the Overbury family went into the Hall. The staff walked away to get on with their jobs. If there was going to be a war, there was nothing they could do about it. For many of the young men, it was the news they had been waiting for. A war - and they would be part of it!

For Devline and Thomas, it was going to be a busy time. The estate workforce would be reduced as men departed for uniforms and glory. They would have to adapt to the new situation.

Later in the morning, Overbury summoned Devline and Thomas to his study.

'Thomas, what are your plans with regard to the war effort?'

'I have not given it a great deal of thought, sir. It is really a matter of priorities. I think a war will drag on; so there will be plenty of opportunity. If all the male staff decided to go, then we would be hard pressed to maintain output on the estate.'

Overbury nodded. 'We need a list of those who are destined to depart for military service to identify their jobs. We can make do with the departure of footmen, valets and gardeners. But we need men for the forests and for agriculture. As long as we have horses, we will require grooms. In those cases, we can make a plea to keep them as essential workers, if men are to be conscripted.'

'Is joining the army not a voluntary thing? If they want to go, can we stop them?' asked Devline.

'We cannot force them not to go, but we must encourage them to remain behind, as their work here is equally as important as fighting in the army,' replied Overbury.

'Perhaps we could look at replacing some of the men with women. Some seem very capable and I am sure they would cope,' said Thomas.

'That's a good point. Can you please look into the possible options,' said Overbury, who then looked at Thomas. 'I am going to ask you to stay on the estate, at least until we are established with viable alternatives.'

'Yes, sir,' said Thomas.

'I suggest we meet every morning until we know what is happening. I shall have to go to London for occasional visits to my regiment. Whilst I am away, you, both of you, will be responsible for the estate and the Hall. As you know, Mr Oliver has been given a commission in the army and is at this moment preparing to join his regiment. This is not going to be easy for any of us. There will be many social changes and we must meet them head-on. Do we have any other matters to deal with?'

'I have one, sir,' said Thomas.

The others looked at him.

'The army will require a lot of horses. They may have to take them from private stables. Should we be prepared for that? And how many are we prepared to release?'

'That is a very good point,' replied Overbury.

'We need to review the inventory of work-horses and riding horses, as I presume they will require the latter. Although the work-horses will pull stores and guns. But we need to be prepared, to ensure we still have enough for working the land.'

'Anything else?'

There were no other matters raised.

With the meeting over, Thomas went to the stables. He sounded out who might depart for the army immediately, and who would leave it for a while to see how the others got on. Some were going nowhere. They would remain as long as there were horses. He found Oliver with his horse.

'You look very smart in your uniform, sir,' said Thomas.

'Thank you, old chap. Have to say I'm not relishing the muck and bullets bit, but they say we will just go over and give the Hun a quick thrashing then be home again. Never sure who comes up with these predictions but I doubt that one is correct.'

'I hope it is a short war, for everybody's sake,' replied Thomas.

'I say, Thomas old chap. I have an enormous favour to ask.'

‘What’s that, sir?’

‘I need you to keep an eye on Clarissa for me. She’s a bit of a tomboy and keeps getting into scrapes. She really likes you and will listen to what you say. Will you do that?’

‘Yes, sir, of course I will.’

‘Good man. I can go now and know she is in safe hands.’

Oliver went to the Hall to finish packing whilst Thomas continued talking to the grooms.

The unannounced visit by Henry Calthrope was not a welcome event. He charged up the drive, forcing his horse to go faster; then he reined it back to a rapid stop outside the front door. A footman and groom came running along the front of the house.

‘Come and get my horse and don’t keep me waiting,’ he shouted at them.

As the groom took the horse, the footman led Lord Calthrope into the house.

‘If you would wait here, please, I shall go and find his lordship.’

‘Overbury? Where are you, Overbury? You have a guest,’ the voice of Calthrope boomed out.

A door opened and Overbury exited his study. ‘What is all this noise about?’

He then spotted Calthrope.

‘You didn’t say you were coming,’ said Overbury, eyeing Calthrope in his cavalry uniform.

‘Didn’t think I needed to. Anyway, not stopping. I just wanted to say that I am prepared to take on that daughter of yours. The one that tries to keep avoiding me.’

‘Is this some form of proposal?’

‘S’pose it is. What do you say? A couple of months with me and I’ll soon tame her.’

'My daughters will choose who they marry: they will not be palmed off to just anybody.'

'Well, I'm the best she will get. She does not act like a lady. So what do you say?'

'I say, leave my house and go and join your regiment. You are not welcome here.'

'Well, I did offer. She must like a bit of rough, fooling about with that gamekeeper of yours.'

Calthrope turned and walked out of the front door. 'Where's my bloody horse?'

Whilst waiting for the horse to arrive, Calthrope paced up and down. When it arrived, he flung himself into the saddle and charged down the drive.

Overbury returned to his study. Soames had appeared and joined him.

'I apologise that we were not ready when Sir Calthrope arrived, but we had no advance warning. He seemed very agitated if I might say so, sir. Is everything all right?'

'Yes, thank you, Soames I was not expecting a visit. He just turned up. Could you please get somebody to ask Lady Clarissa to join me?'

'Yes, sir.'

Clarissa joined her father in what was designated his office.

'We just had an unwelcome visitor in the form of Calthrope.'

'What did he want?' asked Clarissa.

'To marry you.'

'What!' she screeched.

'Yes, he thinks he can get you in line. Make a lady of you. He did comment that there was something going on between you and Thomas. Is that true?'

The question came out of the blue. Somebody must have seen them when she was taking advantage and flirting with Thomas. She quickly gathered her thoughts.

'There is nothing between Thomas and myself. He is a perfect gentleman. I may have flirted with him, but he has not responded. I don't know why the question has been asked; but if somebody is making accusations, then I need to have details. I will say, Thomas has done nothing wrong.'

Overbury did not react. 'I shall also speak with Thomas about it. Until I have done that there is nothing more to be said on the matter.'

As Clarissa left the study, she said, 'I would never marry Calthrope. He is evil.'

Overbury smiled to himself. 'I would never allow you to marry Calthrope,' he replied.

Thomas was summoned to his Lordship's study.

He knocked on the door and waited.

'Come in,' said the voice of Overbury from within the room.

Thomas entered and closed the door behind him.

'You wanted to see me, sir?'

'Yes, Thomas. I have already spoken with Lady Clarissa and now I need to speak with you. We had a rather unpleasant visitor earlier, who made an accusation that you and my daughter were, how should I put it, doing things that her mother and I would find unacceptable. Is this true?'

Thomas thought about the question and what Clarissa might have said and, more importantly what had the visitor seen and said.

'Yes, sir, it may be true.'

'Explain yourself,' said his Lordship.

'I was assigned to escort Lady Clarissa when out riding. Out of sight of the Hall, she insisted that we ride side by side so that we might converse. I did not see this as a breach of your instructions. Among the things we talked about was poaching. Lady Clarissa insisted that I teach her the ways of a poacher. She wanted to catch trout by tickling, to shoot a shotgun, lay snares and then shoot deer with a rifle. Her reasoning was that she wanted to learn more about the estate outside of the Hall. Upon her insistence, and having explained that you would not approve, with great care I taught her about poaching and gamekeeping,' said Thomas, who now waited for the roof to fall in.

'Is that it?'

'Yes, sir.'

'Was there any impropriety between you?'

'Absolutely not,' said Thomas. 'I can assure…'

Overbury had put his hand up to stop him saying more.

'I am sorry I had to raise the subject at all, but I needed to know. Thank you for your honesty.'

Thomas stood waiting for the next move.

'Thank you, Thomas.'

Thomas saw that as the signal to go and walked to the door.

'Oh, Thomas. Thank you for telling me about the hunting activities. I think, in these times, it is no bad thing for a woman to have knowledge and experience of such things; but please be discreet.'

'Yes, sir, thank you, sir.'

Back in his own office space, Devline asked what his Lordship had wanted. Thomas explained. Devline empathised, with the comment that Lady Clarissa was certainly a handful. Thomas agreed.

Oliver Overbury and five of the male staff had donned uniforms and were now en route to training then war. The fighting had begun. News from the front was very restricted; what came through was clearly doctored for public consumption. However, bad news could be curtailed.

His Lordship was often in London and, when at home, was dressed in the uniform of a colonel; he spent a considerable amount of time on the telephone. Devline and Thomas spent hours planning the running of the estate. Rosie still wanted to spend her days off with Thomas and Lady Clarissa continued to make demands on his time. His was a balancing act, in the hope that the two women did not meet when Thomas was with either one of them. With both of them still keen on hunting, Thomas was still able to keep favour with Mrs Brown, through a good supply of game. None of the woman objected to Thomas taking the credit as it avoided exposing their part in it.

5

It was during his return home for his first leave from the front, that the family noticed the change in Oliver. Before his departure into action, he had been outgoing and had enjoyed what many said was playing at soldiering. Having crossed the channel, he had advanced over a few days, not meeting a single Hun. Then he endured the first skirmish, along with the first casualties. Even that was tolerable, as it was generally accepted that in war people died and were injured. Now, progress in slowing the superior Germans had been achieved at a cost. The armies of Britain and France dug in and the conflict became static. It became a war of attrition. Artillery bombardments that lasted hours and even days, followed by a frontal assault with men with fixed bayonets confronting machine guns. The decimation of men, the withdrawal to the lines, the regrouping, the getting back up to strength, then the going back to the trenches to do the same thing again. Now, amidst the tranquil environment of Winslade Hall, Oliver felt safe – but; he knew that the slaughter was continuing, only now it was just happening to different soldiers, different regiments.

Following a disturbed night's sleep, he had breakfast. The family chatted about the things that were important in their particular lives. Occasionally they would ask a question of Oliver, but he was not able to be very forthcoming. How do you talk about masses of dead young men and those with terrible wounds? Nobody round the table would understand. Even his father, who had experienced war in South Africa, had never encountered what was happening now with the mass industrial slaughter.

The room emptied until it was just his Lordship and Oliver sitting at the grand, carved dining-table.

'Is there anything I can say or do?' asked Overbury. 'I have spoken to others of the horror out there.'

'Thank you, father, but it is not something that can just be chatted about. What I would like to do is to talk to Thomas. Would you mind?'

'Not at all; anything that helps.'

When Oliver left the room, Overbury sent a message to Devline to explain that Oliver might seek some support from Thomas. It would take Thomas away from his duties, but it would be beneficial to Oliver, even though they were experiencing a heavy workload.

When Oliver arrived at the estate office, Thomas and Devline had already been briefed.

'Hello, Thomas. Do you have time for a chat?'

'Of course, sir,' he replied, pushing the ledger he was completing to one side.

'We can walk in the garden,' said Oliver.

The garden looked in fine order, considering that many of the younger gardeners had departed for the war.

Thomas didn't speak, but waited for Oliver to open the conversation.

'Thomas, I just wanted to talk to somebody about the bloody mess that is on the other side of the Channel. I hope you don't mind?'

'I think it's good to talk, but I have no first-hand knowledge of what it's like; so I am not sure how I can be of help.'

'Just by listening, old chap. I can't speak to the family; and the others think it's a jolly good show, a big adventure.'

'I can certainly listen, sir.'

'First: when we are alone, you are going to call me Oliver.'

'You are very like your sister.'

'I presume that is a compliment?'

They both laughed.

'Thomas, it's the carnage, the broken bodies, the men who will never come home. In the beginning it was all bravado; but now, leading men who are justifiably terrified to charge machine-guns is really most awful. We charge, sometimes we make the enemy trenches; but then the Hun comes back in force and we retreat back to our trenches. Then there is the noise of the guns, the exploding shells, hour after hour, even day after day. When it rains, there is the mud. Mud like you have never seen. Then, as if all that is not bad enough, your body crawls with lice. Rank and privilege make no odds as far as that problem is concerned. They infest your clothes and eat away at your body.'

They sat on a bench and Oliver held his head in his hands. Thomas said nothing.

'The worst thing is trying to keep up the chaps' morale. Then I have to lead them over the top. I know many are going to be slaughtered - and that includes me. Thomas, people have no idea, absolutely no idea what that is like.'

Tears rolled down his face as he relived the events.

'I am sorry for making a fool of myself,' said Oliver.

'You most certainly are not. I would be most concerned if you enjoyed it.'

There was a silence.

Oliver broke that silence. 'I have to go back and do it all over again. Lead more men to needless slaughter. Don't our military leaders see the futility of it all?'

Thomas sat and listened allowing Oliver to purge all his anger and frustration. When he had reached some degee of stable thought, Oliver expressed his gratitude to Thomas, who was then sworn to secrecy as to what had been said. Oliver would go back - and Thomas knew his time to visit hell was coming very soon.

The telegram boy arrived at the Hall and delivered a buff-coloured envelope. Soames took delivery of it and carried it to his Lordship. Fortunately he was at home, as it would have been intolerable for her ladyship to have been the recipient. Lord Overbury took the envelope and sat looking at it. He knew that the contents spelt bad news; it was just a question of how bad. Soames had remained in the room, waiting quietly. Overbury could not put off the inevitable so, using a paper-knife, he cut open the flap. Inside was a message. He pulled it out and opened it. The contents were in the form of a simple statement: "*Captain Oliver Overbury has been injured in action and is in hospital in France awaiting repatriation to a hospital in England.*"

'He is alive, in a hospital in France, but it does not say where; he is waiting to be sent to a hospital in England, but it does not say where. It does not say what his injuries are.'

'He is alive, sir, that is the important thing. Whatever his injuries, we can deal with them. Should I tell the staff?'

'I need to tell the family first; then we can tell the staff.'

'Very good, sir. If there is anything I can do, please ask.'

'Thank you, Soames.'

By lunch-time, everybody had heard the news about Oliver.

It was two months before the family received the call that Oliver was ready to come home. Clarissa and Thomas drove to the hospital to collect him. They shared the driving and Clarissa flirted with him as usual, but Thomas noted that it was in a more serious way. The hospital was located in a large hall that had been taken over by the military. Clarissa entered, found a nurse and enquired about her brother's whereabouts. The nurse disappeared to find out, leaving the pair of them in the entrance-hall. A nursing sister approached them.

She spoke to Clarissa, 'Are you Captain Overbury's sister?'

'Yes.'

'You must be strong. He is not how he was when you last saw him. He is alive and I am sure your family will be able to take great care of him.'

Thomas who had been standing a short distance away, heard what was said.

'Do you have transport?'

'Yes, we have a car.'

'Very good. If you wait here, we will bring him down to you,' said the nursing sister.

'Oh, before you go. What are the requirements for becoming a volunteer nurse?' asked Clarissa.

'I have some information. It's not much. I will bring it with me.'

They were both taken aback when they saw him. Shrapnel had damaged his left arm to such a degree that he had difficulty in moving it and he had lost his left leg just above the knee. He was wheeled over to them in a wheelchair pushed by a nurse.

Clarissa put her arms round him and hugged him. Oliver just sat and stared into the distance.

'Hello, old bean. It's good to have you back. Thomas is here.'

'Hello, sir, soon have you home.'

'I have a form for you to sign at the discharge of Captain Overbury from the hospital. I also have some information for you,' said the nursing sister, passing Clarissa the documents. 'He has an artificial leg and it will take a lot of perseverance to master using it. We have started the process.'

Oliver knocked the leg with his knuckles to emphasise the point.

Thomas wheeled him out to the car.

'If you decide to join us in nursing, it's jolly hard work, long hours, and terrible food and accommodation. It is very rewarding helping the wounded, but do think about it carefully.'

Clarissa signed the form and handed it back.

'Thank you for all that you have done for him.'

Thomas had lifted Oliver into the back of the car.

'I'll drive,' said Clarissa.

'We'll all probably end up in hospital,' said Oliver to Thomas.

'I heard that, you rotter,' said Clarissa, as she drove away laughing.

The journey to Winslade Hall was tiring and they were all very pleased when they finally turned up the drive, to stop at the imposing front door. Family and staff flooded out of the door to form a welcoming party. Oliver was wearing his Captain's uniform as Thomas carried him into the house to be seated in the parlour. Lady Overbury sat and looked at her son. Tears rolled down her face. A product of the old school they may have been, but on this day she allowed herself to show her emotions. This was her only son.

Clarissa had switched into nursing mode and tended to Oliver's immediate needs. A footman arrived, pushing a newly-purchased wheelchair.

Lord Overbury took charge. 'We were unclear as to your requirements. The hospital gave us no information. If you would like, we can convert a room downstairs into a bedroom. You will have to tell us what you need.'

Oliver looked at his family.

'This is how I am. I am just about getting used to it, and you will in a short time. We will all learn from experience. I have an artificial leg and they say I will be able to walk about unaided, but that it will take some time to master.'

'Nonsense, Oliver: I need you as my tennis partner; so no delaying,' said Clarissa.

They all laughed, and it relieved an uncomfortable atmosphere. Everything was going to be all right.

It was three months since Oliver returned home and he had made remarkable progress. He had mastered walking, although he was still unsteady and used a stick to aid balance. It was all down to the bullying by Clarissa who, in between her voluntary nursing activities at a local hospital, vented her frustrations on Oliver when she got home. He took it in good part and had seen the results. Thomas was still in demand as an escort when she went riding.

Lord Overbury and Oliver were in the stableyard, inspecting their dwindling stock of thoroughbreds when Thomas joined them. When the discussions about equine matters were finished, Thomas saw his opportunity to give a message that would not be well-received.

'Your Lordship, may I speak to you on a personal matter?'

'Of course.'

'I'll wheel myself along to the next block,' said Oliver.

'It's all right, sir. You need to hear what I have to say.'

Oliver stayed where he was and his Lordship looked at Thomas.

'I'm joining up,' said Thomas. 'Joining the army.'

'No, Thomas. Why? I have done enough for the whole estate,' responded Oliver.

'The word is that they are going to conscript soon and I would rather decide where I want to be, than be shunted to some unknown unit.'

'I have been expecting this for some time. You have to do what is right and if I can help, I will. Your home is here and will be as long as you want it. When you return, your job will still be here for you. We will have to manage in your absence,' said Overbury.

'Thomas, Thomas, please think about it. You have no idea what it's like,' said Oliver.

'I have spent hours with you, listening to the reality. But, I have to go, either by volunteering or by being forced.'

Oliver resigned himself to the fact that Thomas was going and that it would need a great deal of luck for him to return unharmed. 'I want to be there when you tell Clarissa.'

'It is not my place to tell her ladyship of my plans to go to war. Perhaps I can leave that to you, sir?'

The farewell at Winslade Hall was embarrassing for Thomas. Rosie was telling everybody that her man was going to be a hero, whilst Clarissa could tell nobody that it was really *her* man going to war.

'Thomas! I shall take you to the railway station,' said Clarissa.

'Oh, good show. I shall join you,' added Oliver.

Clarissa gave Oliver a look that could kill from a hundred paces. He thought it was a great hoot. At the station, Clarissa told Oliver to stay where he was; she would see Thomas onto the platform. He was not alone in joining the train and he endured about fifteen minutes of ogling eyes as he waited with the radiant Clarissa. When the train arrived, he thanked her for seeing him off. But, in front of a mass of heads hanging out of the carriage windows, Clarissa kissed Thomas on the lips. She clung on, leaving him no opportunity to get away from her clutches, not that he had any desire to do so. The noise of the calls and whistles only added to the embrace. On the train, he was allowed to look out of the window and wave back at Clarissa. He wondered how long the news would take to get back to the Hall and the family. He did not want to contemplate whether he would ever see her again. Back at the car, Oliver had a beaming smile on his face.

'I take it the calls and whistles were directed at your farewells to Thomas?'

Clarissa, normally unaffected by such a comment, blushed.

'I may never see him again,' was her only remark.

Clarissa, at Winslade Hall with Thomas gone and Oliver getting about on his own, felt the need to explore what more she could do for the war effort.

'I'm going to spend a few days in London with Aunt Josephine,' she announced.

'I am going up too; so we can travel together, if that's all right with you?' asked Lord Overbury.

'Of course it is,' she replied.

Clarissa remembered the last time she had stood on the station platform and she wondered how Thomas was getting on. His short letters back to the staff said little and Oliver commented that they would never deliver bad news in any event. That was kept for those at the front. She had not received a letter in return for those she had sent him, but she understood the situation. Things would be different after the war.

Seated in a first-class compartment, Clarissa looked out of the window whilst Lord Overbury, dressed in army uniform, read some documents.

'What do you have planned whilst you are with Aunt Josephine?'

'May I speak frankly?' she replied.

'Of course.'

'I am going to see about the possibility of becoming a proper nurse out in the battlefields; and I know Aunt Josephine has contacts.'

'She does, but I understand that the nurses she knows serve right on the front line, where they get shelled and shot at.'

'Well, she can give me some advice.'

'Yes, she can. Have you heard from Thomas?'

'No, he would not write to me.'

'Well, might I just say that things are changing: the "us and them" that we have all been used to will change. It is your life; providing you are sensible, then we shall support you. Thomas is a good man.'

Clarissa was shocked at what her father had just said. Yes, he was moving with the times; but what he said was unexpected.

'Are you saying that I can write to him and he can write to me?'

'Of course. It would be a bit one-sided if he only wrote to you and you did not reply.'

'Thank you, father.'

Josephine was waiting at the station for their arrival; after excited greetings, Lord Overbury took his leave and departed, leaving the two women, who were already in deep conversation.

‘Tell me all the gossip,’ said Josephine.

‘There is not a lot to tell.’

‘Come now, it is me you are talking to. How about young men?’

‘Oh, that is complicated.’

Josephine was intrigued. ‘Come now, tell all.’

Whilst they stood waiting for a taxi, Clarissa divulged the news about Thomas.

‘I have become what you might call infatuated with a man called Thomas. When I had a fall from my horse he rescued me; then, when I was attacked by Calthrope, he rescued me again. Father engaged him as a trainee gamekeeper and the staff took to him. His education developed: he even speaks German! He had to escort me when I went riding, which of course was often. I made him teach me to hunt and trap, as well as to shoot. He is now the assistant estate manager, although he is currently in the army in France somewhere.’

Josephine bundled Clarissa into a taxi and gave the address to the driver.

‘What a wonderful story. Do the family know?’

‘Oliver does and so does father, although he has not said anything directly until today. He has given us permission to correspond.’

‘What about Thomas? How is he dealing with it?’

‘He still sees the class barrier between us, but I know he really cares for me.’

‘Well, I want to have all the details. Is Thomas the reason for coming to London, or is it to see me?’

‘I wanted to see you, but also I want to become a nurse on the front line and I know you know people.’

‘Why a nurse?’

'I volunteer at the local hospital so I have some training, and of course there has been Oliver to look after. Without doctors and nurses out at the front, many more would die. I want to do my bit.'

Josephine did not respond immediately, but just looked out at the London streets. Nothing more was said until they arrived at the house. With the taxi driver paid, they entered the fine, fashionable residence. Staff carried luggage to Clarissa's room whilst the pair retired to have tea.

'Have I upset you, with my wanting to become a nurse?'

'No, not at all. It's just that I have a friend who does just what you are seeking to do, but I don't know if I would be doing the right thing by the family, if I introduced you.'

'If it is of concern to you, call father: I have a telephone number for him in London.'

'I would be happier doing that.'

Lord Overbury took the call from Josephine, who got straight to the point. He took the view that Clarissa was over twenty-one and could make her own decisions. If that was what she wanted to do, then she had his blessing. She had become very self-reliant, thanks to the efforts of Thomas. Having raised the subject of Thomas, Josephine sought the family view as to whether a full relationship should evolve between them. She added that it appeared nothing had happened yet, but that it might well do; although Thomas was keeping his place. Overbury clarified that he considered Thomas to be a fine man and that he would keep an open mind and see how things developed. A lot could happen in times of war. Josephine said she would keep him informed of any developments.

Miss Madeline de Rouche eyed up Clarissa, having already been given a very detailed briefing by Josephine about her abilities and sturdiness to endure life on the front.

Whilst Clarissa sipped tea, she examined photographs that had been taken of the aid post and of the staff. Then the realities were given of life for a woman on the front line. Going to the latrines, washing both clothes and bodies at the post was very difficult yet had to be done. To do a thorough job, they had to wait until they went back to a place of safety and privacy. The uniform such as it was had to endure rough use. Like everybody in the trenches, the nurses; were susceptible to being infested with lice however, care of bodies and clothes helped with that problem. Lice did not like being washed. There was no dressing-up and no make-up. The picture de Rouche painted was that of the raw facts. That was how it was.

Madeline looked at Clarissa. 'Are you really sure you could endure this? There are nurses required in the field hospitals. Conditions might be a bit better there.'

Clarissa did not answer immediately, but examined the photographs one more time.

'Madeline, I should very much like to join you.'

De Rouche gave no immediate reaction. She looked at Clarissa long and hard.

'I am told you know how to poach, ride a horse and shoot.'

'Yes, that is true.'

'Then you have some understanding of what hardship and compromise is about.'

'Yes, but I know I still have a lot to learn.'

'I shall be going back in one week. Two other gals will be coming. We will set up a new aid post on the front line. I doubt we will get very much support from the field hospital; the nursing there is rather regimented. I will give you the date and time as soon as possible. You will need your own money to pay your way. Travel light. What you bring with you, you will have to carry. Obtain two sets of cavalry breeches and officers' high boots. I will arrange for sets of our adapted nurse's uniforms, such as they are: we cannot wear white. We would become targets for the German snipers. The rest you will familiarize yourself with once we get there.'

6

Clarissa could never have imagined what Madeline de Rouche would be like. She found a woman of independent means with a determination that was electric. She not only survived in a man's world, she thrived in challenging it. Over the years, she had travelled extensively to remote parts of the world and had discovered that people everywhere were in need of medical care. She considered her contribution to be miniscule, but had returned home when war clouds gathered as she realized that her nursing skills would be required. She had not joined the established nursing organisations, but attached herself and a few like-minded fellow-travellers to field hospitals. She soon discovered that the field hospitals were well back from the front line and that the stretcher-bearers had little knowledge of first aid. Often, by the time a wounded soldier was carried to medical support he was dead. She wanted to give the wounded a chance, which required being on the front line.

Clarissa was one of three nurses de Rouche had recruited and they all travelled from London to Southampton together. Although they were clearly nurses, their attire was very unconventional. It was only their Red Cross badges that identified them. Whilst waiting to board a boat that would take them across to France, army and VAD nurses were warned by their charges not to associate with them. Even on their arrival in the French port, they were kept separate which caused some complications. A number of railway carriages had been assigned to the "nurses" but there were arguments about their not mixing. Eventually, after much debate, they were all assigned to compartments reserved for nurses, whatever their attire. There was more agitation when the train lumbered into its final destination, a town near the front.

The motorised transport was designated for the army nurses. It was argued that de Rouche's team were not army and therefore not entitled to travel in army vehicles. They were saved by a young woman who approached those who were arguing the point. She was a VAD ambulance driver, who with her ambulance was assigned to de Rouche and her nurses. The two groups parted with the problem solved. The driver introduced herself as Pippa: she was a kindred spirit to the nurses to whom she had been assigned. She led the way to her ambulance which had been parked with all the other ambulances. When they reached it, they were told to move away as quickly as possible. Pippa did not need telling twice and leapt into the cab to activate the switch. She leapt back out and, at the front, swung the starting-handle. As soon as the engine started, she ran back to the cab to press the accelerator and ease the engine into life. With de Rouche in the passenger seat and the others in the back, they were ready. Pippa selected first gear, released the handbrake, released the clutch and, with some acceleration, the ambulance moved off on its journey towards the front.

Their first stop would be a large field hospital where they would collect the medical kits and provisions. As they arrived, the matron came out to meet them.

‘I have a tent for you, Miss de Rouche, and one for your nurses.’

‘Thank you,’ replied de Rouche, but we will share the one tent if there is room. Up on the line we do things differently.’

‘Very well, if you insist. Please follow me.’

Carrying their bags, they all followed the matron. The tent was large, with beds and a side-locker. The floor was wooden and there was a large cupboard that would hold some of their clothing; but then they would only be there for one night. They each selected a bed and relaxed after their journey. That did not last for long. A nursing sister arrived and took them to a tent filled with tables and chairs. On one side were tables where food was served. That was where they ate their first meal within sound of the heavy guns firing on the front line. The faint rumbles they could hear were the guns that pounded the German lines and the shells that the British received from the enemy guns. After the meal, the sister spoke to de Rouche to explain about the quartermaster sergeant. He was a rogue of the premier class; every bandage and dressing had to be checked and counted. Having set the scene, the sister guided them to the stores tent. CQMS Chambers was a long-serving soldier; he knew every fiddle in the book, and some that were not in the book. He was a short man, balding and sporting a large beer-belly. He indicated a number of boxes as being theirs. Clearly he had never met anybody like de Rouche.

‘Open the boxes,’ she declared.

‘Everything is in order,’ he replied.

‘Your order maybe, but that may not necessarily be mine. Open the boxes.’

The debate went on for several minutes; de Rouche won the round. Chambers opened a box. The nurses checked the contents and anything that was out of place was put to one side. Half of the contents were eventually piled on a table. Chambers was squirming.

'I want to inspect every box.'

'Every box?' he parroted.

'That's right, everything in every box.'

Chambers was beaten. He called his two private soldiers who opened the boxes, allowing the nurses to check and to count everything. It took a long time, but eventually de Rouche was satisfied that everything was indeed in order: her order. The nurses carried the boxes and other stores over to the ambulance and loaded them on board. Once loaded, there was little room left for the nurses themselves.

Pippa was concerned that with all of the valuable items now in the ambulance, it would take little effort for the CQMS and his men to raid the vehicle and purloin some of their cargo back.

'I shall sleep in the ambulance,' declared Pippa.

Before anybody else could respond, Clarissa added,

'You cannot do that alone. The CQMS may steal you. I shall stay with you.'

De Rouche did not say anything. She just smiled. Her choice in selecting the right girls was spot-on.

It was dark when the two women climbed into the ambulance with their blankets. Clarissa had found an axe handle, without the axe head. She carried it within her blankets as she considered that it might be needed. They both found a space and made themselves as comfortable as they could under the circumstances. It had been a long day and they were tired so sleep soon overcame them. Clarissa did not know what it was that woke her, but she was awake to watch the back doors of the ambulance open. There were whispering male voices. It was dark inside the vehicle but looking out, the background was dimly lit by the glow of lights from the hospital that was working twenty-four hours a day, as well as by the brightness of the moon. Clarissa grasped the axe handle: as the outline of a head appeared she could not see who it was, but they were obviously either intent on stealing their supplies or on attacking herself and Pippa. She was having none of it and whacked the person. There was a cry of pain, a curse and the noise of somebody falling backwards to land awkwardly on the ground. There were loud and angry whispers before the doors were pushed closed. Then there was silence. Clarissa fell asleep.

In the morning Clarissa said nothing to Pippa until they had returned to the tent to wash and change. First she spoke to de Rouche:

'I was woken last night by somebody trying to get into the back of the ambulance. There was more than one person involved. It was dark, but I think that it was the CQMS. Anyway, I had an axe handle and I knocked him on the head. He fell down and was very cross. Then the doors were closed and they went away.'

De Rouche listened.

'It is not very ladylike, striking a small defenceless older man! But bravo, well done - and we still have our valuable stores and our dignity!'

The other nurses gathered round to give their support. Pippa was flabbergasted.

'I didn't hear a thing. You didn't wake me.'

'I would have done, had they got in!' replied a laughing Clarissa.

Whilst they were having breakfast, Chambers entered. He had a bandage round his head and looked very sorry for himself.

'I don't think that is bad enough for a ticket home to Blighty,' said de Rouche.

‘I fell over in the store in the dark,’ he replied, walking off to the far end of the tent.

Somehow, word spread around the hospital, and whilst some of those in authority were not impressed with the remedial action taken, nothing was said. In any event, they would have to take on de Rouche - and nobody was going to do that.

The officer responsible for the ambulances and drivers joined the nurses as they finished the final packing. He arrived in a vehicle that could carry three nurses and had room for two stretchers at the back. Clarissa was assigned to ride with Pippa, whilst de Rouche sat next to the officer and the two nurses sat behind. An orderly sat at the back with the stretchers. With the officer’s vehicle leading, they headed to the front line. The so-called road was pot holed and churned from the mass movement of men and equipment. It was also a target for enemy artillery and, after a heavy bombardment and a heavy downpour of rain, it became a sea of mud. This day it was dry but very bumpy. If the nurses felt every rut, the patients also had to endure it -and they were wounded. The noise of the guns grew louder and they could see their effects, as shells exploded in the distance. They were out of range now, but would soon be at the mercy of the guns and of the shells they delivered. The road was busy with soldiers: some marching to the front; others, bedraggled and unkempt, were heading away from the front. A steady flow of ambulances, most of which were driven by women, were carrying the wounded to the field hospital. They waved at each other as they passed.

The officer pointed out the remains of a farmhouse in the distance that he thought would be suitable for an aid post. Eventually the two vehicles drove up to it. De Rouche leapt out and, before anybody did anything, inspected the building. It was rough but there was shelter: it would serve their purpose. The equipment and stores were unloaded and placed ready for use. A large kitchen table had survived and would be their operating table. It had to be moved and they were grateful that the officer and orderly were with them. The guns had fallen silent, to be replaced by the sound of machine-guns.

'The men have gone over the top,' said the officer. 'Bodies will arrive shortly.'

Rooms were cleared as best as possible; then they prepared for the first casualties. The outside water-pump was found to be working, which provided them with a vital supply of fresh water. Within a short time, they were ready to accommodate the first broken bodies; they did not have long to wait. News had spread, stretcher-bearers carrying the wounded made their way either to an ambulance pick-up point or, for those needing immediate attention, to the aid post. The aim of the little aid post was to provide first aid that would help keep a man alive before undertaking the journey to receive surgical and nursing treatment at the hospital. Pippa helped in getting those who had been patched up onto her ambulance until it was full; she then began the perilous journey, with her precious cargo, to the hospital.

In those first hours they dealt with bullet and shrapnel wounds. Some had lost a limb; others more than one. Large stomach wounds posed the biggest problem, as a pile of intestines had to be pushed back into the body and held in whilst bandages or large stitches were applied. Either way, it was an almost impossible task. Their frustration mounted when, having got the patient bandaged, he died. Those who died were placed away from their nursing activities, to be removed for burial. The living and the almost-living were always their priority. After several hours, the constant flow of men slowed and they had a chance to start to clean up the place. Then it was quiet. No machine-gun or rifle fire, and the artillery guns were silent. The nursing team worked as quickly as they could, to get ready for the next influx.

The following weeks saw no let-up in the wounded passing through. Between them, they prepared food and often, as dusk descended, when Pippa returned with the ambulance from her last delivery with some additional provisions. It was impossible to drive at night but she could transport wounded back at first light; so she stayed at the aid post overnight. The main room became their living-space. It was where they cooked, ate, rested and slept. It was watertight and some engineers had arrived to undertake some makeshift building repairs. They blocked up the windows that faced the enemy, so that at night when the lamps were lit, the light could not be seen by the Germans.

Wounded men arrived at all hours and even through the night they were treated, but they had to wait until daylight when an ambulance could travel. If there were strong stretcher-bearers available, they could begin their journey back to a pick-up point where ambulances were allowed to go; but it was a long walk in the darkness along a rutted and often muddy road. The nurses slept when they could, but there was always one on duty and one on stand-by to assist. With only four nurses, it was an arduous task seven days a week, twenty four hours a day.

It was during a quiet spell and with all their jobs up-to-date that De Rouche and Clarissa sat looking into no-man's-land. They could see where the British trenches were and, on occasion, make out the German line. It seemed an awfully narrow piece of ground that separated the two sides but had cost such an enormous loss of life in trying to take it each from the other. Their attention was drawn to the noise of aircraft above them. Looking up, they watched two opposing planes attacking and defending as they rolled about the sky. As soon as one had an advantage over the other, machine-guns chattered. Then they changed around as the potential victim became the attacker. The German plane got the advantage and fired. The bullets found their mark: the engine of the British plane spluttered and stopped but, as it glided down, the German one followed. The British plane lifted just enough to drop, tail downwards, onto the ground and then pancake to slide along the ground. They watched for the pilot to abandon the aircraft but he did not move. They heard the Germans cheer at the demise of the British aircraft. Meanwhile the German pilot, keen to watch his target strike the ground, misjudged his height and caused his own plane to crash; this was followed by a cheer from the British when the German struck the ground.

De Rouche studied through binoculars both aircraft that were now settled in no-man's-land. The pilots were alive but did not get out.

'Get the aid bag and follow me,' said De Rouche.

'They are in machine-gun alley,' replied Clarissa as she left to get the bag.

'Well, we can go and have a look.'

They went to the road and followed it to the communication trench, which took them to the main trench. They found soldiers who had watched the spectacle and were now intrigued to see what the nurses were going to do. When de Rouche reached a ladder, she began to climb up to peer over the top.

'You can't do that, miss,' said a corporal. 'It's not safe: you will get shot by a sniper.'

'It's quite all right, young man. They do not shoot at nurses yet. Come, Clarissa.'

The two women climbed the ladder and onto the parapet. They began to walk towards the two crashed aircraft. De Rouche carried a white flag with a red cross on it and made it visible to the Germans. They reached the German aircraft first, where there was a strong smell of petrol. Undaunted, the two women climbed up onto the wreckage to reach the cockpit. They found the pilot alive but with cuts and not fully aware of his surroundings. He was very lucky. They managed to unclip his seat-belt and struggled to lift him out of the cockpit. They were thankful when he did realise what was happening and made an effort to help himself out. Once clear of the aircraft, they sat him down. They were now between the aircraft and the German machine-guns; but there were patients to deal with. Whilst Clarissa checked the pilot over and tended some of his nastier cuts, de Rouche went to the British aircraft where she found the pilot to be in a pretty poor state: he was bleeding from bullet wounds. He had probably got them in the exchange of machine-gun fire that had hit and stopped the engine. As soon as Clarissa had finished with the German pilot, she joined de Rouche. This was a more difficult situation, as the pilot could not really help himself. They had managed to get him half-out of the cockpit when a heavily accented voice behind them thanked them for saving his life. It was the German pilot, who told them that they were much braver than his comrades who had stayed in their trench. He saluted them, then hobbled off towards the German trench.

They managed to get the British pilot out and down onto the ground. With the heavy smell of petrol around them, they got either side of the pilot and lifted, dragging him clear of the aircraft. They rested before continuing their journey back to the British lines. At the steps, willing hands helped the pilot and then themselves down to the relative safety of the trench. A Captain came up to them.

'I have to say that was thoroughly splendid. You ladies should be awarded the VC for that. I shall notify

Headquarters.'

De Rouche smiled.

'Don't waste your time, Captain. We are mere women and nurses at that. We don't get medals. Can your men carry the pilot back to the aid station?'

'Certainly,' he said, ordering men to assist the nurses.

Back in the aid station, the pilot was placed on the table and was checked over. Wounds were cleaned and patched. A note of his injuries and how he had got them was attached to his shirt. Once ready, he was placed aboard an ambulance with two other men who were also waiting to make the journey to the hospital. Then all was quiet again. The rescue was not even a topic of conversation at the evening meal; they knew that the shelling and machine-gun fire would not go away. It was just a matter of time until the next burst.

Two weeks passed, with no end to the causalities passing through the aid post. They patched them up and sent them on to the hospital where the men could obtain surgical treatment. Pippa, returning from an ambulance run to the hospital, had returned with mail, stores and a passenger. The passenger was introduced to those not tending the wounded as Kitty. She came from London and was a member of the VAD. It was explained that she was without an ambulance. This had come about when doing a pick-up close to the front. Whilst stretcher-bearers loaded wounded into the vehicle, she had taken the opportunity to go behind the remains of the wall of a house to "spend a penny". A shell had landed directly on top of the ambulance. She was shaken by the noise and by the shock-wave of the explosion; when she went to look, there was nothing left apart from a large hole with the tangled remains of the ambulance. It was an hour before she was able to get a ride back to the hospital. When Pippa arrived with a load of patients, Kitty would abandon whatever menial task she was doing and go and help. Matron decided that, as she disliked doing hospital tasks so much, she should go and join the ladies at the aid post. In terse terms, she indicated that they appeared not to mind undisciplined behaviour. So here she was.

De Rouche had entered the room unnoticed and listened to the story. When Kitty had finished, she stepped forward and introduced herself.

'I'm Kitty,' she said. 'I did not mean to lose my ambulance,' she added.

'I would hope not,' replied De Rouche.

'I am quite adaptable, miss.'

'Well, as you have been sent and we can desperately use another pair of hands, you are most welcome.'

'Thank you, miss, that is most kind.'

Among the letters was one addressed to De Rouche. It was official-looking.

She opened it. It had come from the General Staff Headquarters. The contents were to the point. They had heard of her exploits with the crashed aircraft and she was summoned to the Headquarters to discuss what she and her nurses were doing so close to the trenches and going unauthorised into "no-man's-land".

In the lull of patients and activity, she sat and wrote a reply, thanking the General for his concerns. She and her "gals" were doing very well, thank you, and saving lives that otherwise would be lost. With very limited resources and being far too busy saving lives, the general would be most welcome to visit her and the team instead, when they were next at the front. It was, of course, a snipe at the generals who never ventured near the action.

However, they did respond and sent a lower-ranked officer, a major, who would be expendable. De Rouche had never given it another thought until a staff car arrived and parked outside the entrance to the aid post. Kitty, who had settled in really well, spotted the car and went outside. She confronted the major who had arrived in his nice neat uniform.

Kitty saluted and he responded.

'He can't park there,' said Kitty.

'I'll say where my driver parks,' stated the major.

A face peered round the doorway.

'No, you won't. It's my aid post and I tell you where to park, so move the car: it will be in the way of the ambulances,' de Rouche had spoken.

The head disappeared.

'Move the car,' shouted the major to the driver.

'You had better come in,' said Kitty.

The major entered the main room. He could see the chaos of living, sleeping, cooking and eating in one room. He sat down where he was told and waited. The noise of men in severe agony could not be ignored. In the end, his curiosity got the better of him and he stood, then strode over to the door from where the noise was coming. He opened the door and marched in.

'Come in,' said De Rouche without looking up. 'Can you give me a hand? That man's entrails have been torn out; if we can get them back in and get him clamped up, we might be able to save him.'

The major looked, then turned and exited the outside door. He was clear of the building when he vomited.

The soldier did not make it. They closed the body up as best they could. He would be removed for burial. De Rouche and the nurse washed their hands and arms, removed their blood-stained aprons and went into the main room. Hot drinks were on the go. The major entered.

'Sorry about that; must have been something I ate.'

He looked at the assembled group.

'Is this all of you?'

'Yes. I'm De Rouche and the senior person.'

He noticed that, unlike the nurses at the hospital, they did not wear white nurse's uniforms but khaki tops and riding breeches. Sturdy high leather boots were worn in place of shoes, and instead of a white head-dress they wore khaki headscarves.

'The General asked me to apologise for not attending himself, but there were more pressing matters to be dealt with.'

De Rouche ignored the statement. 'I will show you round.' She led and he followed. They went into the treatment room.

'This is where we treat the seriously injured patients: those who, without a quick patching-up, will not survive. You saw one earlier. He did not make it but many do.'

He was very careful not to allow his uniform to be contaminated by the excess of blood in the room. She noticed his attitude.

'When we have finished, we will wash the table and floor down ready for the next patient.'

She showed him what equipment they had and how they worked to cover a twenty-four hour period: there were no days off. The visit did not take long. He saw the motorised ambulances arrive, mostly driven by women, load up with the wounded and take a long and very dangerous road to the field hospital.

The major broached the subject that it had been reported to HQ that nurses had actually gone into no-man's-land and recovered injured airmen. She explained that they had little choice, as the pilots were unable to get out of the crashed aeroplanes themselves. They had to be helped; she and a nurse did that. She added that he should tell the

General that the stretcher parties were not of sufficient quantity to deal with the high number of injured.

The major said that he would pass on the message. He then told her that the General required her and her nurses to move back to the field hospital and work there. De Rouche simply looked at the major.

'We will comply with the request when the General stops sending thousands of men "over the top" to be slaughtered and seriously wounded.'

For her, the meeting was at an end unless the major wanted to take his neat, clean jacket off and help them. The major did not and he hastily departed, which was just as she had expected he would. Back in the tiny cramped room, De Rouche commented:

'You have today seen a representative of the General Headquarters Staff on the front line, a very rare sight indeed.'

'He was frightfully sick,' said the nurse who had been assisting in the attempt to return the soldier's innards back to where they belonged.

'Don't worry about him: he will be awarded the Military Cross for his epic exploits today and he will tell a good story back home,' said De Rouche in a sarcastic tone.

The daily routine did not change. Mangled bodies passed through the post until one day there was a difference. More soldiers were going to the trenches. Among them were pioneers who were tasked with the manual job of improving the trenches. Then, a few days later, they were withdrawn, to be replaced by more infantry. Those in the aid post knew that this was the build up to a "big push" and that would mean an overload of work for them. De Rouche had seen it before and asked Pippa to obtain as much first aid supplies as she could. The pioneers were camped close by the post, waiting for their next assignment. After a discussion between their officer and De Rouche, they were soon engaged in transforming a damaged stone barn into a usable treatment area. The biggest problem was the lack of staff to work in it. Kitty had been learning from the others and could look after the more minor injuries. When not driving her ambulance Poppy, helped Kitty.

It had been quiet for a couple of days, with only a few causalities passing through. They made the most of the respite, including catching up on lost sleep. It was just as well because they were awakened when the British guns opened fire. Being night-time, the flashes from the guns lit up the sky. The barrage came from the big guns set well back from the front, then the medium guns in between and the lighter guns which were quite close. The guns fired all night and then all the next day. Shells pounded down on the German trenches. The nurses would, during the daytime, have a glance at the destruction being wreaked on the enemy. They concluded that nobody could possibly survive the bombardment. The shelling continued for three days then, as quickly as it started, it stopped. There was silence.

They heard the officers' whistles, then came thousands of men who climbed out of the trenches and began the trek across no-man's-land. It would be a case of walking over to what was left of the German trenches and then continuing to chase the Hun, who would no doubt have fled in fear and panic. From the highest point of the farmhouse, De Rouche could observe through binoculars the progress of the British advance, on which she gave a running commentary. Then came the dreaded noise. Machine-gun fire. They were German guns and they chattered ceaselessly.

Far from running away, the Hun had managed to survive the massive bombardment and had now manned what was left of their trenches. The mass British assault left soldiers caught in the open, to be cut down by sustained fire from the German trenches. De Rouche described the scene to those below, then climbed down to help prepare for the massive influx of wounded men that was sure to follow.

7

When Clarissa found her place with De Rouche, Thomas was already on the front line in France. Having travelled to London and found that there were numerous recruiting centres for all of the services, he spotted one that just said "Army". He went in to mix with the milling crowd of other men of all ages and backgrounds. They were all looking at the various regiments attempting to entice men to volunteer to join them. Amidst the noise of the recruiting sergeants extolling a particular regiment's attributes, Thomas heard the word "horses" mentioned, not once but several times. He squeezed his way in the direction of the voice. A sergeant was stood on top of a table. Although he wore a khaki uniform, he had on riding breeches and held a riding crop in one hand, which he swung about as he spoke. The other hand rested on a sword in its scabbard. He was a product of the King's Dragoons, cavalry or - as they were described - mounted reconnaissance soldiers. His eyes scoured the men in front of him, looking for a faint glimmer of interest. They, like all of the other regiments, needed men. A man standing next to Thomas, who he did not know, made the comment that cavalry charging machine-guns was sheer madness. Thomas added that thousands of men charging machine-guns using their own legs was also madness. Thomas eased his way past the men standing in front of him, a movement that was not missed by the recruiting sergeant.

'Let that man through,' his voice boomed out.

Men turned to look and see who was going forward. Within moments, Thomas was stood before the table. An officer sat on the other side. Oliver had warned him of the warm smiles and friendly banter until he signed on the dotted line. Then it was orders barked and you were just another name amidst thousands or - as he described it - "cannon fodder".

'Name?' asked the captain.

'Thomas Pierce, sir.'

'Well, Thomas Pierce: can you ride a horse?'

'Yes, sir.'

'Where did you learn to ride?'

'Winslade Hall, sir. The home of Lord Overbury, sir.'

'I know Lord Overbury and his son Oliver. What job did you do at the Hall?'

'I am - was - assistant estate manager, sir.'

'Indeed. You are just the sort of chap we need. The corporal will tell you what to do next. Take this form. You will need it when you reach the training depot.'

Thomas was swept along by the moment; without really knowing it, he had just become part of the war.

'Thank you, sir.'

'Do well, young Thomas Pierce!' said the officer.

At the depot he joined other civilians who had just enlisted. It was the start of six weeks' intensive training. It began with being kitted out in their uniforms. There was one which was called "best" and a working uniform that was used for everyday wear. The new recruits had hair cuts and were shown how to dress like a soldier. Then it was out onto the square, to learn to march like a soldier. Once they had acquired the basics of drill, they were allocated a .303

Lee Enfield rifle for the duration of their training. They did not have bayonets because, as Dragoons, they carried swords instead. Sergeants and corporals took turns at the moulding process. It was never-ending. By the close of each day, every man was exhausted and just wanted to sleep. Then the real challenge began. There were only half a dozen men who had actually ridden a horse before. Those who claimed they could ride were tested: Thomas was by far the most experienced horseman. He was ordered to assist the NCOs with those who could not ride. Visits to the rifle range were, for some, another daunting episode; but for Thomas, this was another skill he already possessed. The time passed quickly and soon he was a trooper in the King's Dragoons, assigned to "D" Squadron. Before departure from the depot he had dressed in his best, well, his only proper uniform, and he had his photograph taken. It took pride of place in the kitchen of Winslade Hall.

Thomas reported to the "D" Squadron Headquarters and was assigned to Headquarters troop. Because of his knowledge of horses and his riding skills, he was given the job of acquiring suitable horses for the Squadron, a job that was normally given to a sergeant. The first pitfall he encountered was due to the fact that the entire British army relied heavily on horses. Following the slaughter of men and horses in the earlier part of the war, horses were now in short supply. In fact most were being shipped from America and Canada. He had just about managed to assemble enough horses when the orders came for the Squadron to mobilise to go to the continent and engage in the war.

The Squadron departed from their barracks and rode at a slow pace through the streets to the railway station. They followed a band which played rousing and patriotic music. People lined the route to cheer them on, as if it was a giant party. Not everybody could get on the train: in fact it took two trains to transport the men and three trains to transport the horses. Thomas travelled with the horses. This had the advantage that the train was not crowded with men. Following their journey to the port, a ship carried the men across the Channel. Another ship carried the horses. Thomas was told that the advantage of being with the horses was that the horses were more valuable than the men. Perhaps that is why they were accompanied by a warship which stayed close by.

Offloading both men and horses on the other side of the Channel went fairly smoothly. Some of the officers rode up and down the quay as if they were preparing for a hunt. Thomas thought that the enemy machine-guns would certainly cool their ardour. He contemplated the fact that many officers had brought their own horses and were not going to be impressed when they had to subject them to front-line action. As the troops assembled and were ready, they began to move off. Headquarters troop followed at the rear. Prior to departure, Thomas had reported that there was a mount for everybody and that there were six spares. He now had charge of them. Although he had listened to Oliver speaking about life and the loss of it on the front line, he had no realistic concept of what to expect. The cavalry had been used as it had for many years: when they saw the enemy they charged, sabres drawn. They were no match for modern warfare when artillery shells began their slaughter, followed by machine-guns which engaged those who were left. The loss of men and animals was incredible. With the growing lack of horses and a dramatic increase in motor transport, many cavalry units found themselves dismounted and serving as infantry in the trenches. The Squadron was, at this time, lucky that it still had horses but it was just a matter of time before they would be fighting on foot.

As they moved into the forward area, they were to stand by; when the infantry had assaulted and gained ground, they would charge forward to chase the Hun as they fled, leaving the infantry to secure the enemy trenches. They would then probe the new enemy defences and relay the intelligence back. The opening event of a battle, as opposed to a skirmish, began with an artillery duel. Heavy guns, well back, lobbing large shells into the enemy. Medium guns in the middle ground; then the smaller field guns closer to the action. The smaller guns and limbers were drawn by teams of horses and could move quickly forward behind the infantry at short notice. The Squadron moved slowly forward, two hundred and eighty men and horses, eager to go. Enemy shells found their mark and gaps appeared in the ranks. Human and horse body parts were scattered about, to fill the mud-filled shell holes. Then silence.

The sound of whistles, then thousands of infantrymen climbed out of the sanctity of the trenches and moved forward. Rifle held at waist height, bayonets protruding forward, they walked into a hail of machine-gun bullets, to be cut down in no-man's-land. The cavalry moved forward, then charged. They had to avoid shell holes and barbed-wire entanglements, but they also met the force of the machine-guns. The slaughter did not take long. Thomas was tasked with catching the horses that had lost their riders. His was not an enviable mission, with animals that were terrified and just wanted to escape. He also had to put down horses that were beyond saving; for that purpose, he had been provided with a revolver. When the action was over and the infantry had retreated back to where they started, the remains of the Squadron regrouped. A roll-call revealed that there remained one hundred and four men, some of which were wounded. The action had cost one hundred and seventy-six lives, those who had paid the ultimate price.

Thomas was sent back to the stores depot to scrounge more horses. His task was almost impossible. Priority for horses was given to the artillery and the service corps, who had to move guns and stores. Men charging about on horses were no longer a priority. He returned to the lines with just two mounts. That news, combined with the new orders that they were to hand over the remaining horses and take up an infantry role, caused all hell to break loose at the Squadron HQ. With no horses to account for, Thomas became a squadron runner. This job came up frequently, as the task of delivering and collecting messages between the trenches and HQ found the runners exposed to enemy fire more than most. Whilst they moved about, they added to the death-toll. He concluded that this was his reward for not obtaining more horses.

Thomas arrived in a trench which had been taken over from an infantry regiment. Men spaced themselves out, with the old hands knowing what to do. Thomas watched and was soon picking up the way to live and survive. The German machine-guns, shells and gas were not the only thing that caused death. He found a dug-out and shared it with another member of the troop.

He surveyed his surroundings. The wall in front faced the enemy. He cottoned on very quickly to the fact that to stick your head above the parapet would provide a target for a sniper, and you would soon be dead.

A sergeant from troop headquarters was close by. He was an old hand.

'A fine mess this is,' he suddenly said. 'When I first joined the Dragoons, we were cavalry. We used the lance and the sabre and we fronted the enemy in dramatic charges. The horses were the finest to be found. Now, we sit in the bottom of a stinking trench. You new boys take heed. Do not put your head above the parapet. The officers are able to see over the top using a periscope. That is a long box with mirrors in it that are angled to provide a view of no-man's-land. The observant among you will have noticed that the bottom of the trench has duck-boards that are raised slightly above the ground. The idea was that when it rains, the mud would be below the boards. They do not work and often the mud is ankle-deep. In winter that means that you are permanently standing and walking in water. That gives you trench foot and your feet fall apart. We have just arrived, but your body will soon be infested with lice that irritate and feed off your blood. You can try to remove them, but you will never succeed whilst in the trench. They get in the seams of your clothes: one way you can deal with them is to run a lit candle along the seams to roast them.' He chuckled at the thought. 'You will see rats as big as cats. They are not a real worry, as they feed off the dead. They can strip a body to the bones very quickly.'

'Where are the ablutions, Sergeant?'

The sergeant began to laugh. 'You wash, shave and scrub your teeth here in the trench. You have to be careful with water use as it has to be carried in. You can either walk along to the crapper which has seen thousands leave their mark, or you can go up behind the trench and squat. You won't be able to hang around at the crapper because of the smell and up the back you could be a target for a sniper. You make your choice and take your chance.'

'When do we go over the top?' enquired another newcomer.

'It's not all action, son. It's ninety-five per cent boredom, two per cent being killed in the trench and two-and-a-half per cent being machine-gunned to death.'

Nobody asked another question.

'Oh,' said the sergeant, 'and when they bring food up to the trench, you may find it has a strange taste. That is because they sometimes use containers that have been used to carry paraffin. They wash them out, but the taste remains.'

There had been five days of idleness and the men were bored beyond belief. The only certainties were the enemy shelling them on a regular basis and the British guns shelling the Hun. Snipers were active at any opportunity. With time, nerves would become frayed and men would seek ways to get out of the front line. Accidentally shooting oneself on purpose was a popular option. That would mean a court martial and possibly facing a firing squad. One of the biggest fears was a gas attack; the men kept their masks with them. In the beginning, there were no proper masks for protection; they only came as time progressed. The sight of a yellow fog rolling across no-man's-land sent sheer panic into those in its path.

Then there was a sense of anticipation. Boxes of ammunition were carried along the trenches and clips handed out to the men. There followed boxes of Mills bombs which were also handed out. Something was happening but nobody knew what. It was a case of "hurry up and wait". Then officers passed through, giving pep-talks that fell on deaf ears. Nobody was going to say anything because soldiers just did what they were told. The word was that there was going to be a push, and that meant crossing no-man's-land to the Hun's trenches. It would be easy, just a stroll in the park: an artillery bombardment would shatter the German defences, both their barbed wire fences and their soldiers in the trenches.

Visits by officers became more frequent and the pep-talks more intense. Then came the noise from the first salvo of shells that screamed overhead to land on the German trenches. The bombardment continued throughout the evening and into the night, only to stop at first light. The men had been given a ration of rum and were massed around the ladders that would take them up to the parapets. Thomas was among them. Then came the call to fix bayonets. Men looked at one another and saw the fear they had in each other's eyes. The shelling stopped.

'All right lads, get ready; we will be back here shortly.'

They waited; then came the sound of hunting-horns and blasts on the officers' whistles and men scrambled up the ladders and over the top. It happened, man followed man.

Thomas was up and walking into no-man's-land. He remembered what he had been told. You only had ten bullets in your gun; so keep them for when you could see the enemy. So far so good: the artillery had done its job. Moving forward around shell holes and past the remains of both German and British soldiers who had perished in previous assaults. Then came the dreaded sound of machine-gun fire, theirs not ours. Thomas, like the others, continued moving forward. Men fell but there was no stopping to help them; they had to help themselves. The remains of the German wire fences could be seen and it looked as if they were still intact. Then, in a moment of madness, those who had made it so far began to charge. The enemy guns were silent. They crossed the wire and reached the edge of the German trenches.

Thomas heard the sergeant shouting,

'Throw Mills bombs into the dug-outs!'

As the men clambered down into the enemy trenches, there was a feeling of excitement. They had charged and won. Mills bombs cleared any hiding-places for the enemy. Then it became apparent that there were no living enemies to be seen.

'They have withdrawn and will counter-attack; so be ready!' shouted the sergeant.

A lieutenant came running along, shouting, 'The Hun is on the run. After them, men!'

'Stand your ground, men!' shouted the sergeant.

The lieutenant came back to confront the sergeant. 'You are a coward. I ordered you all to chase the Hun. Follow me.'

He climbed the ladder and at the top was shot. He fell back into the trench.

'Stand to, men and be ready to withdraw!' shouted the sergeant.

The Germans came in large numbers. The British did not bring machine-guns with them and there were not enough men left to be effective with rifle fire.

The word spread down the trench to withdraw. It was confirmed by the sound of a hunting-horn. The men needed no encouragement and scrambled back up the ladders. It began as an orderly withdrawal, until the Germans regained their trench and began to shoot at the men as they retreated.

The survivors were back where they began and prepared to defend their trenches if the Germans decided to follow them. At least they would have machine-guns and more men who had been moved up whilst they were away.

The Germans did not come on this occasion; the men settled back into a period of boredom. There would be some action when it got dark as they ventured out to locate and bring back any wounded who had managed to stay alive.

Thomas had been promoted to corporal, filling "dead men's boots", and had been on the western front for nine months without home leave. There were rest periods when the troops were moved back to a form of sanctity, generally a town, where they could rest, bath, de-louse themselves and eat proper meals. Often there was time to relax and enjoy some entertainment. Many had endured two years and not been home. So this day was like any other. Smoke drifted across no-man's land and stung Thomas's eyes. There was a smell of cordite hanging in the air. What he could see was an eerie, desolate mud-scape with large, water-filled shell holes. The only safe place at the holes was on the ridges, where care had to be taken not to slip in the mud and slide into the muddy water. Men and even horses had been known to have disappeared by sinking into the mud filled holes.

The assault had been an "over-the-top" as a mass body of men, then a spreading-out and the losses that created a nightmare. He had seen many of his comrades fall to the Hun machine-guns; they lay where they had fallen. It had been a rout; and having survived himself, he wandered about looking for any other survivors. He considered it safe to do so due to the smoke, but he would have to be careful when the smoke cleared away.

He lost his footing at the top of a large shell hole and just managed to stop himself sliding down into the muddy water. It was the wood from part of an old barbed-wire defence that had caught him. He rested, making sure that he had hold of his rifle. He looked down into the murk and could make out a body. It was slumped against the side, but the slippery mud gave no purchase. He saw that the body was moving. Whoever it was had seen him.

'Don't just lay there: get me out and do it now,' demanded an arrogant voice.

Thomas frowned; he knew the voice, but could not place it. From the accent it was clearly an officer. Holding onto the wooden post, he carefully eased himself down to get a better look. The body was immersed in mud to just over the waist. Then he saw the face. Calthrope! Bloody Major Calthrope and he was stuck in the mud.

'Get me out of here, you bastard,' he said, snarling as he spoke.

Thomas pulled himself up out of reach of Calthrope as he flung his arms in his direction.

'You caused a lot of misery for me and Lady Overbury, and in fact to a lot of other people,' said a very angry Thomas.

'Just pull me out. I'm not interested in that trollop. Get me out or you will be on a charge.'

Thomas looked at the now pathetic individual.

'Once the mud is up to the waist it's impossible to get somebody out. Horses have been used to help pull men out in such a situation; but there are no horses here,' said Thomas, matter-of-fact.

'Just pull me out.'

'You're over your waist so there is no chance.'

'Don't talk rot. Give me your hand and pull me out.'

'I have to go and look for any other survivors. They are far more important than you.'

'Damn you to hell. Pull me out and that's a direct order.'

Thomas ignored him and slowly pulled himself up to the ridge. He stood, keeping his balance, then moved on, leaving the mud-filled hole with Calthrope in it.

Thomas found stragglers, some shocked, others wounded. He gathered them up and got them to follow in single file. With the smoke thinning, he decided they should head back to their trenches. He had managed to salvage nine men, although not all of them were from his troop. They passed the hole where Calthrope was trapped.

'There's a man down there,' said one soldier.

'It's Major Calthrope,' said Thomas.

'We have to get him out,' said the soldier.

'Too late,' said Thomas. 'Once the mud gets above the waist, the suction will not allow the body to be pulled out without the aid of horses. He's now up to his shoulders, so there is no hope.'

Another soldier came forward and looked down. 'That's Major Calthrope, commanding officer of "A" Company, the 5th Mounted Rifle Regiment. He turned down a higher rank so that he could terrorise his soldiers. He had three shot for desertion when they were just making their way back to our lines. I know him from old. He raped my sister and when my father complained, he had us thrown out of our cottage. Don't waste your time worrying about him.'

As they watched, they could see the agony that the pressure of mud was creating from Calthrope's laboured breathing. Then he slowly sank below the surface, the mud creating some bubbles as he did so.

'I hope he rots in hell,' said the soldier.

'Let's go,' said Thomas.

The worst part of returning to the lines was encountering the jittery soldiers who would be manning the trenches. With smoke about they could be trigger-happy, thinking that those returning were the Hun. Thomas spotted a marker and signalled to the men behind to get down. They all lay down on the ground. Thomas looked ahead but could not see anything. There was only one option and that was to call out their presence.

'It's Corporal Thomas Pierce, King's Dragoons, "D" squadron. I have nine men. We are coming in.'

There was no reply. He called again.

'Piccadilly?' called an unseen voice.

'Eros,' replied Thomas.

'Advance to be recognised,' said the unseen voice.

Thomas signalled to the men to follow him. In line, with rifles in the trail position showing a passive stance, they moved forward. As they approached the trench they saw the line of rifles pointing at them.

'Welcome back, boys,' called out a sergeant.

They clambered down the wooden ladder into the relative safety of the trench. A lieutenant arrived.

'How many are you, Corporal?' he asked.

'Ten in total, sir,' replied Thomas.

'Right-o, follow along the fire trench and then take the supply trench back and go along the road. You will be met and told where to go.'

'Yes, sir,' said Thomas.

As they moved along the trenches, passing fresh troops who were holding the line, other stragglers joined them. Being at the front, Thomas had no idea how many were behind him. They trudged on, covered in mud, tired and in low spirits and, most of all, very hungry. Those who were uninjured helped the injured. Once clear of the front, he could see ahead what he knew was a field kitchen. It was like a mirage, and even as he approached it, he thought it was just a dream. It was the commanding voice of a staff sergeant that brought reality.

'What have we here then Corporal?'

Thomas looked around and saw the long line of soldiers. 'I am with the King's Dragoons but there are men from other regiments. We took a pounding staff; so I have no idea how many we are.'

'Let's get you all fed, then you can go on to the farm, which is a few miles up the road, where you can be sorted out.'

The soldiers needed no bidding and tucked into the little that was on offer.

Thomas then led the long file to the farm, where a regimental HQ had had it divided into an area for officers, another for senior NCOs and another for the men. A sergeant and two corporals barked orders for the men to go to their respective unit locations. Although it was called a farm, there was only half of the farmhouse remaining; the rest comprised tents which had seen better days. Thomas found men from the Dragoons and dumped his equipment in a tent. Before he could get sorted out, he was summoned to the Dragoon Squadron's Headquarters. He dragged himself over to find his commanding officer, Captain Houghton, and the sergeant-major.

'Good to see you, Corporal Pierce. I understand that you led a fair number of men back, having collected stragglers on the way. Well done. I am afraid that from our strength of two hundred and sixty men, at this time we have only mustered forty-nine men, including two officers. So, we do not yet know how many have been killed or how many wounded. It was a rout and I know that the other units suffered as we did. I hope that we will be pulled back to regroup and get replacements and equipment. In the meantime, can you look after all of our men? If the men can get cleaned up and fed, then we can muster in the morning and I may have more news about what is happening. 'Oh, one more thing: it's Sergeant now. You have just been promoted.'

'Right, sir, I'll get to it, then,' said Thomas. He saluted as he departed.

Outside the tent, the sergeant-major gave Thomas his three stripes.

'Wear these, son - and good work.'

Little had changed by the morning. The squadron had taken a beating and more fresh troops were being sent up to the line to bolster against a counter-attack. It turned out that the number of surviving soldiers had risen to sixty-one. The company had lost a hundred and sixty-six wounded or killed. After a parade to confirm the identification of the men and to assess the state of their uniforms and equipment, they went back to their areas to await orders. It was mid-morning when the news arrived that they were being pulled back to a town for rest and to integrate replacements.

The men collected what belongings they had and prepared to move out. Motorised trucks and trains would provide the transport. The movement of the men to the town was uneventful. Their first port of call was the "cleansing station". Every man had to have a hot bath and remove all traces of lice infestations. Medical orderlies checked that the men were free of the insects and noted their health in general. That was a just a gesture: if you could walk, see and carry a rifle then you were deemed all right to fight. They were then given new clothes, including underwear and uniforms. They were next assembled and given details of their billets. They were warned of the dangers of sexually transmitted disease, and that this was rife in the town. It was also pointed out that catching such a disease was not a ticket home, it was self-inflicted harm and soldiers could be charged under military law for that. They were then given details about the areas and women set aside for officers, leaving the rest for non-commissioned ranks. Once everybody had endured the stern words they were let loose on the town. As they ventured forth, others were departing on their way to the front.

Madeline de Rouche received a letter. Having read the contents, she went to find Clarissa and found her in their treatment room, cleaning and bandaging the wounds of a soldier to prepare him for the journey to the field hospital.

'Clarissa, I have had a letter from two gals who are to join us. They are in the town at the Hotel de Paris. I know it's quite a journey but I would like you to go and collect them. It seems that nobody is willing to take them to the field hospital. They also have with them boxes of supplies; so it's probably as well that they did not make it to the hospital, or the quartermaster sergeant would have helped himself to whatever he could find. Take Pippa and the ambulance. It will do you both good to get away for a short period, and you can make use of the bathroom facilities. I hear they are quite good.'

'When do you want us to go?'

'It's up to you; but do the journey in daylight. Oh, and keep an eye on Pippa: it is said that the men are on a sex rampage and stretching the resources of the local availability, if you understand my meaning.'

Clarissa finished what she was doing and then looked for Pippa. She found her cleaning out the back of the ambulance.

'We have a task.'

Pippa looked up.

'We have to go to town and collect two new girls and some stores. We have to do it in daylight so could we get there today?'

Pippa checked the time. 'Yes, unless we have a breakdown or we meet a lot of traffic on the road.'

'Let's go first thing in the morning, then. By the way, we can get a hot bath whilst there,' replied Clarissa; then she added, 'Madeline said to say that the place will be packed with sex-starved men so to be very careful.'

'I will pack my make-up,' quipped Pippa.

The pair slipped away at dawn, leaving a quiet aid post. The journey was uneventful apart from the movement of vehicles and people along the one road. They were quite pleased to eventually drive into the town. Keeping to the main road, they looked out for the hotel. When it was spotted, they pulled up outside. Entering, they were aware that they looked scruffy in their uniforms and from the dust created by the mass movement of transport. Clarissa went to the reception and spoke to an elderly man. It was at this moment that she was pleased that her French lessons had been forced on her. She found out which room her two nurses were in and that the man could prepare hot baths for them. Clarissa told Pippa to keep an eye on the baths whilst she went to rouse the girls.

Clarissa knocked on the door. Nothing. She knocked again.

'I say, are you in there?' she called.

The door opened and she stood looking at a young woman dressed in a good dress, albeit quite crumpled.

'Hello. I am Clarissa, a nurse with Madeline. I have come to collect you.'

The woman's face broke into a broad smile.

'Hello,' she said. 'It's good to see you.'

Then a head peered round the door revealing the second girl.

'Look, you get yourselves sorted out. The ambulance driver, Pippa and I are going to take our baths. We will see you downstairs for something to eat before we go.'

Two heads nodded. 'See you shortly,' they replied.

Downstairs, Clarissa and Pippa were shown to the hotel's two bathrooms. They had baths with hot water and the luxury of some sort of perfumed bath oil added to it. They had both brought a change of uniform; not that that improved their appearance.

When they had finished, they went to find the two nurses. They were dressed in their de Rouche - styled khaki uniforms. They all went into the restaurant to see what could be obtained. The man who had been on reception came in to tell them what was available. He explained that he got his supplies from his brother who was living in Paris. Orders were placed. Then the new girls wanted to know everything about what was happening at the aid post. It was the last thing that Clarissa and Pippa wanted to talk about and they turned the conversation round to enquire about life back at home. The meal was the best they had eaten for a long time. For the two new girls, it was the worst. They were clearly in for a shock. Clarissa told the girls to go and get the supplies and their bags so that once they were ready, they would load the stores and journey back to the front.

With the girls gone to get their things, Clarissa and Pippa sat drinking what could pass for proper coffee. Then two soldiers decided to impose themselves on them. Their language was crude, as were their suggestions.

'Go away, please,' declared Clarissa.

'Ah, miss hoity-toity. You need a good seeing-to.'

Before anything else could be said, the confrontation was halted.

'Right, lads; move along. Stop pestering the ladies,' said a voice with authority.

The two soldiers were not impressed that they were being ordered to leave what might be interesting conquests consenting or otherwise. But it was a sergeant who was telling them what to do so they slowly stood and departed.

'Perhaps see you later…ladies,' said one of the men.

'Sorry about that, ladies,' said the sergeant.

Clarissa had her back to the sergeant but she knew his voice.

'Thomas? Is it really you?' asked an excited Clarissa.

She had leapt to her feet, turned and, on seeing that it was Thomas, flung her arms round his neck and hugged him. Then, in her usual way, she kissed him. In his excitement he responded and they stood for several moments in an embrace. When they separated, Clarissa remembered she was with Pippa.

'Thomas, this is Pippa: she drives our ambulance. Pippa, this is Thomas.'

'I have heard a lot about you,' said Pippa with an impish grin.

With introductions accomplished, they exchanged general information about what they had been up to. Pippa felt she should leave them to chat; she went to find the two girls and then to load the stores into the ambulance. Clarissa could have stayed forever, but they had to get back. With everybody loaded into the ambulance, Thomas stood and waved them off. He waited until they turned a corner and were gone.

He had begun to walk the length of the main street when a soldier came to find him. He was summoned to the Squadron HQ to meet Captain Houghton.

Thomas reported and was ushered into a tent situated on the edge of town which contained the HQ. He saluted.

'You wanted to see me, sir?'

'Yes, Sergeant Pierce. I have some unfortunate news for you. I understand that you speak damn' good German.'

'Yes, sir; not too bad,' answered a puzzled Thomas.

'Right, well: up at the front they have captured a number of the Hun but there is nobody who speaks the language. You are required to go back to the line and translate during the interrogations. I know that you have only just got here, but they are desperate and you are the nearest German-speaking solider we have or that they could identify. I have written out your orders.'

Thomas was numb. He took the document and put it in his jacket pocket.

'I'll get my things and get going, sir.' He saluted.

Thomas collected his kit. The only thing that buoyed his despair was the meeting with Clarissa. That had been wonderful.

Thomas had to get to the front; he was making his way to the edge of town when he came across some Royal Horse Artillery men with a number of horses that were destined for their unit at the front line. He had no transport organised so volunteered to help them get the mounts to the gun teams. The ride was uneventful, and he parted company with both men and horses close to the front. He diverted off the main road and followed a smaller road as he began the trek to the trenches, fully aware that as he got closer he would be more exposed. There was a small amount of comfort and safety to be gained when he reached and entered the communications trench. He was now less exposed to machine-gun fire, but artillery shells could drop in and send their deadly contents along the trench, shredding everything in their path. When he reached the main fire trench, he asked where the officers were located. Soldiers pointed along the trench and so he plodded along in that direction. He eventually found two officers and told them that he was seeking out the captured Germans. They told him that they had been taken back to a location away from the trench and gave him directions. He continued to make his way along the trench until he met a corporal who had been sent to guide him to the dugout where four German soldiers were being held.

When Thomas arrived at the dugout, a major and a captain were standing outside; he reported to the major.

'Thank you for coming to help us out, sergeant. We know you should be back resting, but we are in a frightful muddle. We understand that you speak German.'

'Yes, sir, I do.'

'We have four Huns that we managed to capture; we want to find out what we can about them and their plans. So what I suggest is that I ask a question, then you translate what I say and then tell me what they say in reply.'

'Yes, sir.'

The major led the way. It was cramped inside the dugout. The four Germans sat on the floor and two large British soldiers guarded them. The major crouched down in front of them. He spoke to one man.

'What is your name and what is your regiment?'

Thomas asked the question in German.

The German soldier answered. He gave their names. He said that they would not give any other information. Thomas repeated what the German had said.

'What is your unit and how many men are there?' asked the major.

Thomas translated. The same soldier replied. They would only give their names and numbers. The major did not need a translation.

Thomas looked at each man in turn, then at the major. He realised that the major did not recognise the ranks of the captives.

'Can we speak outside, sir?'

'Of course.'

Outside and away from the dugout, Thomas explained the situation:

'The one who is answering the questions is of equivalent rank to a captain. The one with the large moustache is a corporal; the others are private soldiers,' said Thomas. 'Nobody will say anything with the officer there.'

The major called his captain outside to confer.

'If it would help, I will just have a general chat with them and see how that goes,' said Thomas.

The major nodded, 'All right.'

Thomas went back in and chatted to them. His questions were general, such as: how long had they been in the front line? Did they have families? Where did they come from? The two private soldiers relaxed a little and began to answer. That was until the captain snarled at them to be quiet. Thomas went back outside to speak to the major, leaving them under guard.

'Sir, if they can be separated I may be able to get the privates talking. The captain is of the Prussian school and will never speak. The corporal may also hinder their talking.'

The major agreed and the German captain was moved to a separate dugout along with three guards. The corporal was also moved outside under guard. Thomas went back inside with the two privates. He sat down again and offered them cigarettes and gave them coffee. The coffee was more for his benefit than for the Germans'. They chatted for about fifteen minutes before Thomas was called outside again.

'Have they said anything?' said the impatient major.

'They are part of an infantry division, new to the front line. It has been moved up ready for some sort of big push. They have been told that it will be the last big battle and will decide the war. The one interesting point is that they say ammunition is low and that there are complaints about the lack of food. I think they are telling the truth.'

'Thank you, sergeant,' said the major. 'We will recommend a plan for a full-scale defence and be ready to counter-attack. It will not do any harm; meantime we will send the Hun back to our HQ for a full debrief by the intelligence people in due course. You can return to your unit. Good luck; and thanks again.'

The ambulance drove into the area in front of the aid post. Clarissa could see how busy they were and that they had arrived back just in time. Pippa was left to unload the ambulance whilst the new girls were given aprons. Without any discussion, Clarissa led the two girls into the foray of their treatment rooms. Damaged bodies were everywhere and those they could not treat were loaded onto the constant convoy of ambulances to be moved to the field hospital.

In between treating patients, de Rouche welcomed the two new girls to the reality of the Western Front. They had been selected as "the right sort" and, as expected, had got stuck in. Fortunately, they had been working in a London hospital; but this was a totally different situation. De Rouche asked Clarissa about the trip and was told about the soak in a hot bath. Pippa walked in at that moment and regaled them with the story of her meeting Thomas. It was, amidst the death and gore, a moment of light relief. Then reality returned. Bodies needed treating.

'There is some bad news,' said de Rouche.

Clarissa looked at her, in anticipation of the news being expanded upon.

'Kitty was taking water out to the walking wounded who were on the road. An artillery shell landed amongst them. She never stood a chance. It is a sad loss: she was a nice gal.'

Clarissa momentarily stopped, closed her eyes, then regained her composure and carried on bandaging a soldier.

'How long is it going to go on for?' was the question she asked herself, as well as anybody else who could hear.

'Until it ends, my dear,' replied de Rouche. 'Then we wait for the next one; which will be equally bad, if not worse than this.'

Then, as always happened, the last casualty was sent off; and a sense of sanity, as far as they knew it, began to return to the post. The new girls were introduced to everybody and shown the ropes of surviving in the primitive conditions. The two nurses who had initially travelled out with Clarissa could now return to England for a well-earned rest. For the time being, de Rouche, Clarissa and Pippa would remain at the post with the two new girls.

8

Having completed his first interrogation, Thomas did not want to delay in the trenches. He had done his bit, as far as enduring hours and even days of boredom went; as well as the suicide over-the-top charges against the machine-guns. He quickly made his way back through the trenches the way he had come, where he was, to a degree, sheltered from enemy fire. Passing along the fire trench, he noted that the soldiers were already alert and that there seemed to be an awful lot of them. The German prisoners were probably right: there was going to be a big push by the Hun. He had reached the communications trench when the artillery bombardment started. He took cover as earth mixed with shrapnel blackened the sky. Unless there was a direct hit, he thought he would be all right. He could hear the noise of the wounded screaming in agony back in the main trench, where some shells had landed.

As he crouched in a dugout, a soldier scurried along and joined him. He was also heading away from the Front. At first, Thomas thought he was somebody who had cracked under the pressure of trench warfare and was running away. The soldier explained that he was a company runner, who had been tasked with getting a very important message back to his battalion HQ.

'Keep down or the shrapnel will get you,' said Thomas.

'I have to get a message through,' he replied.

He then left Thomas and moved forward through the trench as fast as the conditions would allow him, then climbed up onto the road where he was exposed.

Thomas watched him depart; he heard the scream and realised that the runner had been hit. Thomas knew that the message had to get through so he scrambled along the trench to the place where the runner had left it. He climbed up cautiously to assess the situation. He saw the soldier lying on the ground. Choosing his moment, he scrambled along the ground to reach him. The runner was alive but had serious wounds. The shells seemed to land in a sort of pattern and, as soon as there was a gap, Thomas picked up the runner, draped him over his right shoulder and moved along the rutted and shell-holed road as fast as he could. The shells that pounded the earth were not as frequent, but adrenaline was still pulsing through his body and that drove him on. A shell landed close by and the shock wave blew him over. He had to summon every ounce of his strength to get up and lift the soldier back over his shoulder. It was then that he felt a burning sensation in his left leg; but to stop, he reasoned, would mean certain death so he carried on. He did not contemplate the fact that continuing was equally risky.

He carried the soldier to the aid post, but it had been evacuated. Looking around, he could see that it had suffered from enemy shell fire. It was a question of survival and, with the runner still over his shoulder, he continued along the road towards the field hospital. He knew it was a long way but he had no other option. He could feel a warm wetness on his leg but he felt no pain. He knew that he was wounded, but had no idea how badly. He had to get to them both to safety as he had no field dressings to undertake any first aid. His brain told him that he was alive and so he pressed on. He remembered staggering to reach the hospital, and seeing the lines of bodies outside the numerous tents that served as wards and surgical theatres. In front of some orderlies who were running towards him, his body shut down and he just collapsed. The blood-soaked injured runner collapsed on top of him.

At the field hospital, the huge volume of wounded were assessed. Those who were considered to have little chance of survival were made comfortable, leaving the surgical teams to concentrate on those likely to survive. Thomas, who was covered in blood, was laid down in a line of men who were all seriously wounded. Because the medical staff were unable to cope with the influx of broken bodies, it was a matter of luck as to who got treated. The hundreds wounded had to wait until a doctor could attend to them. In the meantime, the orderlies and nurses did their best with the wounded men. They made a list using their identity tags, and they recorded the types of wounds they appeared to have.

De Rouche and her nursing team at the aid station endured the artillery bombardment until it became unsafe for them to stay. Shells were falling very close by so they escaped, accompanying their patients back to the field hospital. The matron, who despised the part-time nursing heroines, accepted that they would be accommodated at the field hospital, and that they would do their job nursing the injured arriving from the front until it was safe for them to return to their aid post at the Front. Clarissa was passing the rows of wounded when she heard an orderly call out the name Thomas Pierce. She stopped: had she heard right?

'What name did you just call out?' she asked the orderly.

'Thomas Pierce, miss.'

She stood looking down at the soldier covered in blood.

'Not a lot of hope for him, miss,' said the orderly.

She moved closer and could see that it was indeed Thomas, her Thomas.

'Help me get him into the surgical tent,' she shouted at the two orderlies.

'He hasn't been assessed yet, miss.'

'I have assessed him and I know him, so help me move him.'

The orderlies picked Thomas up and carried him to the surgical tents, with Clarissa leading the way. She checked each tent until she found an empty one.

'In here,' she commanded the orderlies.

The surgeon had just finished an operation and an orderly was washing things down.

'Dr Bloom, will you please look at my friend? He's badly injured. said Clarissa.

Bloom smiled. 'What's his name?'

'Thomas Pierce. In the past, he saved my life twice; I need to save his now - with your help, of course.'

Bloom nodded to the orderlies carrying Thomas, who then lifted him onto the operating table.

Clarissa looked at the two orderlies: 'Thank you very much.'

Whilst they returned to identifying the wounded, Clarissa stood by to assist Bloom. They both looked down at the blood-saturated body of Thomas. He was not awake. In an automatic action born out of long practice, they both began to cut away his clothing. They were astounded not to discover any life-threatening wound. He was alive and breathing. Further investigation revealed the rather nasty shrapnel wound in his leg. Clarissa cleaned away the blood and then Bloom examined the damage.

'I will remove the shrapnel and then the wound can be

sterilised. I will leave the stitching-up to you. If infection can be kept out, then he may well keep his leg,' said Bloom.

They set to and Bloom removed three pieces of steel. An orderly came past and asked how the soldier was doing.

'He is doing fine,' said Bloom. 'Do you know him?'

'No, I dealt with him when he arrived. He had carried an injured runner from the line to get him here, but the runner had bled to death. So he was covered in the other man's blood. Anyway, the runner's message got through. I think he's just collapsed from exhaustion. Hope he's all right.'

Bloom looked at Clarissa.

'That explains why he was out for the count: he's actually asleep.' He then added, 'Let's keep this Sergeant Pierce between us. No need for Matron to know. Don't want to rock the boat. You know how she hates you independent Madeline de Rouche nurses.'

'We know she doesn't like us; so we avoid her like the plague,' replied Clarissa, smiling.

'Well, we doctors admire the work you do and it has certainly saved a good number of lives which otherwise would have been lost.'

Clarissa was the happiest she had been in a long while. Their efforts were appreciated by the people who mattered most, the doctors; and Thomas, who she left a few days ago in the town, was going to be all right. She wondered why he was at the front instead of resting in the town.

When Thomas awoke, he was unsure where he was. He realised that he was in a bed and in a tent, a large one. He thought it must be late as it was not very light. He saw the figure of a nurse passing and called to her. She explained that he was in a field hospital, having had surgery on his left leg. Now he was awake said that she would let his guardian angel know. When he asked who that was, she just smiled.

He had no idea of time, but it was only about fifteen minutes later when another nurse attended his bed. She was unlike the other one, who wore a white uniform with some evidence of wounded soldiers on her apron. This one was in khaki, and wore riding breeches. She hovered over him.

'Well, Thomas Pierce: I left you safe in a town away from the front and now I find that you've got yourself into a right mess.'

Thomas stared into the gloom.

'Lady Clarissa, is that you?

'Yes, Thomas; and it's just Clarissa. You have had an operation on your left leg to remove shrapnel. It will mend and your leg will be all right. But for now, you have to take it easy. You will have some scars, but that should be all. You will keep your good looks.'

'I remember carrying a soldier back. He had a message for HQ. Is he all right?'

'He did not make it and he absolutely covered you in blood, which caused us some alarm; but the message got through.'

'Is this where you work?'

'No, I work on the front line in a forward dressing station. That's why we have to dress like this. A normal nurse's uniform would be impractical and we would stand out as targets for enemy snipers. We got shelled out and came back here. We are waiting to go back so we can carry on.'

'Bloody hell, that was the place I went to on the way back,' was all he could say.

'Rest now and we will chat later.' She leaned over and kissed his forehead.

Clarissa was confronted by the matron of the hospital on her way out of the ward.

'Nurse, I know you are not one of my nurses, but fraternisation with patients in this hospital is forbidden. I know your nursing under Madeline de Rouche is unconventional and that you may not adhere to the standards of propriety that we do; but I must insist that when you are in this hospital, you abide by our rules. Your actions could influence my nurses and give the soldiers the wrong message. Have I made myself clear?'

Clarissa glared at Matron for a moment, then answered,

'You have made yourself perfectly clear. However, the soldier in question is Thomas Pierce. I have known him for many years, in fact he saved my life twice and is a part of the family. He resides at Winslade Hall. In fact I know him so well that after the war, if we both survive, we intend to become even better acquainted; that would be officially, of course.'

The two women looked at one another, neither wanting to give ground.

'Consider what I have said or I might have to speak to Miss de Rouche on the matter.'

'I will visit Sergeant Pierce each day I am here. I will not interfere with his medical or nursing care; if you have any other concerns, then please speak to Miss de Rouche.'

Clarissa then turned and walked away. She felt she had held her ground.

Having seen Thomas every day, it was on the third day when Clarissa came to see him to say that she was returning, with her fellow nurses, to the aid station. She gave him letters to post for the family and one for an Aunt Josephine. If he was allowed to go home straight away, then he could hand over the letters personally. She leaned over to bid him farewell and kissed him, much to his embarrassment and the delight of those around him. He told her to take great care.

His next visitor was an older woman, dressed in the same khaki nurse's uniform.

'My name is Madeline de Rouche: I am in charge of the aid post and have heard a lot about you from Clarissa. She's a great gal. I just came by to give you this.'

She handed him a photograph of Clarissa in her uniform at the aid post. To Thomas she looked more like a soldier than a nurse.

'Thank you,' said Thomas. 'Thank you very much.'

'That's quite all right. Get well and take care of yourself: you will have a great future together.'

Then she was gone. But Thomas had a memento to treasure.

Three days after Clarissa had departed for the front, a doctor did his rounds to decide which patients would be transported home and which ones were fit enough to go back to their Battalions and Squadrons. He inspected Thomas's leg and noted that he had been mobile, albeit with the aid of crutches.

'How long have you been out here?' asked the doctor.

'I think it's ten months or a year,' replied Thomas.

'All right, back to Blighty and get the leg checked out properly.'

Thomas did not argue.

His next visitor did. Major Crisp arrived in his nice neat uniform and confronted Thomas.

'Sergeant Pierce,' he said, the plum-stone in his mouth almost making the words inaudible. He did not wait for a response.

'You have been difficult to track down. Now, staff at General Headquarters understand that you speak good

German and did a splendid job interrogating some captured Hun. The situation is that we have a growing number of prisoners, but not enough people to interrogate them. So, staff at HQ require your presence to undertake interrogations. What do you say?'

Thomas opened his mouth to raise an objection, but Crisp continued.

'We have good medical facilities at HQ, so you will be looked after and we can get you kitted out in a proper uniform.'

'I am going back to Blighty, to a hospital to get my leg checked and then some home leave, sir.'

'Oh, I've sorted that out. That is all postponed for now. A car will pick you up in the morning and bring you to HQ. Carry on, sergeant.'

'Not as nice as the nurse,' said a grinning soldier in the next bed.

Thomas laughed. 'Bet this is the closest he's been to the front line. He soon scampered back to safety.'

After breakfast Thomas said cheerio to as many people as possible. He had written a short letter to Clarissa, telling her what was happening. An ambulance orderly returning to the front promised to pass it on. The car was waiting as arranged and he joined the driver, in the front passenger seat, having reassured him that he had been deloused and scrubbed top to bottom with disinfectant. The driver was an older man and keen to get going: even the field hospital was too close to the front. He obviously preferred the HQ to being closer to the front line. Little conversation passed between them. They passed medical transport returning from the channel ports, where they had delivered Blighty-bound wounded, as well as lines of soldiers going towards the front. They were constantly held up by the slow progress of ambulances taking the wounded to the ports. In any event, Thomas shared the view that if you hadn't been there, you couldn't talk about it.

The journey for Thomas was uncomfortable, as the car seemingly found every pothole on the thirty-mile stretch of road. So he was pleased when the driver steered the car into the grounds of a very elegant-looking chateau that had been commandeered as a Head Quarters. They did not go to the front entrance but went round the back and stopped at a door which, by the time Thomas had alighted from the vehicle, was open and filled by a fearsome-looking nursing sister, in a very neat pristine white uniform. She marched across to greet him.

'Are you Sergeant Thomas Pierce?'

'Yes,' said Thomas.

She told the driver to put Thomas's bag in her office, then directed her next command to Thomas.

'Right, follow me,' she said, leading Thomas across the courtyard to an outbuilding. She entered and he followed. In a room was a bath which she began to fill with hot water.

'Undress and put your clothes in that bin: you won't need them again. Then get in the bath and scrub yourself from top to bottom. Get rid of any lice. Do a good job or somebody will do it for you.'

Thomas did as he was biden, removing personal items from the pockets. Once he was in the bath, he had to admit that it was a really welcome feeling, to relax and feel properly clean. He had scrubbed and dried himself by the time the sister returned carrying a new army uniform for him.

'Let me look at your wound,' she said.

After careful inspection and some prodding, she wound a fresh bandage on it.

'It's mending well,' she remarked.

She then told him to get dressed.

'You can use one crutch to help you move about, but we need to get the leg working again,' she commanded.

Once he was ready, she led the way to the kitchen.

'Right, cook, would you give this man some food,' she said as she marched away.

Thomas got on well with cooks and he was soon being well looked-after. He was amazed at the quantity and quality of the food. He was pleasantly relaxed when an orderly arrived to take him to meet the Brigadier. In the outer office a sergeant inspected him, tut-tutting the whole time.

'I suppose you'll have to do. Do you really need that crutch?'

'Sister told me to use it, Sergeant.'

'Well, if Sister said so, then you had better use it.'

The sergeant knocked on the door.

'Enter,' boomed a voice.

Both men entered what was, in more normal times, a large dining-room. Now it served as the Brigadier's war room. He noted that a captain was in the room and stood away from the Brigadier's desk.

'Ah, Sergeant Pierce, come in. Take a seat. I trust you have seen Sister and been fed?'

'Yes, sir.'

'Good. Now, sorry to spoil your leave prospects, but we have a problem. We have captured a number of the Hun, but we do not have enough German speakers to interrogate them. Our biggest problem is the officers: of course they have the vital information we need. So we need you to interrogate those we are holding. It may be best if you start with a private soldier and see how it goes. Are you up to having a crack at it now?'

'Yes, sir.'

'Good man. Captain Goodbody will take you to the holding place and you can begin. Anything you need, just ask.'

'Yes, sir.' Thomas saluted and followed the captain out of the room. The sergeant was waiting for them.

'You had better have this until we can get the stripes sewn onto the uniform,' said the sergeant, handing Thomas an armband with three stripes on it.

'Thanks.'

The interrogation room was in fact a stable area, and it had a faint smell of manure which instantly reminded Thomas of Winslade Hall which in turn reminded him of Clarissa. His day-dream was soon disrupted when he was brought back to reality by Captain Goodbody.

'It's pretty basic but it serves its purpose.'

Thomas surveyed the place. It had a table with a chair at either side. A light bulb hung down over the table. There was a pen and paper on one side of the table.

'I shall remain in the room without being involved in the interrogation, unless you need my input. We will wait outside until the Hun is brought in.'

A German private soldier was escorted into the room and seated on one of the chairs. A well-built British army private stood guard. Captain Goodbody and Thomas entered the room. Walking over to the table, Thomas looked down at the German. He was young and, judging by his uniform, had not been on the front line for very long. Thomas sat down opposite him. There was no reaction from the German and Thomas realised that he was just terrified, having been drawn into a war and told bad things about the Englanders and what they did to prisoners. He was clearly worried about his fate. Thomas offered the man a cigarette and then a light. The soldier thanked Thomas.

Thomas let him draw on the cigarette a couple of times before asking him his name, rank and number in German. That put the man slightly off his guard. He had been told that German officers spoke English but that the Englanders did not speak German. He now sat opposite a sergeant who spoke very good German. The soldier replied with the information. Thomas made notes. As they progressed, the tension relaxed and the interrogation became more of a conversation between two friends. The German knew that neither of the other two men in the room understood what was being said and so this was a personal conversation. It was between two men, thrown into a conflict that neither wanted. Whilst the man gave information, Thomas continued to note it down.

Eventually Thomas decided that they had reached a point where there was little else to add, so the session was ended. Whilst the German was taken back to the holding area, Thomas went back into the chateau to an office where four females manned typewriters and telephones. He was introduced to one of them and the process of producing a report began. He gave her his notes and where needed he dictated; she, using shorthand, scribbled on a pad then typed up the result. Thomas edited it, it was retyped and passed to Captain Goodbody. He departed for a meeting with the Brigadier. They were pleased with the information that had been obtained. It gave a clear picture of the state of morale of the other side.

The following morning, Thomas returned to the interrogation room and confronted a German officer. From the moment they met, the German threw obscenities at Thomas. He would not communicate with a common soldier. He was an officer and his superior class told people like Thomas what to do; they did not tell them what they wanted to know.

Captain Goodbody stood and watched the spectacle as Thomas tried to communicate. Then he interrupted Thomas and asked what the German was saying.

'He says that he is a German officer and does not speak to common soldiers like me. He will only speak to a fellow officer.'

Goodbody ordered the German to be taken back to his cell. Thomas could relax whilst Goodbody was off seeing the Brigadier. Thomas went and saw the cook, who gave him coffee and some sort of local bun. An hour later, Thomas was summoned to the Brigadier's office. He arrived and the sergeant checked him to ensure that he was smart enough to enter, this being part of the formalities of HQ. In the room there were about eight officers, of varying ranks and regiments, standing round the table and examining a large map.

The Brigadier looked up. Thomas saluted.

'Ah, Sergeant Pierce, come in. Please relax; this is an informal meeting.'

The other officers all looked at Thomas in such a way that he felt really out-of-place amidst their smart uniforms.

'Your interrogation of the German soldier yesterday revealed some interesting information. Well done. I understand that the officer is not playing the game?'

'That's right, sir. As an officer he will only speak to an officer.'

'That is not a problem. As of now, you are Lieutenant Pierce. That should stop his nonsense. So, can you have another crack at him?'

'Right, sir. Yes, sir, be pleased to.'

'Sergeant Reilly,' boomed the voice of the Brigadier.

The door opened and Reilly entered. 'Yes, sir?'

'Sergeant. Pierce has just been promoted to Lieutenant so can you take him to be kitted-out and accommodated. He has already been groomed in the ways of a gentleman, so there should be no problems there.'

'Very good, sir.'

'If you would follow me, Mr Pierce.'

Thomas followed, quite lost for words. They arrived at a store where he was provided with a uniform. One of the other officer's servants was summoned to show him how to dress. He would be provided with his own man in due course. He then moved his scant belongings to a room allocated to him in the officers' quarters. Once he was sorted out, he lost no time in returning to the interrogation centre and having the German officer brought to the room.

The German entered and sat down. He glared at Thomas.

'So, you have changed your uniform and you now appear to be an officer. Of course you are not a real officer, not a gentleman, not from a proper family.'

Thomas did not take the bait. He was, after all, a poacher at heart.

He asked questions, and when the German answered he made a note. He was looking for any weak spot which he could focus on. The interrogation had been going on for about an hour when the German asked why they had promoted Thomas, and not simply found a German-speaking officer.

Thomas saw an opportunity to target the man's vanity.

'We have so many prisoners - hundreds in fact - that we have run out of German speakers. I was brought from hospital to take up duties here. They assessed you all as being all low-key soldiers of little value being held here, and judged that I would be able to deal with you.'

As Thomas predicted, the German flew into a violent rage, thumping the table. The guards moved forward but Thomas motioned for them to stay where they were. He let the officer rant and sat back to observe. At any opportune moment, he fed the man's anger with comments about his low standing. The German responded with odd statements comments, purporting to show that he was important, somebody to be reckoned with. Slowly information flowed, a bit at a time. He claimed that they had been successful in Russia and had been withdrawn to serve on the Western Front. They were an elite battle-hardened unit, and would easily crush the Englanders and the French. After two hours there was a lot of information to digest; Thomas stopped the interrogation and the officer was taken away, still ranting. Thomas would leave him to stew until the following day.

Whilst the first day's interrogation was being typed up, Thomas continued questioning the German officer. This continued for three days. The German started each session in control of himself then, when bated with information that the Germans were losing ground with considerable losses of men with the consequent downgrading of the German officer class, he began to rage. They eventually reached the point where Thomas had taken the interrogation as far as he could. His notes were typed up. He edited the proof copy; when he was satisfied that he had covered all the options, he handed the report to Captain Goodbody.

The following morning when Thomas went to the prisoner holding centre to interrogate his next prisoner, he found it deserted. No prisoners and no guards. He returned to the main building and searched for Captain Goodbody. He was nowhere to be found. As a last resort, he went to Sergeant Reilly.

'Good morning, sir,' he said, as Thomas stood in front of his desk.

'Your report has really stirred things up.' Nodding towards the closed door, he said, 'We've got more generals in there. Been at it all night, never seen anything like it.' You, sir, are a bleedin' marvel. If I may suggest it, sir, you might go and wait in the mess until they have finished.'

'Right-o, sergeant, thanks.'

It was mid-afternoon when Thomas was summoned. The Brigadier told him that his work, whilst unconventional, was invaluable. He was handed an order to attend a hospital in England for a check-up, then to take two weeks' leave. He was also given a letter confirming his promotion. He would be notified about a new posting in due course; being an interrogation officer was certainly an option.

Before his departure he wrote a lengthy letter to Clarissa, explaining what had happened. The following day, Thomas began the journey back to England, a hospital and then Winslade Hall.

9

Thomas had notified Lord Overbury of his pending arrival and Oliver was at the railway station to meet him. They hugged each other as friends as well as comrades-in-arms, each knowing what the other had endured. Thomas was impressed with how well Oliver was walking and indeed how well he looked in general. As the car made its way to the Hall, they laughed and joked about things of no importance. Thomas was given all the local gossip and news of the changes that had taken place since he had been away. Both men considered the contrast between the war zone on the continent and England, where-on the face of it, the conflict did not seem to have had any great effect. The twenty or so miles between England and the continent was a true divide.

As the car travelled along the drive, Thomas reflected on the past when he had escorted Clarissa on her riding ventures. The necessary protocol when he rode behind her, compared to the closeness when they were out of sight. He was here now, but she was still in a living hell. As they approached the front door, the family stood on the steps and the staff stood on the driveway, all waiting to greet him.

Lord Overbury welcomed him back first, followed by the family then the staff. Soames, formal to the end with his greeting; Miss Smith, the housekeeper who had done so much to help him, behaved like a proud mother. Rosie flung her arms round his neck and kissed him on his cheek. Mrs Brown said he needed feeding up. Bert Moore shook hands and welcomed him home and Thomas asked how Mrs Moore was. Then there was a warm greeting from Devline, who said that he had been missed and that the estate office was not the same without him.

Miss Smith led the way to his new room, explaining that his Lordship was responsible for the change. Thomas was now an officer in the army and therefore was to be treated as such. He was embarrassed at the situation, but was consoled when Smith told him that although he might have the uniform, he was still the same Thomas wearing it. The room was more than he could ever have expected. Smith went to the wardrobe and opened it.

'Mr Oliver selected some clothes for you and we hope they fit. When you change, we shall arrange for your uniform to be cleaned,' she said, smiling.

'Thank you.'

As she was leaving, she said, 'Oh, Thomas, one more thing: the family expect you to dine with them this evening. If you are worried about anything, please let me know.'

She was gone before he could respond. He really had landed in another world.

The three men met in his Lordship's study prior to dinner. Thomas was full of thanks for the welcome he had been given and for the changes to his status, which he said he would try to adapt to as quickly as possible. Overbury and Oliver went out of their way to make the transition as smooth as possible. It was Oliver who asked the questions about the Front; when information from Thomas was slow in forthcoming, Oliver quietly understood. Thomas changed the subject by handing Overbury the photograph.

'This is a photograph of Lady Clarissa in her working attire. It was given to me by Miss de Rouche when I was at the field hospital. I can't begin to tell you what a good and valuable job she is doing. Of course, she fits very well into that type of nursing. You will have news of her through the letters I posted.'

'She doesn't say much; not allowed to, or more probably does not want to worry us. She says it's all going well; like one of our picnics,' said Overbury.

Oliver laughed. "Well, our picnics have never been that adventurous.'

Overbury held out the photograph to Thomas.

'The photograph is yours, sir,' said Thomas.

'I am sure she would prefer you to have it. Anyway, it looks a bit too dramatic for her Ladyship to see.'

'Thank you, sir,' said Thomas, smiling. He put it carefully in his pocket.

Before anything more could be said, Soames announced that dinner was served.

Thomas survived dinner, and after an early breakfast Overbury suggested that they take a walk. The grand views of well-kept grounds were a pleasure and the war seemed a million miles away.

'How do you think Oliver is doing?' asked Overbury.

'Very well. In fact, much better than I expected.'

'He really likes having you around. You have something in common that none of us who have not experienced it can begin to comprehend.'

'I would agree. It is difficult for those at home to understand.'

'Do you have any idea where they will post you? I presume you will go back to the front.'

'When I left, I was told that I might become an

interrogator, because I speak German and seem to have a knack of extracting information.'

'That would be an interesting job.'

'May I speak frankly, sir?'

'Of course.'

'I don't understand trench warfare. We send thousands of good men over the top against machine guns. We make very little progress and have causalities beyond real description.'

'It's all new and very unfamiliar. Warfare has changed and become mechanised; the generals are having to learn and adapt. Many of the senior officers led soldiers in the old ways and do not want to change. As you and Oliver have said, you cannot use a cavalry charge against machine guns,' replied Overbury.

'I understand that, but once you learn that you cannot charge machine guns either on horse or foot you do not continue to do so. It just means wholesale slaughter; new ways have to be found.'

'The problem is that changes have to be formulated and that takes time. The higher echelons do not work very quickly. They are used to horse-and-cart warfare.'

Thomas was still impatient.

'When I interrogated prisoners, the one thing all the Germans said was that they are generally well-supplied. The allies have to haul equipment over long distances and have to cross the Channel. One thing I did learn was that a main German supply line is along the river Rhine. One soldier opened up and told me that before the war, he worked on a boat moving goods up and down the Rhine. He said that there were arms depots sited along the river, with railway lines running towards France and Belgium. This meant that the armaments factories put their equipment in boats and transported it to a depot. Once at a depot, it could be stored and either sent to the front line or moved to another area where it was needed. This means that boats carrying goods to supply depots on the river could be vulnerable to attack. My thoughts are that a small, specially-trained unit could use the river: to infiltrate Germany, to seek out and destroy supply depots and even to attack the armaments factories sited along the Rhine.'

Overbury did not answer immediately but thought about what Thomas had said.

Overbury, a colonel in the City of London Rifles who were tasked with guarding important places in London, was aware that in political circles, there was a great deal of concern about the losses and the stagnant situation of the war. He thought that Thomas had the makings of an idea that needed to be explored. The Boers operated effectively behind the lines in South Africa: why not an operation in Europe? He knew a prominent MP who might be interested in such a venture.

'Thomas, you may have a point. I have to go to London tomorrow and I will speak to some people I know. In fact, why don't you accompany me, and if anybody is interested then you can answer any questions. We will, for the time being, keep this to ourselves. It may come to something or it may not.'

10

Overbury and Thomas departed Winslade Hall before any of the family were awake. After a hasty breakfast and car journey to the railway station, they were ensconced in a first class carriage. Overbury spend most of the journey engrossed in documents whilst Thomas admired the passing scenery and pondered on the possible prospects of his idea. London was busy, but it had an air of doom and gloom even though the war was a long way away. Newspapers recounted the mounting death tolls in the various campaigns.

In London, Overbury hailed a taxi and they went to the Officers' Club. Thomas was signed in by Overbury as a guest, following which they went in search of a very senior officer who Overbury knew. He was found reading a daily newspaper. Looking up, he saw that it was Overbury, and after warm greetings between two old comrades he beckoned him to sit. Thomas sat close by so that he could listen.

'General, I have something that I would like to discuss with you as I value your opinion.'

'Fire away, old chap.'

'This is Lieutenant Pierce. When not at war, he is my junior estate manager. He has just completed a long tour on the front line, as well as being involved in the interrogation of German prisoners. As a result of his experiences, he has an outline proposal for a plan that would involve taking a ship down the Rhine with a small group of well-trained soldiers, to attack armaments stores and fuel depots as well as armaments factories.'

The general listened until Overbury was finished.

'I have been in the army for most of my life and I have never heard of anything so preposterous. It's not proper war, not playing the game: it's just not British.' He turned to look at Thomas. 'Get back to the front line and do your duty. Don't meddle in military planning.' He looked back at Overbury. 'I am surprised that you even contemplated the very thought of such an endeavour.'

'I am sorry you feel that way,' said Overbury. 'I apologise for disturbing you.'

Overbury stood and shook hands with the General as gentlemen did. Thomas followed Overbury back onto the street and into a taxi. The Houses of Parliament was their destination. From the gatehouse office, a telephone call was made to the office of Ian Boswell, MP. The question was simple: Lord Overbury wanted to meet urgently with Mr Boswell. The answer was straightforward: his Lordship should enter the main hall of the House where he would be met and taken to Mr Boswell's office.

Overbury had been at school with Boswell and they had remained firm friends over the years. In the office they chatted generally about their respective families. Boswell looked at the clock.

'We should get on. What can I do for you?'

'It's more about what I might be able to do for you.'

'Right, you have my attention. I do hope it's better news than what we have been experiencing lately.'

Overbury gave an overview of the plan that Thomas had proposed. He explained that it was more of a thought process than a detailed plan at present. He focused on the points of a daring military success, albeit of limited proportions. In such a situation it would be a morale-booster. He then produced a document providing the information he had imparted, with more details of the concept. He finished with the view that there seemed to be little feeling in the country, aside from doom and gloom. The losses of men were high, the Germans had more of everything as well as quicker production and supply. A strike at the Hun in the Fatherland must be good for all concerned.

Boswell sat through the briefing without comment. He contemplated what had been said.

'Would you propose that Lieutenant Pierce lead this operation?'

'I would. He is very capable and speaks excellent German.'

Overbury had Boswell's full attention and, having heard the idea, he commented: 'We had considerable experience in the Boer War of unconventional warfare and its successes. I am very intrigued by the concept. I am seeing the Prime Minister this afternoon and would like to discuss the matter with him. Where is Pierce now?'

'I left him at the gatehouse. They would not let him enter with me.'

'How long are you in London?'

'We were going to travel back tomorrow afternoon, but we are avail able if required. Oh, just one point: Pierce is due to return from leave in a few days' time and return to the Front.'

'Do you have his details?'

'Yes.' He handed over a note of them. 'I prepared the information just in case. I have also included contact details for us whilst we are in London.'

'Thank you. If the Prime Minister is interested, I shall get Pierce transferred to your company. That will stop the body grabbers sneaking him away.'

At the gatehouse, Overbury found Thomas talking to the gatekeepers. It was something he had noticed: no matter who a person was, Thomas was at ease with them. He had no airs and graces: he was who he was and people just had to accept that. He admired that trait in the man. Overbury acknowledged the gatekeepers as Thomas bid them farewell and joined him. He did not speak until they were clear of the area.

'Good meeting?' enquired Thomas.

'The proposal is going to be put before the Prime Minister this afternoon. So we will have to see what happens,' said a smiling Overbury. 'I think we should go to the Company Headquarters, then we can go for a spot of lunch. I can show you round the HQ because, if this plan goes ahead, you will be transferred to the Company.'

'I'm with you all the way, sir.'

Boswell had already sent a briefing note to the Prime Minister's office as an agenda item for their pre-arranged meeting. When he entered the office, the formalities were already in place. The Prime Minister wanted the proposal to be discussed first. He had taken the time to read the document himself rather than have an aide provide an overview.

'I am impressed with this brief outline proposal. It would be a small price to pay for a potentially substantial outcome in terms of possible destruction; and it would of course, be a morale-booster.'

'Those were my thoughts, sir.'

'We need, as a matter of urgency, to get the proposers of the venture in to provide more information. We will also have to get the chiefs of Staff to have representatives here to listen to them and give us their views. Because it is not a normal type of operation, I am sure there will be opposition. Can you contact these people quickly?'

'Right away, sir. If it can be done, do you want to meet today, sir?'

'Yes; otherwise we meet first thing tomorrow.'

The Prime Minister's aide stood in the background. 'We can move things round in the morning if required, sir.'

'Good; let's say ten o'clock in the war room, unless we can do it today,' replied the Prime Minister.

As soon as the meeting was concluded, Boswell contacted Overbury.

'Be ready to come this afternoon at short notice; otherwise it's at ten o'clock tomorrow morning. It will be in the war room.'

'Thank you for the update. We are ready: young Thomas just has to sell it.'

'Oh, the Prime Minister is onboard so to speak: he thinks it's a great caper. See you later; if not today, then tomorrow.'

After lunch, Overbury and Thomas spent the afternoon refining the proposal and awaiting a call. It was a forgone conclusion that the military staff would reject the proposal out of hand. But if the Prime Minister said it was going to happen, then happen it would.

It was the following morning when they entered the war room; for Thomas, like entering the lion's den, it was a dangerous and daunting place. Thomas was formally introduced to the Prime Minister. Then each of the senior army and navy officers and government figures were introduced. The mood of the room was cold, but Thomas knew that he had the stage and just had to present the proposal and answer any questions. Mr Boswell asked Thomas to brief those present on the proposal the he had first explained to Lord Overbury.

Thomas explained the concept of taking a small group of soldiers aboard a ship, down the river Rhine, to locate and destroy armaments and storage depots which would disrupt the flow of stores to the front. He was stopped by the noise of the senior military officers who poured scorn on the proposal. Their response was made very clear: there were no men who could be spared and there was no suitable ship available. They argued that, even if they could get to the river, they would be challenged then sunk and all would be lost. Thomas kept calm and, when he could, continued to outline the plan. The Prime Minister watched every move, and in particular how Thomas dealt with the situation. Having seen his calm reaction to the opposition, the meeting was called to order. The PM explained that he and his government needed some good news to counter the heavy losses on the various fronts and the growing public discontent. They wanted to avoid the problems that the French were having, with the mutiny that was occurring in their army. Their view was that, in the worst case, the loss of a few men would be nothing compared to the overall losses that were occurring with very little being gained. However, if the operation had any success, it would be good news, especially for the troops on the front line. It might even hinder Germany's war effort.

By the end of the meeting, the military had not provided a single sound reason why the operation should not go ahead, so the PM directed that the unit be formed. As Lieutenant Pierce had the right background for such an operation, with his fighting experience having been on the front line and speaking excellent German, he was the obvious person to lead it. The Prime Minister ordered the army to promote Thomas to Captain and provide him with up to thirty soldiers, plus equipment and facilities. His new unit would be attached for administration purposes to the City of London Rifles. The Prime Minister then ordered the Navy to find and provide a suitable vessel with a crew. The meeting was over. The Prime Minister thanked Thomas and wished him well with the project. He also asked to be kept informed of progress.

11

The ruling élite who provided the foundation of the British Army's officer corps were in a rage. The Prime Minister was allowing a common gamekeeper to be promoted to a position beyond his standing in society: the tradition of generations was being swept away. But worse, he was being allowed to head up some foolhardy plan that was destined for failure. The War Office dug its heels in and took the view that he could have his thirty men. However, no unit would allow any of its good men to be transferred. The Navy did not have a vessel or a crew to spare so they would seek out an unwanted craft and find some "unwanted" sailors to send on the folly.

Overbury was aware of the backlash befalling the project, but Thomas seemingly remained oblivious. When they arrived back home, Oliver was at the railway station. On the journey to Winslade Hall he wanted to know every small detail of what had happened. Later, the three men met in Overbury's study.

'Well, we now have to find you a place to operate from. The army will not be very forthcoming and my HQ in London is not really appropriate. Too many loose tongues,' said Overbury.

Oliver came up with a proposal. 'What about the old house, down by the river? It's not been used since our aunt died, but it's not in bad condition. It has outbuildings and stables, as well as the advantage of being out of sight and alongside the forest, which would be ideal for training.'

'What a splendid idea,' replied Overbury. 'It used to be where my sister lived until shortly before the start of the war. She never married and when she died, it reverted back to the family. We have not got round to doing anything with it yet.'

'What do you think about that, Thomas?' asked Overbury.

Thomas pondered, but only for a few minutes. 'Are you sure about this idea? Having all these strangers around?' As an afterthought, he added, 'We would make the Hall and grounds out of bounds.'

'That's not a problem. It's far enough away that I doubt it will cause us any issues. So that's settled then. We will go over in the morning and have a look at the place,' said Overbury.

'Oliver,' said Thomas, 'I know you are unfit for overseas service due to your injuries, but would you consider joining with me to put this plan together?'

'Would I? Oh yes, I am with you all the way; well, probably to the docks when you sail.'

The two men shook hands.

'Just one thing,' said Oliver. 'I want to make it clear that you are in charge.'

Lord Overbury was as pleased as he possibly could be under the circumstances. Oliver was needed; he was no longer just another wounded soldier with little or no future.

The following morning, they piled into a car and drove to the house. It and its outbuildings were found to be ideal. Devline organised local labour to remove furniture, clean up the property and prepare it for habitation. Overbury spent the rest of day on the telephone, organising the equipment that would be needed. That left Thomas and Oliver to begin the process of finding the men that would form the unit, as well as preparing a training plan.

Thomas did not want what the army calls “good men”, who just blindly follow orders; he wanted men who did not fit that profile. He wanted men who would think for themselves and not just wait for orders. Men who could think unconventionally, but still operate as members of a close-knit team.

Oliver declared that he would take on the task of finding potential unit members.

‘I will use the old school tie to try to open doors,’ he said.

‘I doubt that many of your old school chums will be the sort we are looking for,’ said a laughing Thomas.

‘Very true, but they have a network of contacts that we can tap into.’

Oliver began his quest at the War Office military personnel procurement office. After being passed to a number of people, he eventually reached a quiet-spoken man whose task it was to place those who were not out of the standard mould. He listened carefully as Oliver explained what he required.

‘We need poachers and/or gamekeepers, as well as men with knowledge of the countryside. Good shooting or explosives skills would be an added advantage. They do not have to be able to march well, or be very smart in their dress. They need to be able to sneak up on the enemy unseen and unheard, and they need to be able to survive off the land if necessary.’

With this picture painted, the man explained,

‘What you seek is what most units do not want. Those types who remain in units are used as snipers or runners; if not used, they are discarded as not really suitable for front-line trench warfare. This means that there are suitable people, they just need to be found. The biggest problem is recruiting for a dangerous job without but being able to say or even hint at what the job is.'

Two days later, Oliver answered the telephone. It was the man from the War Office.

'I have located a Scottish ghillie and two of his people. They were assigned to a highland regiment but there were problems and they were returned home. They are at a holding centre, awaiting assessment and re-allocation to a new unit. At the same centre there are two brothers from the East-End of London. They are described as wide-boys and scroungers. Complaints were made about equipment going missing, by other regiments and indeed companies. In the spells of inactivity when there was no fighting, these boys were at their most active.'

Oliver made careful notes.

'If you want to interview any of these people, then you will have to go to the holding centre sharpish.'

'We shall indeed want to see these chaps. When can we do that?'

'I shall telephone the centre and let them know you are coming. Do not delay, as they could get a posting any day.'

'Right-o, we will get to it. Thank you.'

Thomas and Oliver caught the very next train; after two changes and some waiting-about time, they arrived at the holding centre. They had to wait at the guardhouse until the duty officer arrived and escorted them to a room where they could speak to the men. The first to arrive were the three highlanders. They entered the room and stared at Thomas and Oliver.

'Sit down, please,' said Oliver.

The three men walked across the room and stood behind the chairs still not speaking; nobody sat down.

Oliver felt uneasy but Thomas understood their reluctance.

'We are not here to assess you, but to talk to you about a new unit that is being formed,' said Thomas. 'It will be unconventional and will certainly not involve trench warfare.'

The reaction of the men was instantaneous and they relaxed.

'I'm Donald McLeod, a ghillie on the Earl of Rockshire's estate. These two are Hamish and Dougal, who are part of the team.' The men then sat down.

'I can't tell you anything about the operation. It's dangerous and the risk of harm and even death is very high. But it needs men with your skills in fieldcraft and shooting. There are no trenches where we are going,' said Thomas, who then added, 'I was first a poacher, then a gamekeeper on the Winslade Hall estate. The owner, Lord Overbury, is our Colonel and this is his son, Captain Oliver Overbury who was injured on the Front. We have to find about thirty men of a similar mind.'

McLeod who had been almost aggressive upon entering the room, responded:

'On the estate we are generally left to get on with our work, much of which is in the hills, in all weathers. We have struggled in the army. The marching, the trenches and the stupidity of charging across open ground and being exposed to machine-guns,' said McLeod. 'What you are talking about could be where we need to be.'

Thomas nodded. 'How about you, Hamish and you, Dougal?'

'If I go, they go,' said McLeod.

'We don't work like that. Every man has to know what is expected and agree himself.'

The two men both confirmed their request to join the new unit.

'Before we agree, there are some rules,' said Thomas.

There was a distinct change in the three men's faces as they awaited the clause that could keep them at the centre.

'By joining us you will agree to obey commands given. Avoid drunkenness, not get into fights and not enter the grounds of Winslade Hall or associate with any of their staff. If you fail to keep to any of these, you will be returned here. There are no second chances. If you accept this, then you will be the first to join the unit.'

'We understand and accept,' said McLeod. The other two also voiced agreement.

They were told to go and pack and be ready to leave.

Next to be interviewed were the brothers Harry and Alfred Cooper who hailed from the East End of London. Oliver was at a loss to know how they would fit into the unit, being city boys. He was alone when they arrived and having told them to sit, he shuffled papers about, hoping that Thomas would hurry up.

Oliver could wait no longer.

'Well, chaps, the situation is that we are forming a new unit that will undertake a special operation. I cannot tell you anything about it, other than that it will be dangerous. There is a high probability of being wounded or even killed,' said Oliver. The two men stared at him expressionlessly.

'Have you been to the Front, sir?' asked Harry. 'Both the enemy and our lot do their best to kill us. It's just a matter of time.'

'I was wounded earlier on and have an artificial limb for my efforts. We plan to reduce the risks of being wounded or killed, but this is war.'

Both men nodded.

At that moment, Thomas entered the room. He introduced himself and joined in the interview process. It was discovered that what the two brothers lacked in fieldcraft skills, they made up for by their ingenuity and procurement skills. If they could sneak into a quartermaster's stores and procure items, then they could surely do the same in Germany. After agreeing to the terms of joining the unit, they were told to pack and be ready to leave.

When they had gone, Thomas looked at Oliver's notes.

'Sorry I was delayed getting here, but I was accosted by Sergeant-Major Alan Hall. He was posted here to help set up the centre and now that job is done, he is looking for a new billet. He has seen plenty of service and action and is just the man for us. He had to get permission from the CO to join us. That's been granted, so we have another good man. I think we should go and eat before we decide what to do next.'

Having eaten, they arrived back at the room they had been allocated to discover a queue of men. Word had got round. Thomas told them that they would speak to each man in turn. It would delay their departure however: they would not be getting away that day. Sergeant-Major Hall arrived and took charge of the waiting men. He paced the line and identified those he knew, from years of experience, who were looking for an easy number, preferably away from the front line. The number of volunteers dwindled, but Thomas and Oliver selected two gamekeepers, a quarryman who had skills with explosives and a forester. They were pleased with their day's achievements and made preparations to get the men and themselves to their base camp early the following day. Sergeant-Major Hall arranged travel documents and railway passes.

12

At the quaint little railway station in rural England, a truck complete with driver that had been procured by Lord Overbury awaited them. He had been stood proudly beside it, but when Oliver and Thomas came out of the station, he walked over and greeted them. He was then introduced to Sergeant-Major Hall who, following years of military life, stood to attention and saluted. Overbury returned the gesture. He then gave a quick look at the new members of the unit and welcomed them. With the three officers in the car, the truck followed on behind as they made their way to the unit's base.

At the house, the men climbed out of the truck and stood in a group, taking in the location. None of them had been to an army camp like this before. Overbury, Oliver, Thomas and Sergeant-Major Hall went inside and met Devline, who showed them round. They went to one of the stables and saw that it had already been transformed into quarters for the men. Hall left them and went to collect the men and get them ensconced into their new abode. He was tasked with organising the men to assist the local workers in getting the other stables and outbuildings ready for habitation.

Overbury, Oliver and Thomas went to the Hall. Entering Overbury's study, Oliver and Thomas were astonished to see Clarissa sitting behind the desk. Having abandoned her khaki nurse's uniform, she was dressed in what would be considered a more conventional long dress. She leapt up and rushed round the desk to hug her father, then Oliver, followed by Thomas. The questions flowed fast and furious from the men who wanted every minute detail of her adventures. She brushed them aside and demanded a full report on the new unit.

Whilst the three of them went out into the garden to chat, Overbury checked the rather long list of messages. He was then joined by Soames who announced that the kitchen contained six - at the last count - men in army uniform looking for a military unit in the area. Mrs Brown had taken it upon herself to make sure that they each had something to eat and drink. He told Soames to speak to either Oliver or Thomas, who would sort things out and get the men moved to the house.

The first of the two that Soames met was Oliver.

'Excuse me, sir, there are six or more men in the kitchen, all looking to join your unit. Mrs Brown has fed them, but could you arrange for them to move to the house?'

'Certainly, Soames, I shall get right to it. Sorry if they have been a bother.'

'No bother, sir, yet.'

Entering the kitchen, he actually found eight men all in uniform. When they saw him, they all stood.

'Right, chaps: outside, as quick as you can.' He followed them. 'Oh, thank you Mrs Brown, for looking after them,' he said as he was leaving.

Outside, eight men stood in a line. Oliver walked along, obtaining names, former units and particular skills.

Soames had also seen Thomas, who telephoned the house and arranged for the truck to come and pick them up.

He joined Oliver outside the Hall, where they had a brief conversation.

'Right, men. A lorry is on its way to collect you. You will be under the watchful eye of Sergeant-Major Hall whilst you stay the night at the house. You will be interviewed first thing in the morning. If you are suitable, you stay; if not you go back to wherever you came from. For future reference, this Hall and its grounds are out of bounds, as are the staff.'

The truck departed with the men in it.

Oliver spoke. 'I think we may have some suitable chaps there, but some may be looking for a cushy billet.'

'How did they know we were looking for people and where to find us?' asked Thomas.

'It appears that they were on the train and spoke to a couple of our chaps. They were going on leave and went to the next station before deciding to get off and come and find us.'

'Well, we'll see what we have in the morning.'

When Thomas and Oliver arrived at the house, Sergeant-Major Hall was on hand to greet them.

'I have had a look at the eight men you sent over and they seem to have fitted in all right. I have them all busy working, but will call them over when you are ready to interview them.'

'Thank you, Sergeant-Major, we will have the first one when you are ready,' said Thomas.

That was the form for the remaining men; all eight seemed to meet the requirements. It had been noted that some of the men had been on the front line for a long time and that this was their first home leave. Each was advised to have their leave first and then to join them. Four rejected that and opted to stay; the other four, having wives and children, took the leave option and would be back in two weeks. Meantime, Oliver was tasked with getting each man officially transferred to the unit.

Hall had identified an oversight in the unit. It had become evident that they needed a proper cook. Oliver went back to the kitchen at the Hall. He located Mrs Brown.

'Mrs Brown. We have a bit of a situation. The unit at the house needs a cook. Do you know of anybody who could fulfil the role and who most importantly, is available?'

'I don't know anybody. But I will have a think about it.'

'I overheard what you said, sir. I can do it, you know I can cook. But that's if I can be spared from the Hall,' said Rosie.

'That sounds splendid, Rosie. What do you think, Mrs Brown?'

'I don't know, sir. A pretty girl amongst all those men.'

'Oh, yes, I see what you mean,' said Oliver.

'I can look after myself,' said a defiant Rosie.

'I think we have to ask the master before we decide anything,' said Mrs Brown.

'Quite right,' said Oliver. 'I shall go and find him and enquire.'

When Oliver arrived back at the house, he broke the news to Thomas. He was not best pleased but at least it solved the problem. They had to work out how to keep her safe in the company of a number of men cooped up in a remote location. The next step was when Sergeant-Major Hall presented the refined training programme. Thomas had explained in great detail that the focus had to be on fieldcraft, as the men had to move without being seen or heard, both during daylight hours and at night. The poachers and gamekeepers already had these skills, and they added their own to the instruction. Thomas had told Hall to promote to NCOs those who had leadership qualities.

Three days later, Oliver received a telephone call from the quiet-spoken man at the War Office.

'I have made requests to a number of places and have made a preliminary assessment of a good number of volunteers. I have the names of ten men who you could interview.'

'That would be good. Are they in one place or spread about the country?'

'They are all in the Southampton area, awaiting their return to the continent.'

'If you let me have the address and contact details, we will get down as quickly as possible.'

With the details noted, Oliver telephoned the appropriate officer in charge. He agreed to hold the men until they had interviewed them. There was no delay and Hall was left in charge whilst Thomas and Oliver departed for Southampton. Being quite practiced in interviewing by now, the ten men were quickly assessed. Only eight passed; they were directed to pack and be ready to travel in one hour. Thomas was pleased. They had the key elements of the fighting unit in place.

Back at the Hall the following day, the new men had been dispatched to the house to join the others whilst Oliver and Thomas joined the family for dinner. The formality of pre-war life at the Hall was diminished, much to the horror of Soames. Her Ladyship found it a little unsettling, but she generally said nothing. She had seen her daughter Clarissa with Thomas and knew that their relationship would develop, no matter what her opinions were. She really liked Thomas, but for her it was still a matter of one's place in the order of things.

With the meal finished, Clarissa announced, 'I have something to tell you. Something very important.'

She smiled as she produced a letter. 'I have a letter from the King. He informs me that I have been awarded the Military Medal for saving a pilot who had crashed in no-man's-land, as well as the Albert Medal in Gold in recognition of my work in rescuing and saving wounded soldiers, both on the front line and in no-man's-land. The awards will be presented in London. I will be notified of the date in due course.'

She lowered the letter, beaming a radiant smile as the family erupted in joyous celebration. Her ladyship cried, her sisters squealed with delight, his Lordship was overwhelmed as he knew what was required to earn such an award. Oliver and Thomas stood clapping. Soames and the footman also joined in by clapping. One of Clarissa's sisters went to the library to find a book about medals. She located a picture of the medal and returned to show the family.

At an opportune moment, Thomas gave his congratulations on the well deserved recognition of her time on the Front, especially at the forward aid stations. She thanked him but said that there had been other nurses, not just herself, and that she hoped that they also received recognition. Her Ladyship's voice broke into the excitement.

'I hope we shall all be able to come and see you presented with the medals.'

'Mama, only one person can accompany me.'

'I see. Who shall that be?' she asked looking at the rest of the family.

'Well, I know you would all want to come, but I have decided that it shall be the person who served on the Front where I was, and who understands first-hand what was involved. I should very much like Thomas to accompany me.'

There was silence.

'I think that is a splendid idea,' said Overbury.

'Oh, I second that,' said Oliver.

'If that is what you want, my dear,' said her Ladyship, not impressed at her daughter's choice.

Thomas still stood, lost for words and looking very flushed, amidst her family.

Oliver was informed that two men who had previous wounds were causing concern. He telephoned the Hall and spoke to Clarissa, explaining the situation. She said she would be over as soon as she had changed. It was just the opportunity she had been waiting for: she had her front line nurse's uniform all ready. Taking one of the cars, she drove to the house. Most of the men were out training and she went inside and found Oliver.

'My, you've come prepared,' he said, looking at her khaki uniform.

'You've got your uniform; I've got mine,' she replied, smiling. 'Where are my patients?'

Oliver led the way to a room where the two men were waiting. Oliver departed, leaving Clarissa to open up her medical bag. She examined the two men. One had shrapnel wounds that looked very raw. She had some of the ointment that was prescribed in the aid stations when wounds played up. It was applied and the soldier was told to return the next day. The second man had slight shakes. This was a case of talking and delving into what was causing them. He had endured a pretty rough time in the trenches, with constant artillery bombardment; this had taken its toll, but fortunately only to a small degree. There was no first aid treatment she could give him but she promised to talk to and monitor him over the coming days.

At that moment Rosie arrived with a cup of tea. They sat and talked. Clarissa was quite relaxed but Rosie sat on the edge of her seat, feeling quite out of place, just chattering. Relief came when Thomas entered the room. Rosie excused herself and departed.

'So what brings you to the house?' asked Thomas, already knowing the answer.

'Tending the men of your unit.'

'How are they doing?'

'One man has wounds that need ointment, but he will be fine. The other has what is called "shell shock", but it's very mild. We will need to keep an eye on him, especially if we are going somewhere where there are no aid posts.'

'We?' said Thomas, smiling.

'Your unit needs medical care and I have all the skills required,' she replied, looking at Thomas in a manner that showed him the decision was made.

He smiled. 'Good to have you along, thanks.'

There was a knock at the door. Hall entered.

'Excuse me, sir, there is a Royal Naval captain on the telephone, wanting to speak to you.'

In the room that had been designated the company office, Thomas picked up the telephone.

'Captain Pierce speaking.'

'Captain Spooner, Royal Navy, specialist branch, speaking. Understand you are looking for a boat?'

'Yes, sir.'

'Right, get yourself to the port of Felixstowe and meet with Lieutenant

Victor Gould. He has been appointed captain of the boat that we have found for you. She's not the most gracious of our fleet, but she is of German origin and will fit the bill. Can you take down his telephone number and arrange a rendezvous with him? I suggest you do it pretty quickly: our officers are very valuable. If the boat is no good, we need him back. Goodbye.'

The telephone line went dead.

Oliver had come into the office, along with Hall and Clarissa; Thomas announced that they had a boat. Oliver was pleased. Hall raised his eyebrows; nothing had ever been said about a boat, and Clarissa just introduced herself to Hall.

13

It was an overcast sky when Thomas arrived at Felixstowe and made his way to the Harbour Pub. Inside, he looked around the old building with its bars that had served thousands over the years. The regulars eyed him up and down. Uniforms were common place, but not that of an army captain. A smog of cigarette smoke hung from the ceiling and he began to feel the effects. He spotted the blue of a naval uniform and made his way towards it. The wearer looked up.

'Ah, Captain Pierce,' said Lieutenant Gould.

The two men shook hands.

'A drink before we go and have a look at the old girl?' asked Gould.

'All right, the same as yours.'

Gould caught the eye of the barmaid. 'Two rums, if you please.'

Two rums were delivered. They toasted the future, whatever that was going to be. Gould led the way as they left the pub. Out of earshot, he spoke in a low, serious voice.

'The boat is in the navy berths. We have destroyers and minesweepers based here so the place is a possible target for the Hun should he ever leave port. The boat we have been given had been used to move cargo on the Rhine.

When war began, the German captain, along with some his crew, decided to take the boat and escape to Britain. They arrived off Felixstowe and the crew were arrested and interned for the duration of the war. The boat had been moored and forgotten about.'

'Have you seen her?' asked Thomas.

'Yes. Had a good look over her yesterday.'

'And?'

'She floats and I presume the engines work. I have not been briefed on what you want to do with her, just assigned to captain her.'

'Your first command?'

'Yes. I upset a number of senior naval officers. They seem to forget that slavery has been abolished.'

At the port gate they were searched and then issued with passes. The formalities completed, they entered the world of the Royal Navy, at the time the greatest navy in the entire world. As they walked through the port, it was a hive of activity with warships coming and going as well as men and equipment moving in all directions. Then they stopped and looked at their prize, the *Schwanhild*. Walking along the dock wall, Thomas took his time to absorb the boat. A black hull, complete with rust marks. A centrally located bridge and accommodation cabins, painted white but now showing the signs of neglect. She had a single funnel, and cargo areas to front and at the stern. Most remarkable was the fact that the cargo areas were filled with planks of timber.

The men went aboard and Gould led the tour as they examined the boat in detail. The first place to inspect was the bridge, where they found an elderly man who identified himself as Jed Rankin. He was engaged by the navy to keep an eye on a number of out-of-commission boats, to stop people going aboard and removing items. He was expecting visitors. It transpired he had spent his life on the sea and knew a great deal about boats such as the one they were on. He even knew that the captain and his crew had been taken to an internment camp which was located just outside of the town. Rankin showed them the accommodation. It would not house the whole company and Thomas noted that the issue would have to be addressed. Then they went to an important part of the boat, the engine-room. Gould carefully inspected the boiler and the machinery that would provide the propulsion. It was of German manufacture and appeared to be in good working order. Thomas was pleased that Rankin had joined in the walkabout: he exuded a wealth of information about the workings of such vessels. The one thing that Thomas had not allowed for was the need for stokers to keep topping up the boiler's fire with coal. That was a round-the-clock operation. Back on deck, Thomas raised the fact that the timber was still on board and had not been removed. Rankin told them that the navy had not got round to removing it. Their focus was on keeping the warships operational.

Whilst Thomas and Gould took a final look at the bridge, Rankin disappeared to the captain's cabin. The two men looked at each other.

'What do you think?' asked Thomas.

'She floats, she's watertight and her propulsion looks in good order. So long as you don't want to take on a German battleship, she should do most things.'

'What do you think of Rankin?'

'A very knowledgeable chap. He knows about these types of boats.'

'I was thinking of asking him along for the ride.'

'Good idea. I presume that where we are going, there will be no friendly port to call into for repairs.'

'That's exactly right,' said Thomas, smiling.

Rankin arrived on the bridge. He handed Thomas a book.

'A naval officer gave it to me to hand over to you. It is the captain's log. It's dated up to when the navy brought her in here. It's in German so I don't know what it says.'

Thomas took the book. 'Thank you. I have somebody who can look to see if there is anything of interest.'

'Do you need to see anything else?' asked Gould.

'No. It's been very worthwhile.' He then turned to Rankin. 'Thank you for showing us around; your knowledge is most valuable.'

As they were about to leave the bridge, Thomas turned. 'Mr Rankin, we are taking this boat on a special mission. Would you be interested in joining us on our venture? It will be highly dangerous.'

There was a very definite twinkle in Rankin's eyes as he absorbed the mere thought.

'I have no family and love boats. It would be a great privilege to take this old girl to sea, wherever that may be.'

'Then, Mr Rankin, you shall join us. Keep an eye on her and we will keep you informed as to our plans.'

Their departure from the boat left the three men very pleased with the outcome.

The navy had provided accommodation for Thomas and Gould, which was where the two men were now headed. Close to the port was a large house, now under the control of the navy, that provided accommodation for its officers. They could eat and sleep as well as have private conversations away from prying eyes and ears. It was ideal. When they signed in, Thomas asked about the internment camp, explaining that he needed to meet an inmate. The Petty Officer on the desk said that he would enquire, and if possible get them access the following day.

In private, Thomas divulged the outline plan to Gould. One spoke whilst the other listened. Then, with all his cards on the table, Thomas sat back.

'What do you think?'

'We have the boat, you have the men, I just need to get a crew and we are set. I do have to say that it sounds bloody marvellous.'

The two men toasted the pending venture, each with a glass of rum.

The Petty Officer had worked a miracle: they had an appointment at the internment camp and he had even arranged transport to take them and to bring them back. Driving through the town and out into the countryside, there was little evidence of the massive conflict that was causing such destruction on the other side of the Channel. They turned off the road and went down a narrow lane into a wooded area. They had gone about a mile when they reached a road-block. One soldier covered them with his rifle whilst and another came to the vehicle to check them over. Peering into the car, the soldier saw their uniforms and saluted. He checked their ID cards then signalled for the barrier to be raised.

They travelled on, to turn in to face the gates of the centre. A barbed wire fence surrounded the entire site, with double-entry barbed wire gates to allow access and egress. Once inside, they followed the driveway to a large country house. Stopping outside, a soldier came out of the front door and led them into the large reception hall. They reported to a corporal at a desk. They were expected and they followed the soldier to the office of the Officer-in-Charge. Like all of the soldiers they had seen so far, he was an older reservist. A major who had seen action in many parts of the world, he was now the guardian of aliens who were seen as a potential threat to national security. It was not a job he relished, but somebody had to do it. He was quite pleased to have visitors and made the most of it.

He had the files on his desk. The first one he opened was for Captain Günther Hartmann. His notes showed that he spoke English and was very cooperative. He had brought the *Schwanhild* to England to escape the madness of the German empire. The second file was for Hans Leitz, the engineer who was responsible for the engine room. He also was cooperative. The third file was for Johan Dieter, who was the first officer and responsible for the deck. Again, he had been cooperative. The other files were in a separate pile. They were the files for the remainder of the crew who were definitely uncooperative. The major had arranged for them to meet the three who were responsive. They could meet the others if they saw any value in going so. Thomas opted for the three men the major had identified. They were responsible for the key operational areas of the boat.

Thomas and Gould were taken to a wooden hut and shown into a room that had a table and four chairs. Whilst they waited, they looked out of the windows at the other huts and could see that was where the internees lived. They knew that many of these people had been in England for years and ran successful businesses. Only their Germanic accents gave them away. Even the Royal family were related to the Germans. It was a sad outcome for people who had adopted England as their home. The door opened, allowing a soldier to enter. He saluted and said that he had brought Captain Hartmann. Thomas told him to allow the captain in. He moved to one side and the captain entered. Thomas looked at the man before him. Standing just over six feet tall and of slight build, he was unkempt and unshaven, probably not from his own choice. Thomas held his hand out and Hartmann took it. He then shook hands with Gould.

'Please sit down,' said Thomas, in English.

Hartmann sat. Thomas handed him a cigarette. He took it and accepted the light. He drew in the smoke and savoured the moment.

Thomas noted the reaction. 'Do you not get cigarettes?'

'Yes, but the guards take them when they arrive and then sell them to us. We have little or no money and so cannot afford them.'

'That is appalling,' responded Thomas.

'It is as if we are prisoners of war. I with my crew escaped and voluntarily sailed the boat here. We were then imprisoned. I understand that they may think we are spies, but we get called names, spat at and terrible food.'

'The problem is,' said Thomas, 'that your country started a terrible war, and the people here only see you as a German: you are the enemy so you pay the price. We all hope the war will be over soon so that we can all get on with our lives. In the meantime, we have to deal with your fellow-countrymen.'

'Why did you ask to see me?'

'We are going to use your boat and we are exploring the possibility that you may be interested in being captain of the boat once again. It will be very dangerous. You will be under the overall command of Lieutenant Gould.'

'Where are you taking the boat?'

'I cannot tell you that, security reasons.'

'You do not trust me?'

'Even I do not know where the boat is going,' said Gould.

Hartmann looked at Gould.

Gould shrugged his shoulders. 'Secrecy,' he said.

'I come from a town on the river Rhine, a quiet part of Germany. I followed my father working on the river, starting as deck-hand and working up to become captain.'

'Always on the river?'

'No, we would use the river to transport cargo to England and other countries.'

'You decided to escape from Germany. Why?'

'Germany was and is militaristic; for those of us who are not so inclined, it can be difficult. When the army came to my town looking for recruits, I told them I was already serving my country as a merchant sailor. They would not accept that. They said I had to don the uniform of a soldier. I argued that I would volunteer for the German navy. They beat me up. My father stepped in to stop them and they shot him. They said we were traitors to Germany. My mother had already died and my brother had moved away so I had no real family left. An officer stepped in and took the soldiers away and after I buried my father, I went back to the boat. Those in the crew I trusted, I asked if they wanted to escape what was happening. They agreed. I took the boat up the river. I landed those who did not want to escape in Holland. With only a few men aboard, I made for England. The rest you know.'

There was silence in the room.

'Your own people shot your father for no reason?' said Gould.

'Yes.'

'So would you be interested in joining us?'

'What do I get out of it?'

'I can't promise anything. You would get out of here for a period of time; but after that, all we can do is put in a good word for you in the right quarter.'

'What about my crew?'

'It seems that only Hans Leitz, your engine-room man and Johan Dieter, your first officer have been selected as being interested. The others have been un-cooperative. We can speak to them today and consider if they are suitable.'

'As you say, joining you will get me out of here so yes, I will join you.'

'Thank you, Captain Hartmann. We will speak to the authorities and get you transferred to the boat.'

When Hartmann had gone, Thomas raised a question with Gould.

'How many men do you have as part of the crew?'

'As we speak, none. I have to report back when we decide to have the boat and then they will find us a crew. Do not build your hopes up that they will be very good. They will probably get them from the naval prison.'

'Well, the boat is all right - and we have two captains and an old sailor to look after her. That's a good start.'

They interviewed Leitz and Dieter who told similar stories to Hartmann's. They agreed to join the boat on its secret operation, on the basis that there were no guarantee's about what would happen to them after the operation. He told them the conditions and also that if things went wrong, they could be shot as spies.

The transport that had waited took them back to the accommodation, where the two officers agreed a plan of action regarding the boat. Then Thomas departed to catch a train, leaving Gould to raise a crew and get the three Germans transferred to the boat.

14

When Thomas arrived at the house, he was greeted by Oliver, who was pleased to see him back but was very agitated. Thomas had already noted the presence of police officers.

'Thomas, good to have you back. We have the police here. You remember that chap Manson. Well, it turns out that he is a deserter from the army and they found him dead by our weapons store. It appears that he had been struck by something heavy.'

'Do you know who was here at the time?'

'Everybody was at the shooting-range. Clarissa was here, sorting out her medical equipment. Rosie had gone to the Hall to see her mother.'

'Just Clarissa?'

'Yes. She knew nothing about it until the men had returned and found the body. They called her to look at the body.'

A police inspector came out of the front door. He looked at Thomas.

'Are you Captain Pierce?'

'Yes,' said Thomas.

'I'm Inspector Turner. A dead body was found here today. Understand you have been away?'

'Yes, at a place called Felixstowe.'

'What were you doing and can anybody corroborate that?'

'I was on secret War Office business and yes, there are a number of people who can vouch for me.' Thomas did not take his eyes off the inspector. 'Do you know who the unfortunate person was?'

'A chap called Manson who is wanted by the army for desertion. He was found by your weapons store. What are you people doing here?'

'I am afraid you will have to address that question to the Prime Minister.'

'I see. Well, the only person who seems to have been here at the time was your nurse, Lady Clarissa Overbury. She claims that she knows nothing about the incident.'

A timely intervention came in the form of his Lordship, in the uniform of a colonel. Introductions made, they entered the house and went to the office which Thomas and Oliver shared. The inspector went over events as he saw them. Overbury thought that it was a matter for the army and that they should be informed. The inspector returned to the fact that Manson was struck by an object and that he needed to find out who had done that and what item was used. They reached an impasse. The training needed to continue and Clarissa was needed at the camp.

The body was placed in a police van and was driven away, the inspector following close behind. Overbury, Thomas, Oliver and Clarissa were left in the room. Overbury spoke.

'Clarissa, something happened and we must know the circumstances. What can you tell us?

She looked at the three men in turn. Then she gave her version.

'I was in the room that we use for first aid. I was preparing a box of first aid equipment for the operation.

Anyway, a man came into the room holding a knife. As he grabbed hold of me I realised that it was Manson.He held on to me and told me to be quiet. He said I had to open the weapons store. I, of course, said that I was a nurse and so did not know about such things. He shouted at me to take him to where the officers kept the keys. He was now holding the knife against my throat so I had no choice. He found some keys in the office and he seemed to think that they were the ones. He started to drag me out of the room towards the front door. The next thing I know is that he is slumped on the floor. Standing behind him is the soldier whose injury I had dressed earlier.'

'Who was that?' enquired Overbury.

'Do I have to say? He may get into awful trouble.'

'We need to know.'

'It was private Alfred Hill. He had a piece of wood and had struck Manson. He checked that I was all right, then picked up Manson and took him to the door of the weapons store, placing him on the ground. I checked Manson and found he was dead.'

'Where is Hill now?'

'I told him to go and hide until the others returned and to say nothing.'

'We will stick with the story that the police have been told,' said Overbury, 'I will get in touch with people in high places. The police inspector could jeopardise the whole operation.'

Overbury turned to Thomas. 'By the way, how did it go?'

'We have a boat, a German captain and two German crew members, a Royal Navy man to run that part of the show and an old hand with such boats, who is a watch-keeper over a number of boats. When I left, they were going to get the boat ready. This means that we have to finalise the plan.'

'The men are working well together and I think they are ready to go,' said Oliver.

'It all sounds very good. Can we start the final planning tomorrow morning. Here, say at ten o'clock. Oh, and we keep the lid on the other business,' said Overbury.

Thomas sat and chatted to Clarissa until the men returned. He wanted to ensure that she was unharmed. He knew that she was made of stern stuff and that her main concern was not to get Hill into any trouble. Thomas put her mind at rest and when he saw Hill in the camp, he took him to one side and spoke to him. He reassured him that he had done the right thing and told him that he should never speak about what happened to anybody.

Overbury, Thomas, Oliver, Hall, McLeod and White, the latter two having been promoted to sergeants, assembled in the office. Rosie brought drinks and some of her fine buns. As they ate and drank, Thomas, who would run the meeting, asked Hall what the men were doing.

'They are having intensive first aid training from Lady Overbury, sir.'

'Good, that is useful.'

He opened up a map and laid it on the desk.

'Gentlemen, this meeting is top secret and I do mean that. If word gets out, it will be very dangerous for us; we could enter a trap. Now, you will see that this is a map of the Western Front where we have been bogged down, often quite literally, for a long time. The Germans are well-supplied along the entire length of the line. They had planned for this conflict and there are railway lines that run across Germany, east to west. This means that they can move thousands of men and equipment from one front to another. Now, added into this equation, is the river Rhine. It runs from Holland to Switzerland,' he said, pointing out the route of the river. 'This means that the Germans can move men, equipment and supplies up and down the river as and when they want to.'

Thomas looked at those in the room. They were transfixed by his every word, whilst looking at the map.

'We, gentlemen, are going to sail across the water to the entrance to the Rhine, here. This first part will have neutral Holland on either side of us. That means we will be reasonably safe. Then, we enter Germany and will have the enemy on either side of us, all the way to Switzerland, here,' he said, pointing to the map.

There was absolute silence in the room. Each man was absorbed in his own thoughts, particularly those who had no previous inkling as to what the venture was to be. Thomas continued:

'We will travel along the river to attack key targets such as fuel dumps, ammunition and weapons stores. If the opportunity arises, we will blow up railway tracks and factories.'

'I think this is the best thing I have heard in this war,' said Hall, 'but how are we going to just sail down the river, behind enemy lines, and attack them. Has that question been addressed?'

'Yes, Sergeant-Major, it has. The boat we are using has plied the Rhine for years, moving cargo. It is a German ship. The captain is German and he brought it to England to escape his own people. Also with him is a chief engine-room man and a deck officer, both German.'

'So we have three Germans in key positions aboard the boat. Is that wise, sir?' asked sergeant McLeod.

'I have interviewed the three of them and consider them safe. We are about thirty strong so we are the more powerful force. What they do not know is that I speak German; so I will listen to what they say amongst themselves. There will also be a Royal Navy crew onboard, looking after the ship.'

The furrowed brows of concern were now replaced by smiles. This was going to be one big party, a chance to get their own back for the pals that had been lost in the stupidity of trench warfare.

'The unit will be divided into two groups, "A" and "B", which can undertake separate missions. If we find a large target or get into real bother then we can amalgamate into one group. Myself, with the Sergeant-Major and a runner, will form a headquarters so that we can go ashore as well. Lieutenant Gould, Royal Navy, will be the captain of the boat; he will remain with his crew aboard at all times.'

'Because the boat has a captain who has intimate knowledge of the river, I propose to put men ashore, attack a target then move to a location to rejoin the boat and continue on our way. If we are stopped, the German speakers will do the talking and we will only intervene if we have to.'

Thomas waited for comments. None came.

'I propose that we take four Lewis machine-guns, along with plenty of ammunition.'

'Already requisitioned and confirmed,' said Oliver.

'Our plan is to do as much damage as we can without actually firing a shot. Once we shoot, we give ourselves away. Sergeant McLeod, what is the situation regarding ghillie suits?'

'Every man has one; those who are unfamiliar with them have been practicing moving and hiding wearing them. We are in good shape, sir.'

'Good. Have we had any joy with the "coloured" capes?'

'I found a place that said they could make them. I went to visit and they had already made up an example. It's a random mix of shapes and colours including browns, greens and black. They will be rather grand. Anyway, I ordered thirty-five and should hear any day that they are ready,' said Oliver.

'Thanks, Oliver. Can you chase them up?'

'Of course. Will do so when we finish.'

'The plan is that once we have all of the equipment, we will move the unit over to the boat. In the meantime, as soon as we can, I will send a working party over to help get the boat ready. At this time, just the names of who we are sending, but no details of where.'

Thomas looked at each man.

'No doubt you will have many questions in due course, but does anybody have any pressing queries right now?'

There were none. The first meeting was at an end. The operation was coming to fruition and the atmosphere was electric.

Thomas was outside speaking to Lord Overbury when a car pulled up at the house. Inspector Turner got out.

'Good morning, gentlemen,' said Turner.

'Good morning, Inspector,' replied both men.

'I thought I would come and update you on the situation. The army has spoken to my superintendent and he has directed me to take no further action. It appears that the man Manson would have been arrested and court-martialled. He would then probably have been shot for desertion.'

'Well, he should have had his day in court; but then the outcome would have been the same anyway,' said Overbury.

'Quite so, sir. Well, we are busy looking for German nationals who should be in internment camps. So I shall take my leave of you. Good-day, gentlemen.'

'Good-day, Inspector,' said the two men.

'Well, that's one less thing to concern ourselves about,' said Overbury.

Overbury climbed into his car. 'Can you let Clarissa know the outcome of the inspector's visit?'

'Yes, sir, of course,' said Thomas.

Clarissa was instructing the men on life-saving techniques for stopping blood flowing and the dressing of wounds. Where they were going, there would be no friendly aid stations or field hospitals. There would be German ones, but it was not known how they would react to soldiers operating a long way behind the front line who had just done considerable damage to their war effort.

At lunch time, Rosie served food. Nobody was late and nobody complained. In fact, Rosie could do no wrong. She took food to Thomas and Clarissa who had remained in the office. Oliver had gone to inspect the special capes.

'How did the meeting go?' enquired Clarissa.

'Very well indeed. We are getting closer to starting the actual operation. I think the men are ready.'

'Are you able to say what the operation is? I have a vague idea.'

Thomas gave an outline of the plan, the boat and the key players. He reinforced the message that Oliver was invaluable and was playing a full part in the unit.

'Take him with you,' said Clarissa.

'Take who?'

'Oliver, of course. You are going on a boat, so he would not have to walk far. He could be part of your headquarters, as he is at present.'

'Oliver has endured more than most. I could not impose more conflict on him.'

'Ask him. Let him make the decision.'

Thomas was caught off his guard. The question had crossed his mind a few times, but he always dismissed it.

'All right; I shall ask him.'

Clarissa then delivered her dramatic piece of news just when Thomas had taken a mouthful of food.

'I think it right and proper that I sail with the boat to tend any wounded men. They will not get treated anywhere else, because it would expose you all to capture or death. The other thing is that you have a limited number of men and you need to keep as many as possible active.'

Thomas swallowed the mouthful, 'It's out of the question.'

'No, it's not. I have been on the front line and picked up wounded in no-mans-land. I have been shelled and machine-gunned. I am a valuable part of this unit. So there is no argument.'

'How do you think I can go to your father and tell him that you are going behind enemy lines?'

'You don't have to. I shall go and do that.'

He was clearly not going to win the argument; so unless his Lordship countermanded it, she would have to be found a berth on the boat. After lunch, she departed to inform her parents of her plan to join the operation.

Oliver returned with the truck and thirty-five capes. They were, in his words, 'splendid creations' that would help the men blend into the country side and give them some protection against the wet and cold.

'Oliver,' said Thomas. 'What are your thoughts about partaking in the operation? You would be based on the boat and run the headquarters.'

Oliver's face lit up. 'Are you really sure? I'm game if you are. It would be splendid.'

'Only if you are absolutely certain. You endured terrible suffering in your front line actions and I would never wish to expose you to further anguish. You must make the decision.'

'I am with you. Thank you so much, Thomas. I must telephone father and tell him the news.'

Thomas waited whilst his Lordship received the news that his wounded son and eldest daughter were going on the operation. He anticipated a visit and some strong words. The fact that both siblings made their announcements and did not bring down the might of his Lordship's powers came as a complete surprise. Perhaps the recriminations would come later, if either or indeed both of them did not return home safely.

The final planning meeting was held the following day at the house. Thomas met Over bury as he arrived. Anticipating an exchange of hard words, he saluted Overbury in his colonel's uniform.

'Well, Thomas, all seems to have gone better than expected, so far.'

'Yes, sir. You will have been given the news about…'

'If you are referring to Oliver and Clarissa going on the operation, then my view and that of the family is that they are both adults and make their own decisions. As I pointed out to her Ladyship, if Clarissa was not going with you, she would be going back to the front line. This way, we know that she will be in good hands, whatever the outcome.'

They walked into the house and joined the sergeant-major.

'We have reached the point where we have almost finished our preparations. I propose to take a working party to the boat to help get it ready. I would like Oliver to run things here, with Sergeant McLeod looking after the men. Sergeant-Major, you will join me. I will take the Cooper brothers, who may be of use procuring things. I will also take Long to sort out storage for the explosives. I would like Clarissa to join us so that we can accommodate a first aid facility. We can decide, after the meeting, who else will be of value on the boat at this point. Sergeant-Major, do you have anything to add?'

'All the equipment has arrived and been distributed. The machine-guns and ammunition will be delivered to the boat, as will the explosives. Colonel Overbury organised that. Thank you, sir.'

'Good, we are all set,' said Thomas, wondering what, and when, things would go wrong.

Arriving at the boat, the soldiers were quite shocked. One man asked if they were being transferred to the navy. They knew that going to war involved a boat journey, but they appeared to have their own boat. Lieutenant Gould bounded down the gangway.

'Good morning, Thomas,' he said. 'This must be the famous nurse you were speaking about. Good day, ma'am.'

She shook hands with him and smiled. 'Good day.'

'This is Sergeant-Major Hall,' said Thomas.

Hall saluted.

'Good to meet you,' responded Gould. 'I will get my man to show you round and to your billets. You will see what has been done.'

'Thank you, sir.'

'We have had some weapons and explosives delivered. I have put them aboard,' said Gould, addressing Thomas.

'I have an explosives man so he can decide the best place for it to go.'

A petty officer, who had volunteered for the operation, came down the gangway.

'Can you show the sergeant-major and his men around the boat and where they are billeted. They will soon find where everything is,' said Gould.

When the men had gone on to the boat, Thomas asked how Hartmann and his men had been. Gould reported that they had just adapted and got on with the job. Rankin the watch-keeper came to the boat each day and was keen to go. Gould had managed to obtain six stokers and four seamen to help on the deck. They were waiting for more coal to be delivered. He was pleased to say that the port's naval detachment had been most helpful. They had the use of a truck with a driver.

'Come along,' said Gould. 'I will show you round.'

Thomas was amazed at the transformation of the boat since his visit. Perhaps the biggest change was to be found in the fore and aft deck cargo of wood. It had in effect been hollowed out. The aft area was for storage, and that was where the boxes of explosives had been stacked. The forward area provided additional accommodation. To the outside world, it looked just like a cargo of planks of wood. Inside, bunks had been - and were still being - made. It was waterproof and provided more comfort than the trenches. In the engine-room, everything was clean and well maintained. The boiler was ready to be lit, supplying power to the vessel. Clarissa was provided with a small cabin, which would be the aid post and also where she would sleep.

Thomas, Gould and Hartmann crammed into what was known as the captain's cabin. Thomas unfolded a map that showed the German borders with Holland, Belgium, France and Switzerland. Hartmann gazed at it.

'I was right. You *are* going down the Rhine,' said Hartmann.

'Yes,' said Thomas. 'We will pass through Holland, then down into Germany. When we find a target, we will attack it. If we cannot get back the way we came, we will go to Switzerland and surrender.'

Hartmann grinned. He pointed to the map.

'Just here is a really big military depot. It has ammunition, weapons and fuel. It is alongside the river and there is a railway line that goes towards Belgium and France. I have delivered loads of timber there when they were building it. Because of where it is, the guards will be old and not well trained or led. Their main task will be to guard against civilians stealing things; they will not be expecting experienced enemy soldiers.'

'We cannot just moor at the jetty and undertake a raid,' said Gould.

'Unless they have been removed or damaged, there are some additional jetties just past the main one. I would propose that we stop at one of those. Your men can then go and do what they have to do. Once they are ashore, we will sail on a bit further, where it will be safer to wait. Once the men are back onboard, we can continue on our journey.'

Thomas and Gould listened to every word.

'So you think there will be no real guard?' said Thomas.

'I don't know; I cannot be certain, but I doubt it. They will never expect an attack to come from the river.'

'Once we have attacked the depot and caused damage, won't they be looking for us?' asked Gould.

'No; why should they? They will look internally. Unless we are inspected by water patrols who might discover our secrets, we should be all right,' replied Hartmann.

'Are there other possible targets?' asked Thomas.

'All along the river. Down here, for example,' he said, pointing at the map, 'there are armament factories.'

'All right; so we will plan to attack the depot first, then seek out more targets further along the river.'

Thomas looked at Hartmann. 'Please do not tell your men about the operation until we are ready to sail. Our own men do not yet know,' said Thomas.

Hartmann nodded. 'I agree. Oh, one thing. We need a cook and we could do with somebody who can speak German. If we are challenged, we have to look and sound as if we are German.'

'I will look into it,' said Thomas.

A sailor came to the cabin door.

'Lieutenant, sir, we have another delivery of coal. The main bunker is full. Where do we put it?'

Hartmann stood, 'Come with me and I shall show you.'

When Hartman had gone, Thomas folded the map.

'We need to keep an eye on the Germans. I think they are all right, but you never know. Our lives rest on our security.'

'I agree,' said Gould.

'How long do you estimate before we are ready to go?' asked Thomas.

'Say three days. That gives us some time to spare if there are any problems.'

'I will get the rest of the men moved over so that we are ready as soon as we get the go-ahead.'

Thomas went to the port office to use the telephone. He spoke to Oliver and appraised him of the situation. He raised the question of finding a cook who also spoke German. The captain was demanding one, and in fact Thomas agreed that a cook was an essential requirement. Food would be important on a crowded boat. Thomas asked

Oliver to inform his father that they would like to depart in three days' time. No doubt some War Office wallah would want to come and poke their nose in, but that was to be expected.

Oliver arrived with the remaining men. The sergeant-major took charge of them and they began the process of getting settled in. He saw Oliver in deep conversation with Clarissa but gave it no thought. It was the meal-times when the well-prepared food was served up, that Thomas asked Oliver if indeed he had managed to find a cook.

'I did find a cook; it took some negotiating, but it turned out well.'

'Does our cook speak German?' asked Hartmann.

'Yes,' replied Oliver.

'That is good. Very good,' said Hartmann.

Thomas looked at Clarissa, who had a blank expression on her face. He turned to Oliver.

'The cook is Rosie.'

'What?' said Thomas. 'What were you thinking?'

'It was our only option and she volunteered,' replied Oliver, in defensive mode. 'She has been part of the unit for some time and the chaps put up a good argument for her to do the job.'

'Does her mother know?'

'Yes. My father was the problem. He did not want her exposed to danger. But you know Rosie: she argued her own case.'

'Well, we can see that she can cook and Clarissa can keep an eye on her. She also speaks German. What's the problem?' said Gould.

Thomas knew he was not going to win the argument, and there was now no time to get anyone else.

'Clarissa, can you keep her under your wing?' asked Thomas.

'Of course.'

'I take it that the German-speaking cook is a woman?' asked Hartmann.

Before Thomas could answer and as if on cue, Rosie entered the mess to enquire if everything was all right with the food. Great approval was expressed.

Thomas noted that her flowing curly hair had been cut short and that she had deliberately given herself a dowdy appearance. The one thing that had not changed, though was her radiant smile. Hartmann spoke to her in German. She replied in German. Hartmann smiled.

'Excellent. I fully support her and she can be part of the crew,' he said.

It was early morning three days later when Lord Overbury arrived at the boat, followed by a car carrying a lowly War Office official, accompanied by an equally junior army staff officer. The men were lined up on the quay. The army unit, then the naval unit, such as they were. Clarissa and Rosie had gone into town and were not allowed to come back until the visitors had gone.

Thomas greeted the visitors formally, then introduced them to his men. They walked the ranks of the motley band of soldiers and sailors. Some wore a large cape of patchwork, made from a waterproofed material comprising browns, greens and black. Others wore ghillie suits. The remainder, standard army uniforms. The War Office men made negative remarks about the non-standard attire. Thomas explained that this would help them to blend into the countryside, as they had to watch from makeshift hides and move about unseen. They then did a quick tour of the boat, before they departed with the vague words, 'Good luck'. It was about an hour later when the two War Office men got in their car and were driven away. Lord Overbury spoke to the men.

'The military call this great adventure absurd: you saw the reaction of those who have not actually seen any form of front line activity. However, the government deems that if this operation is in any way successful, it will be good propaganda: the people need some good news. The green light has been given. I wish you Godspeed, much success and a safe return home.'

The men cheered. Thomas knew that they were ready. That afternoon the *Schwanhild* would sail for the river Rhine.

15

Thomas, Gould, Hartmann and Hall the sergeant-major crammed into the captain's cabin for the final pre-operation briefing. The pace onboard had slowed down as all of the preparations had been completed. This was the final act of confirmation by all concerned. Thomas asked each of those present if there was anything that had not been addressed. Once they sailed, there would be no turning back. Each man was keen to show that all was in order and that they were ready to sail. They had fired up the boiler and were still testing the engine and its myriad of pipes. Hartmann reported that there were no problems and Gould confirmed this. They discussed the question of whether a sea-trial was necessary, or if they should just go to sea since everything was working and just get on with their mission. The view of those in the engine - and - boiler rooms was to opt for the latter. Thomas was satisfied: it was now a question of when to sail. Gould had spoken with the naval people at the port. The weather was favourable and due to become even better. It was decided that they would sail that afternoon, which would allow them enough time to arrive at the mouth of the Rhine in darkness. They would sneak in and hopefully be well on their way when daylight arrived. Gould was to confirm the plan with the navy, whilst the sergeant-major would ensure that everybody was accounted for.

With a full head of steam and everybody in their place, the two captains - along with Thomas and Oliver - were on the upper open bridge. The coxswain was at the wheel below them in the closed bridge. Also there for the departure were the sergeant-major and Clarissa. Dieter was at the chart table. His task was to navigate the vessel to its initial destination: the river Rhine.

Gould, who was technically the official captain, stepped back.

'Captain Hartmann, please take your ship to sea.'

'Thank you, Captain Gould. It will be an honour.'

Hartmann blew down the communication tube. He heard the whistle and then the voice of Leitz respond:

'Are we ready to sail, Hans?'

'Yes, Captain, we are ready in the engine – and - boiler rooms.'

Hartmann ordered the mooring ropes to be released.

Shore crews removed the ropes from the bollards and the crew on the boat hauled them aboard. A small harbour tug used its tow-rope to gently pull the bow of the *Schwanhild* round to face the river which led to the sea. There was no rousing send-off, just the shore crews and the lonely figure of Jed Rankin, whose health had let him down at the last moment so that he was unable to sail. He gave a wave and shed a tear at missing his last opportunity for adventure.

Hartmann cranked the handle on the telegraph that indicated to the helmsman and the engine-room that slow speed was required. The signal was confirmed. The men and women aboard the boat just stared at the port area, each lost in their own thoughts. In the engine and boiler rooms, the men checked the dials and pipe-work. Stokers shovelled coal. Hartmann cranked the handle on the telegraph to half speed and gave orders to the helmsman, who altered the heading of the boat as it took its course to head out into the river and on its way to the open sea. A sailor was stationed each side of the bridge: equipped with binoculars, they began their task of lookouts. Hartmann called the engine-room and boiler-room for an update on how everything was working. Gould had taken the precaution of taking a morse code operator as part of his crew. He ordered the sending of a message. It simply stated, "catch the poacher". The recipients in the War Office and Admiralty would know that the *Schwanhild* had sailed. The message was passed on to Overbury.

As the boat entered the open sea, Hartmann cranked the handle on the telegraph to full speed. The men below checked all the working parts, as well as the pipe-work, for any sign of problems. They knew that they were now at sea by the motion of the boat as it moved through the gentle swell. If anything went wrong now, they would need help from the small tug that had followed them down the river. Once at sea, they were on their own.

On the bridge, they could feel a greater motion from the boat as it reacted to the movement of the sea. Some soldiers had already felt the effects of the movement and had placed themselves at a guard-rail. Ahead of them was a friendly destroyer waiting to accompany them across the open sea. A lookout advised that a destroyer was closing up to shadow them as a guard boat. Hartmann looked into the late afternoon light and noted that she was not one of the new class of fighting ship, but one that had seen better days.

As land was left behind, checks of the boat were continually made to ensure that all was well. They were at sea with no problems. Thomas ordered the sergeant-major to assemble everybody not engaged in sailing the boat in the mess-room. It was a jam; those with most need of the boat's side because of sea-sickness remained by the door: Thomas addressed them.

'Men and ladies, I can now tell you that the operation we are embarked upon is to reach and then sail down the river Rhine. For those of you suffering from the effects of the sea at present: once we are on the river and the boat stops moving about, you will feel better. The plan is that as we travel down the river into the heart of Germany, we will search out military targets and attack them. This has never been done before and so they will not expect us, or afterwards, suspect us. You have the skills and equipment to carry out this operation and, if in the worst case we have to abandon the boat, the ability to evade capture should the situation arise. This is one adventure where we can strike at the Hun and damage his supply of war materials destined for the front line. As we progress, you will be given more information and full briefings before going ashore. Our plan is not to engage the enemy unless we have no other option. If we are forced to fight, then we have the weapons with which to do so. For now, leave it to the navy boys to get us to the river and make yourselves as comfortable as possible.'

Thomas left them as the room erupted into excited chatter. Outside, he asked Clarissa to keep an eye on those suffering the worst effects of sickness. He then went to check on Rosie who had returned to the kitchen. She had anticipated that there might be problems at sea and had already prepared food for cooking. She was not sure how many would want to eat. Thomas next called at the chart table where Hartmann, Gould and Dieter were pouring over a chart. They were estimating that if everything went well, it would take about eight hours to reach the river. Fortunately the weather was holding.

Progress was steady but sure and eventually the lookouts shouted that they could just make out the coastline of Holland. They would soon be entering the danger zone. When they could see Holland, the Dutch could see them. Whilst the Dutch would not give them away, the Germans would, without doubt, have people in the country spying and observing shipping movements. Fortunately, the darkness would cover their approach. Then a lookout reported that the destroyer was closing up alongside them. When slightly ahead, it flashed a signal. It wished them Godspeed and signalled it that they was going home. As quickly as it had arrived, it veered off at a sharp angle and departed. They were now on their own.

There were four sailors on the open bridge on lookout duty. Although it was night, watchful eyes still had to peer into that darkness and look for anything out of the ordinary. Lights shone in Holland, which gave them a rough idea of how far away the coast was. Hartmann gave the order to "darken ship" and the navigation lights of the *Schwanhild* were turned off. Those not on duty were doing their best to sleep. At the entrance to the river, the lighthouse light still operated, providing some aid to their navigation. It seemed to take for ever, but eventually the movement of the boat eased as they entered the calmer waters of the mouth of the river. Eyes strained to spot navigation buoys and lights ashore that they could use for reference. The Dutch were neutral and so displayed lights to aid their own ships that were plying the oceans. In the vastness of the mouth of the river, they knew that on either side was Holland, a safe haven.

On the open bridge, Hartmann, Gould and Thomas stared into the darkness. The only noise came from the boat, the dull sound of the engine as it pushed the boat forward, her bow parting the water. A sailor and an army signalman acted as runners. Hartmann whispered orders to them, which they took to the coxswain below. In the engine-room, a man stood by the open hatch; the communication pipe for the telegraph was not to be used because the noise might travel across the water, which was a risk they could not take. The boat continued on its course. Rosie and Clarissa appeared with steaming mugs of hot chocolate for everybody on watch.

They continued unchallenged and then, with the first glimmer of dawn, Hartmann calculated that they were past the critical area where vessels bound for Rotterdam followed round to the port side. They now had a mix of open countryside and villages spaced out on either side. Hartmann looked for an area that he had used before, to anchor the boat and allow the crew to rest. He spotted the location ahead. It was where the river widened and had virtually no habitation on either side. He ordered the engine-room: "slow ahead". As they approached the location, he ordered: "dead slow". A signal to Dieter who was at the bow, and the rumble of the anchor chain told everybody aboard that they were at anchor. Hartmann ordered the engine-room to "stop" and the boat gently came to a halt, swinging round on the anchor.

Soldiers who had rested and slept during the crossing replaced the sailors on lookout. Hartmann, Gould and Thomas found a place close to the bridge to sleep. Oliver was the senior officer in charge and sat on a chair on the open bridge. As the morning evolved, boats became evident on the river. They just travelled in either direction, paying no attention to the *Schwanhild,* where the Union flag had been replaced by the German one. She was, as might be said, a round peg in a round hole.

It was mid-morning when the alarm was raised. A small Dutch warship was coming down the river. The word passed through the ship and all those not required on deck went to the secure hiding-places. Hartmann, Dieter and Leitz, who had left the confines of the engine-room, were on the open bridge. Rosie, who had managed to get some rest, was in the galley area, aware of the approaching vessel. Thomas was on the bridge, but kept out of sight. He knew that if they were boarded and searched, there could be problems. At least it would test the security of the vessel. Within the wood-piled cargo areas fore and aft, men waited, weapons ready. Rosie climbed up the steps, mugs of coffee grasped in one hand, the other grabbing the handrail to help her climb. She was in full view as the warship moved to become level. At the top of the steps, she looked at the boat and at the numerous faces looking in their direction. She waved. There was no response. She continued up the steps to the open bridge. Hartmann walked over to the wing and looked at the vessel. It had slowed almost to a stop and was close. He could see men scanning the ship with binoculars. A voice shouted:

'What vessel are you?'

'The *Schwanhild,'* replied Hartmann.

'What are you doing?'

'We have a cargo of timber. We collected it and now we take it to Mannheim. We have anchored to allow the crew to rest: it was a long night.'

Hartmann could see men on the bridge in discussion. He noted that the single gun mounted in front of the bridge was manned and that there were machine-guns located at other points, with men standing at them. He leaned on the bridge wing and drank the coffee Rosie had brought. He affected a casual appearance, but in reality he was sweating. An officer came out and wished them a good trip. The warship then gained speed and with a plume of black smoke spewing from its stack, veered away from them and continued on its journey. Hartmann waited for it to be well away before he gave the all-clear. Throughout the boat, men breathed a sigh of relief.

Thomas was pleased that they had endured this inspection because it had not been by the Germans. This would have caused a diplomatic rumpus, but once they were in Germany, it could well erupt into a shooting match. They could also learn from the experience and be more prepared next time. For now, the men would have to remain hidden during daylight hours. They could emerge after dark.

The noise of the anchor chain running over the steel of the boat signalled to everybody that they were getting under way. Below decks, stokers shovelled coal, men lubricated moving parts, then the telegraph signalled "half-speed ahead". Smoke emitted from the single stack as the fire below did its work. Once speed was up, "full speed" was ordered and the boat ploughed through the water. They were heading towards enemy territory.

They timed the crossing of the border into Germany to be under cover of darkness. Those aboard the boat prepared themselves and all lights were extinguished, including those used for navigation. Hartmann ordered half-speed and silence. The river was still wide and they ran down the middle. Lights could be seen on either side. Then Hartmann pointed out that they had just crossed the line. They were now in Germany. With those on board split into watches, soldiers and sailors worked together to keep the boat functioning. The plan was to keep going until they reached the first target.

When dawn opened a new day, the landscape had changed little. Hartmann was in his element, as he knew every inch of this waterway. The look-outs took their jobs a little more seriously as they scoured the land and water for any sign of armed threats. They passed other boats, but none were military. Those on board ate in shifts as Rosie, with help, prepared food to keep everybody going. Thomas visited every part of the boat to check on the soldiers and sailors. Those who were working below in the boiler-and-engine rooms were informed that Germany was now on either side of them. He checked on the soldiers who had to remain unseen in fairly cramped conditions, waiting for nightfall when they could come out on deck. Some took up duties as look-outs or helped in the galley. They checked and re-checked weapons and equipment. Complacency and boredom could become the biggest problem and there was little Thomas could do.

16

It was raining and night was closing in when Hartmann ordered the boat to move at half-speed. They moved slowly past a loading jetty on the starboard side. Hartmann explained that it was a military arms dump. He had transported timber and equipment to it during its construction. It had grown in size since his first visit. He pointed out a store for ammunition and explosive materials, then another for weapons and a final one for fuel to feed the growing number of mechanical transport vehicles. Thomas, Oliver and Gould were glued to their binoculars whilst Sergeant-Major Hall, McLeod and White just used their eyes to look. There were no vessels at the jetty and nobody could be seen guarding the place. Hartmann explained that the guards were not front line material and would probably be sheltering from the rain. After all, they would conclude that no-one would be at the dump at night who did not need to be there. It was a place you had to intend to go to, not a place you just passed by and dropped in on. It was a long way from the front line, which had extended well into Belgium and France.

The boat almost drifted past, allowing a good view of the dump and the surrounding area. Moving at slow speed, they continued for about a mile, when they came upon another jetty. Hartmann told them that it was just large enough to take the *Schwanhild*. He had moored here before to unload cargo that was manhandled to horse-drawn wagons on the road. This had then been taken to the arms dump. Hartmann gave orders first to the helmsman, then to the engine-room, to reverse the thrust of the propeller. The boat gently drew up alongside, allowing sailors to jump onto the jetty where the mooring-ropes were passed to them. They were looped back so that, in an emergency, they could cast off without requiring anybody to be on the jetty. Once they were in place, the main engine was shut down but the boiler kept fired up, to allow the ancillary motors to provide power to the boat.

As soon as it was dark enough, Thomas, McLeod and his two ghillies prepared to undertake a reconnaissance of the route to the dump and then of the dump itself. They each carried a rifle and a back-pack containing food. Ammunition and Mills bombs were stowed in their webbing. In addition to their capes, they carried ghillie suits tied to the back-packs. They would stay out as long as required, leaving those on the boat prepared to deal with any inquisitive uninvited visitors. Whilst Thomas went to look at the dump, Sergeant Major Hall would take a separate patrol of men ashore to act as a rearguard. The plan was that Thomas would return and rejoin the boat as soon as they had sufficient information to enable them to carry out a raid. If the boat had to be moved, then they would meet up with it further down-river. On board, Oliver was in charge of the remaining soldiers whilst Gould was in charge of the sailors. They were both in charge of the Germans.

The four men felt good to be on land and although the rain was unwelcome, it did keep the enemy out of the way. They moved in single file at a fast pace, along the road that followed the route of the river, heading towards the dump.

There was not a lot of cover, apart from a shallow ditch on the opposite side of the river. Either would provide some shelter if they came under fire. Behind them, Hall led eight men ashore and up onto the road.

Following the same road as the smaller team, they reached a wood; Hall entered it and set the men up in defensive positions, so that they could observe the road. They had no time-frame for how long the recce group would be out; so they settled down in the rain, to endure the night. It was still better than being in the trenches. Those on the *Schwanhild* prepared for a nerve-racking wait. A military boat travelling the river would probably want to know what they were doing, so close to a military dump. At least they were dry and Rosie was looking after them with her culinary delights and hot drinks.

Thomas and the men approached the perimeter's barbed wire fence. It was not a serious fence or like the barbed wire entanglements found at the trenches. They peered into the darkness. Nobody could be seen. One of the men cut through the wire, creating just enough space to allow the men to crawl through. On the other side, they split into pairs. Thomas and one man went in one direction, whilst McLeod and the other man went the opposite way. They would gather information and meet back on the far side of the wire. Moving carefully because the rain was creating muddy areas, they headed towards the buildings. Thomas was close by a wooden building when the door opened, casting light outside. Nobody exited, but it became evident that somebody was urinating out of the door. It was clearly too wet for those inside to venture out. There was a shout from inside the building then a grunt from the man at the door which then slammed shut.

Part of the training programme had been for the men to observe and gather detailed information. Then they had to remember what they had seen, until they could commit the information to paper later on. The doors for the weapons and explosive stores were locked but clearly marked. The fuel was stored in barrels outside. They found the railway track that entered the dump and had its own platform. It was the end of the line, but it carried the war materials to Belgium or to France. Beside the platform were crates of artillery shells, ready for loading and movement to the front.

The men checked the locations and potential routes for the explosives' command wires. There were no guard posts identified. In fact, there was nothing that gave them cause for concern. Everything was straight forward; having passed back through the fence, the four men secured the wire they had cut. They then crept away from the dump to take shelter under some trees. The men discussed what they had found. Thomas regretted that they had not brought the explosives with them, but they were venturing into the unknown. The option they considered was whether they could get back to the support group and get them to return to the boat, then return to carry the explosives to the dump. All of that leaving enough time for these to be placed at critical points and detonated whilst allowing them time to make good their escape before dawn.

They agreed that they would have sufficient time. In the worst case, they could hide up during the day; after all, that was what they had been trained to do. Thomas scribbled an order as best he could. Hamish was the youngest and a fast runner: he was tasked with sprinting back to locate Sergeant-Major Hall to inform him of the change in plan. They needed to send a runner back to the boat to alert them so that they could get the boxes of explosives, command wire and detonating boxes ready. Their only worry was whether the support group could be located.

Hamish ran as fast as the conditions would allow. The cape hugged his legs so he dragged it up to free them. He was used to working in foul weather in the Scottish Highlands, so that did not concern him. As the rain streaked down his face and generally soaked him, he stared into the distance; as soon as he spotted the wood, he slowed down. That was where he would have expected to find the support group. He moved cautiously, and once he had reached the edge of the wood, he crouched down. He called out:

'Sergeant-Major, it's Hamish.'

A cockney voice responded:

'Hamish, it's Alfred. Come forward.'

Hamish moved forward and almost stood on Alfred.

'Where is the Sergeant-Major?'

Before Alfred could answer, a voice announced the Sergeant-Major's presence.

'I'm here, lad. What's happening?'

Hamish recounted the orders from Thomas.

'Right, Alfred, run like the wind back to the boat and get them to get the explosives, wire and detonators on deck ready for us. Give this to Captain Overbury. We will be following you; so get going, this is urgent.'

Alfred could run fast. He had learned to do so when getting away from the police, following dodgy deals in the back streets of London. Adrenalin pumped through his body as he pounded the road in the driving rain. He ran down the ramp to the jetty. At the boat, he gasped in breath as he approached the look-out. He got on board and located Oliver who read the note; this started a chain reaction, getting everybody up and galvanised into action. Men moved boxes of explosive, wire reels and detonating boxes onto the deck. Those with explosives experience were ordered to get dressed and to join those ashore. By the time Sergeant-Major Hall arrived with his men, some boxes were all ready to be carried away. The high activity was maintained as Hall organised the men, who had been joined by four others. Some would carry the boxes of explosives and wire reels. The explosives men carried the detonating boxes. The others would act as a guard, should they encounter any of the enemy. As soon as they were ready, Hamish led the way up to the road and headed towards the dump.

Oliver was more than impressed with the way everybody had reacted to the situation. He watched as the file of men departed from the boat, many of them loaded down with boxes of high explosives and equipment. Now, aboard the boat, life reverted to a waiting game. Hartmann and Gould were appraised of the change to the plan and they made the boat ready to sail at short notice. As soon as the last man was aboard, they would slip the ropes and move down-river.

Thomas was impressed with how quickly the men had got back to the boat and then, weighted down, had made it to the dump. Whilst the men regained their breath, Thomas briefed the NCOs. These would form three groups; each had an explosives man with them. They were assigned specific target locations. A ghillie would lead each group, having already explored the site.

The first group, with the furthest to go, passed through the wire. Thankfully, it was still raining, which kept the guards inside their quarters. Boxes of explosives were placed amongst the shells that were destined for the Front. The explosives man placed detonators into small charges, then linked them to the primer charge with a small section of electrical command wire. When he was happy that all connections were made, a thin electrical wire held on a spool was connected. The men then began to return to the fence, spooling out the wire as they went. The second group had entered and placed their explosives on the outside of the weapons store. They found a pile of sandbags and carried them to place on the outside of the explosives, to help direct the explosive detonation into the store rather than out into the void. They connected them and returned, running out their wire. The third group placed a small amount of explosives against the drums of fuel.

As they passed through the hole in the wire, Thomas had counted them in; now he counted them out. The three explosives men waited at the wire. When the Sergeant-Major came through the wire, he said that one man was missing. Checking the wire was in place at the shell storage area, one of the men had seen the shape of a soldier. It was not a friendly one, but a Hun. He drew his bayonet out of its scabbard and waited, but his route was blocked. The Hun moved and became visible. How long had he been in the shadows, and had he seen anything? There seemed to be no urgency in the Hun's movements, but there was a need for the man to hurry up as he knew time was short. He slowly moved forward, shielded by the rain. The Hun moved closer to the soldier until they were almost touching. With all his strength the soldier drove the bayonet up under the Hun's ribs. Death was silent and instantaneous. The body fell to the ground; the man did his best to hide it, then made good his escape back to the wire.

Those waiting by the wire helped to haul him clear. With everybody now accounted for, the three electrical wires were joined. Whilst the explosives men worked with the command wires, Thomas looked at Hall.

'Get the men back to the boat as fast as possible. Once you are on your way, we will set the charges and blow the place sky-high.'

Hall went to organise the men and get them moving back to the boat.

Thomas remained with the three explosives men. They then linked up what was now a pair of wires to wires on another reel. That done, they moved back to and then along the road, spooling out the wire as they went. They had practiced this so many times in training that it was now second nature; but they were not complacent. They checked and double-checked everything. They continued until they came to the end of the wire. None of them were under any illusion as to the destructive force that would be let loose when the dump went up. A detonating box was prepared and the wires connected. They were ready. Thomas ordered two of the men to return to the boat.

The German guard had not returned so a colleague put on a rain cape and his helmet and went to look for him. As he walked in the pouring rain, he called out the missing guards name. There was no response. The guard kept walking and made it to the railway line and the stock of shells. He called out the name again. There was no reply. Then he saw something on the ground. He moved closer to examine it. It was dark and he was confused. It took several moments for him to realise that it was his colleague. Kneeling down, he shook him. The man did not stir. He then managed to turn the body over and felt it. He touched the hilt of the bayonet. The shock delayed his reaction. But he was soon getting onto his feet. He had to get help, and quickly.

Sidney Long, a quarryman in civilian life, was the most experienced in the unit where explosives were concerned. He pulled the plunger up.

He looked at Thomas.

'Do it,' ordered Thomas.

Long pushed the plunger down. An electrical charge passed down the wire to the primer charges.

There was no sound.

Thomas was concerned. Long just grinned. Then there were three distinct "crumphs" from the primers, before the main detonation. Thomas and Long were on their feet and running like madmen towards the boat. Long held on to the detonation box which was dragging the wire, that was still connected, behind them. They had not gone far when the main detonation occurred. The explosive force from tons of ammunition, explosives and fuel sent out a blast wave, impacting everything in its path. Thomas and Long were flattened and the air sucked from their lungs. The noise from the blast was deafening. As soon as they were able, they got to their feet and staggered along the road.

When they reached the wooden ramp leading to the boat, the two other explosives men were waiting. They grabbed the trailing wire and pulled it. It fell into a tangled mess. Thomas and Long continued to the boat and were hauled aboard. The two men with a large pile of tangled wire were then dragged onto the boat, as Hartmann gave the order to cast off. Those on the boat had felt the blast wave too; even down in the engine-and-boiler rooms, they had felt the impact of the explosion-wave. As the boat eased out into the river, the night sky above where once there had been an arms dump was lit up, and the enormous column of fire and smoke could clearly be seen spiralling upwards. Everybody not involved in the sailing of the boat found a place so that they could see the most enormous ongoing explosions of shells, bullets, weapons and fuel. There was no noisy celebration, but all were boosted by their success.

Clarissa had waited at the point where the men climbed back on board the boat to check for any injuries. Thankfully, there were none. Her concern was for Thomas and Long who had endured the blast wave; she insisted in checking them out. Content that both men had only been winded, she gave a clean bill of health to everybody. As had become her routine, Rosie had been busy and had prepared hot food for the men as they returned from the operation. Thomas joined Oliver, Hartmann and Gould on the bridge. They watched the fire and erupting fire-balls that still lit up the sky. Sergeant-Major Hall arrived on the bridge to report that everybody and their kit had returned to the boat. He added that two of the explosives men had stayed ashore to gather up the command wire so that when the Germans investigated, they would not find it and would therefore not immediately realise that the explosion was a deliberate act of sabotage. They were the last to get on board. Thomas commended them for clear thinking at a time of high action.

The Handley Page 0/100 bomber powered up its engines and taxied over the short-cropped grass airfield, following small fires that had been lit to show the route of the runway. As the aircraft gained momentum, it lifted off from its base in France. Once airborne, it headed for the front line. There were, in fact, four such aircraft in the formation; but because dawn was just a faint glimmer, they were well separated to avoid collision. Their task was to bomb German trains as well as the roads that were filled with mass troop movements. The weather had been overcast, but they had not had rain. Heading towards the front line, they had been briefed that they could expect dark clouds and possibly rain, not a welcome message for those in open cockpits. The task for now was to press on, but the plan could change. The front gunner and observer was exposed to the full force of any inclement weather, which made his job operating the machine-gun very difficult.

Then, on the horizon ahead of them, a bright light grew, followed by heavy rumbles. They were witnessing an explosion like nothing they had ever seen. The glow and noise just grew. The crew knew that what they were looking at was in the direction of the river Rhine. They had crossed the front line and began looking out for German fighters, but at that moment, all was quiet as they continued onwards. Dawn opened up a new day and the crew could start to see around them and the ground below. The front gunner used binoculars to scour it. But the glow on the horizon did not diminish. Their first target was a train. It moved slowly towards a station where both motorised and horse-drawn transport waited. The observer in the front relayed the information to the pilot, who banked the aircraft round for a better look. Those below knew what was above them and opened fire with whatever weapons they had.

The aircraft flew a steady course until they had both the station and the train in line as targets. Bombs were dropped, some from special devices fitted under the lower wing; others were dropped over the side of the aircraft by the crew. It was a primitive system, but sometimes they got lucky and today, four aircraft delivered their maximum loads onto the one target. Arriving back at the airfield, only three aircraft landed: one had succumbed to enemy fire. It was not known if any of the crew had survived but the fatality rate for aircrew was very high. With the aircraft parked, the first task was a post-flight debrief. The crew described the attack on the rail depot. It appeared that they had had some luck as there was an explosion which had caused a fire and considerable damage. They then reported what they had seen: the fire on the horizon. Whilst the flight crews departed for an English breakfast, the intelligence officers prepared the reports for relaying to England.

The air force department in the War Office received three reports from the crews of three aircraft, about the glowing fire in the night sky. They separated this information from the normal mission reports and forwarded it to the general military intelligence department, where it was almost lost in the mass of information that was being sent there. Enquiries were made, but nobody had any similar reports. In case it had any importance, the information was added to the next intelligence meeting agenda.

Prior to the main intelligence meeting, Ian Boswell MP was in communication with a member of the air force intelligence department. He had heard rumours about the sighting of the most enormous explosion in the area of the river Rhine. There had been no communication from the *Schwanhild,* although that could be expected as they would want to be very careful. He was given the details of what had been observed. Later in the main meeting, intelligence officers brought the attendees up to date. For Boswell, the meeting involving representatives from all parts of the armed forces seemed like a schoolboy's parade of "look how good me and my people are". Much of it was done to hide the bad news: the loss of life, no progression in overcoming the enemy and the lack of ammunition. The list went on. Then, almost as an afterthought, there was a brief resumé of the bright-burning light in the area of the river Rhine. The air force confirmed it, the navy ignored it and the army said it was probably searchlights. Boswell asked the question as to whether it could have been down to a successful attack by "Operation Poacher". The senior army officers laughed and drew upon the words "preposterous", "damned impertinent to suggest such a thing" and "they will be prisoners of war by now, even if they made it across to Holland". The naval representative stated that they had escorted the boat to the mouth of the Rhine, so he could confirm that they had made it that far. The air force representative added that what his aircrews had seen were not “searchlights”, but a very large explosion and fire. His people dropped bombs and could tell the difference.

Boswell’s next meeting was with the Prime Minister. It was always an uncomfortable experience for both men. But this morning this meeting, was different and he gave a report of the sightings by the aircrews. There was no other credible explanation than it being a massive explosion inside Germany. Generally, there were just the two men but a messenger had arrived with an urgent message. Shown into the room, the young officer was quite flustered as he passed on the important information. There had been a report from a Dutch contact who supplied the intelligence people with information. He stated that further up the river Rhine there had been an explosion like no other. The explosion was heard and felt, along with the fire, many miles away. The fire had lit up the night sky and the whole area of a military arms dump was said to now be just a big hole. The person sending the report was a very reliable source. Boswell and the Prime Minister looked at each other. “Operation Poacher” had made its first kill, but they could not say anything about the mission officially as the men were still operating behind enemy lines.

The duty officer at the German General Staff Headquarters for the area where the arms dump was located was woken with the news that a report had been received stating that there had been an enormous explosion and fire at the military store. His first reaction was that the NCO who had called him was exaggerating. However, after a few telephone calls, he understood that the entire supply dump had been destroyed. Once he had confirmed the situation he called the “Oberst” who was in charge of major incidents, who in turn had to explain to the colonel in great detail - twice - before it became clear to him. During the conversations, nobody asked how this could have happened. It was only during the "Oberst's" call to the General der Infanterie to inform him of the situation, that the question as to how it had happened was finally raised.

The general summoned all appropriate staff to an emergency meeting. The first issue on the agenda was to determine exactly which weapons, ammunition and explosives had been destroyed. The second issue was to get replacement materials for those lost to the places where they were needed. The third issue was to determine how such an incident could have occurred. Officers were given orders to find answers to those questions. With the office cleared of those tasked with actions, the general spoke to the head of intelligence who had remained. They considered the possibility of bombing by aircraft, but that would have required a night flight over a very long distance and then very accurate delivery of bombs; at that time, there had been no reports of aircraft in the area. Another possibility was that a bomb had been dropped by one of their own aircraft by accident. But the German air force had nothing flying at night. Perhaps German people who were not happy with the progress of the war had decided to attack the dump. The front lines both east and west were a long way away; so it would not be possible for enemy military action. They were fast coming to the conclusion that one of the guards may have been sheltering from the rain and had perhaps decided to have a cigarette in the wrong place; but nobody at the dump was alive to answer that sort of question. Everybody at the site had been vaporised. They would have to wait and see what the investigators came up with.

17

The *Schwanhild* moved slowly down-river, the night sky still bright with flashes and explosions from the demolition of the arms dump. The look-outs on the boat were being as unobtrusive as possible in their posts, whilst maintaining a very careful watch over any activities, both on the water and land. Hartmann was concerned about moving at night; when they were a comfortable distance away from the scene of the devastation, he guided the boat to one side of the river and dropped the anchor. The map showed that there was relatively open country on either side of them; they would wait until dawn, then lift the anchor and get under way. Thomas, having ensured that all of the men were sorted out and wet clothes hung up to dry, crashed out on the floor in a corner of the bridge. Clarissa had provided a pillow and covered him over with a blanket. She sat on the floor alongside him. The noise of the anchor being raised woke everybody on board. Those on duty went to their assigned posts; others, not required, grabbed a little more sleep. The look-outs were watching for any sign of trouble, but to the outside world, the boat looked like a German cargo carrier, with its decks full of timber, going about its business. Whilst on the inside, it was a miniature military unit at war.

Stokers shovelled coal and the boiler was up to full steam. The propeller cut into the water and pushed the boat along. Gould had control of the bridge and determined they should travel at half speed. A look-out spotted a boat heading in their direction. Judging by the black smoke being emitted from its stack, it was moving at full speed. Using binoculars, it could be seen that it had what appeared to be a gun on the bow. Although the vessel was a considerable distance away, Gould took no chances and called, "action stations".

The men and women knew what to do and did so quickly and efficiently. Clothes that had been hung up to dry were removed and then checks were made to ensure that nothing was out of place. German speakers were in their positions. Rosie was in the galley, ready to provide drinks to any "visitors" if required. Thomas had put on an old pair of overalls, reflecting his position as a deck hand. Everybody else went to the secure hides inside the timber cargo where they waited. Weapons were ready so that they could take action, should anything go awry.

The two boats closed in on each other. Hartmann, who had arrived on the bridge, studied the boat and stated that he could see men manning a gun on the foredeck. The bow wave and the smoke pouring from the stack indicated that it was still moving at full speed. Hartmann kept the *Schwanhild* on course so that they should pass well clear of the gunboat. Then the gunboat's bow wave reduced and the black smoke dropped away. It had changed course and was now heading straight for them.

Word was passed to everybody on board to expect unwanted visitors. Pre-empting the actions of the gunboat, Hartmann changed the telegraph to "quarter speed". The *Schwanhild* slowed down. The gunboat was now very close and still holding a course directly for them. Hartmann reduced their speed still further, in fact to just sufficient to be able to maintain steerage. Then the gunboat suddenly swung out to move beam on and run down their starboard side. The bow gun swung round to follow them. The machine-guns could now be seen, which were also pointed at the boat. Hartmann knew that the *Schwanhild* was seriously out-gunned and could be outrun by the gunboat. Alongside, numerous eyes on the gunboat studied the *Schwanhild* and those who could be seen on board. Hartmann moved to the side so that he could hear if any instructions were given. There was a waiting period whilst they were in discussions, then there was a wave from an officer on the gunboat as it speeded up and ploughed ahead, leaving thick black smoke behind it. Those who knew what was happening breathed a sigh of relief, but that was premature as it swung round and was now heading in the same direction as the *Schwanhild*. The gunboat came alongside for just enough time to allow three sailors to jump across. Once they were on board it eased away to maintain pace alongside, machine-guns firmly trained on the *Schwanhild*.

An officer made his way to the bridge, followed by two sailors. All were armed.

'Who is in charge?' demanded the officer.

'I am. Captain Hartmann, welcome to the *Schwanhild*.'

The officer looked him up and down. 'Papers,' he demanded.

'I will get them from my cabin,' said Hartmann.

The officer looked at Gould, who was at the wheel and who stared straight ahead.

'What is your name?'

Gould ignored the officer.

'I asked, what is your name?' repeated the officer.

'He is deaf and almost dumb,' said Hartmann, returning to the bridge. 'He serves his country well aboard the boat.'

'Good,' said the officer.

He took the documents from Hartmann.

'My men will search the boat.'

'Do you need one of my crew to show them round?'

'No. They will find their own way.'

The two sailors walked around the crowded deck. Inside, they inspected the cabins, the mess and the galley. Rosie had made herself as unattractive as possible and just grunted a few words when they spoke to her. They then went to the engine-and-boiler rooms. The engine-room was empty; entering the boiler-room, they were met by Leitz who started to explain about the workings of the machinery. After a cursory look round, they departed and went to the bridge. They reported that everything was in order.

'Did you hear the explosion and see the fire down-river?' asked the officer.

'Yes, we had just gone past so we were quite close. We kept going to get well clear. It looked very serious and we were very alarmed.'

'Did you see any boats in the area?'

'No. It was dark and I was trying to make up time. We are busy with the war effort.'

The officer handed the documents back. He stood looking at Hartmann then turned and left the bridge, followed by his two sailors. Once they were back on deck, the gunboat moved alongside and they jumped across to their boat. With its engines powered up, the gunboat swung to the starboard to turn round and head down-river. As soon as it was well clear, everybody on board was informed that the emergency was over.

Life on board returned to normal. Rosie began to prepare a meal; Clarissa checked to see if anybody was suffering any ill effects from the earlier operation, then helped Rosie. Men in the boiler-room continued to shovel coal and the soldiers cleaned weapons and equipment for the umpteenth time.

Thomas, Gould, Oliver and Hartmann crammed round a small chart table. Hartmann pointed to a place on the chart.

'There is a very large and important heavy armaments factory at this location,' he said. 'I have been there many times with cargo. This is the industrial region where they make steel and build big guns and make ammunition. It is also where there are many coal-mines which keep the furnaces going. This is a particularly valuable target but there are lots of workers: we will be attacking a place that has many civilian workers. The majority will be German. If they find out that the places have been attacked they will hunt us down without mercy. It will not be like the arms dump.'

Hartmann then drew a rough sketch of the factories and the landing jetties. Thomas asked a multitude of questions. Hartmann explained that with the country at war, things might have changed. There would undoubtedly be guards, but of an unknown calibre. The options were: men too old to serve on the Front; boys who had not yet been sent to the Front; or men who had been wounded, but who had recovered sufficiently to be commandeered back into limited military service. Either way, there would be an armed defending force.

The key question came from Thomas:

'Let's just say we are able to lay charges and set them off. We will have to make good our escape. Which direction do we take?'

'We are more than half-way along the *Rhine* so it's a long way back to the safety of Holland or England,' said Hartmann.

'But we do have Holland to the north and Switzerland to the south. We could surrender in either,' said Gould.

Thomas produced a larger-scale map and added,

'When we left England, the front line was as shown in red. You will see that down here, towards Switzerland, the French front line is much closer to the river. We may be able to escape across to the French lines,' replied Hartmann.

'I doubt we could go that way. We would be shot by either side if we got caught,' replied Gould.

'It would be too far; I doubt we could get everybody through the German lines and if we did, we would have to cross "no-mans-land" and risk being shot by our own side,' said Thomas.

'So the best option will be Switzerland,' said Hartmann.

'Did you ever look inside the factories?' asked Thomas.

'Yes. This one is the biggest,' said Hartmann, pointing at his drawing. 'It makes the guns for the battleships and the heavy artillery. This one makes shells. You will see that they are some distance apart. They did that in case there was an explosion.'

'If we go for these two as targets, you will have to drop us off and move away. We will conceal ourselves as best we can, place the charges and detonate them. Then we will have to make our way to meet up with you at a safe location. Would that be possible?' asked Thomas.

'Yes. Because we used to call at the factories quite often, I have a detailed chart of the area and the landing jetties. I will locate them and we can discuss the situation in more detail.'

Finding a quiet place on the boat, Thomas and Clarissa sat looking at what was a peaceful landscape. It was difficult to believe that they were in enemy territory and that millions of men, women and children were being slaughtered at that very moment.

'What do you think about doing after the war?' asked Thomas.

Clarissa, being as bold as ever, answered: 'Well: marrying you; living at the house we used as our base which I just adore; possibly having children. I want to do something useful, not just sit about. What would you like to do?'

Thomas was not so bold. 'I am not sure your father would allow us to marry. There is a big social divide. But what you describe sounds really good to me.'

'Daddy would approve. Mother might not, but then she has two other daughters to marry off to the "right people"; losing me will not be a problem.'

Thomas laughed, 'Well, we have to get out of this mess first.'

'I have to say it's a real adventure. It seemed more dangerous on the front line, perhaps because there was continuous shelling and machine-gun fire,' said Clarissa, who seemed to just absorb the dangers. 'Here, we have peaks of tension; then, like now, it's all different and calm.'

A head popped round the corner. It was Oliver.

'Sorry to interrupt your private moment, but there is another gunboat heading towards us.'

The action to be taken in such events was now well-drilled and everybody knew what to do. On the bridge Hartmann, who had been getting some rest, assumed control from Gould who departed to his hiding-place. The gunboat was heading towards them at speed.

'This looks serious,' said Hartmann.

Thomas agreed. They had rigged up a telephone from the captain's cabin to the accommodation hidden in the wood cargo on deck. They were able to warn the men there of the approaching gunboat and keep them updated. Four Lewis machine-gunners prepared their weapons. The plan was that if their hideaways were discovered, the gunners would surprise the enemy by putting down a hail of machine-gun fire in, the hope that it would give them some advantage. They had seen numerous cargo boats on the river, plying in either direction; the gunboats could not stop every boat. It was a game of cat-and-mouse. The gunboat moved closer. People could be seen on the bridge looking through binoculars at them. Hartmann ordered half speed. The gunboat kept coming. Then, in an instant, it changed course slightly, just enough to deflect the two boats' being in a head-on collision course. It steamed past at speed, its bow wave impacting on them. Hartmann and Thomas waved to the enemy crew as it passed. Then it was gone, leaving only its wake behind.

The message was sent round, and weapons were made safe. Everybody relaxed once again. Rosie, knowing the impact on the nerves of everybody on board, had prepared a large urn of coffee. It was a welcome respite, but nobody was under any illusion that it would be the last such alarm. With full speed regained, the *Schwanhild* continued on her course, deeper into the enemy heartland.

18

Thomas woke up and realised that the engines had slowed down. He was instantly wide awake and made his way to the bridge. Like everybody else on board, he spent most of the time dressed ready to spring into action at a moment's notice. The only time anybody relaxed that situation was to shower or change their clothes. Showers and additional toilets for the men had been rigged up at the stern of the boat, whilst the ladies used those inside the accommodation. Neither could remotely be described as luxurious. Hartmann and Gould were on the bridge when he arrived.

'Ah, Thomas,' said Hartmann. 'We were just about to send for you. It will soon be dark and we are going to anchor for the night. But, most importantly, you will just about be able to see, on the other side of the river, the weapons and ammunition factories. We have a little time to observe them, but we must be very careful as they will also observe us. We must not raise any suspicion.'

Hartmann had just finished speaking when the noise of the anchor chain rumbled throughout the boat. "Stop engines" was ordered and the boat came to rest on its anchor. When Thomas looked through his binoculars, he could not see much of either factory as they were set back from the river. But he could get an idea of the surrounding area. Morning would reveal more but, in the meantime, the look-outs needed to keep a very careful watch.

Once everybody had been fed and the dining area cleared, it became the operations room and the key players assembled for a planning briefing. Hartmann began by pointing out where he would moor the boat to allow them to get ashore. It would be about a mile further up-river. He would stay as long as he could but, if he had to move, then he would continue upstream to other locations he pointed to on the map. Those ashore would have to make the journey on land, passing through hostile country - with the added complication of built-up areas - so as to meet the boat. Hartmann then added one important point. The boat could not wait for long as it would raise suspicion and, once the targets were attacked, boats on the river would be suspected and scrutinised. He would continue towards Switzerland and stop for as long as possible along the way. Apart from enemy inspections, he warned them that there was only so much coal on board and that they could not re-supply in Germany.

Thomas looked at everybody around the table.

'We shall operate in the same teams as before. I will go with Donald, Hamish, Dougal and Sidney, with his knowledge of explosives, to carry out a recce of the two targets.

When we have the information we will brief the two groups. The plan is that we will blow the ammunition factory first; then once that has gone, the arms factory will follow. If we find that there are a lot of guards around the factories, this may pose logistical problems for getting more explosives to the site and placing them so that they cannot be seen. What I propose is to start a small fire in the area of the ammunition factory so that it is evacuated of the workers. We do not want to kill civilians even though they are making the weapons to use against us. Once the ammunition starts to explode, the arms factory will be evacuated if this has not already been done. Then we bring it down. Again, there are workers, working in shifts over 24 hours; so this way, we keep any harm to the civilian population to a minimum.'

'Why are we concerned about the people who make the munitions and arms?' asked one.

'If we run into problems, it will not help us if we have killed a number of civilians. Our targets are the factories themselves.'

'How long do you anticipate the recce to take?' asked Sergeant McLeod.

'It will depend on what we find and how well we are able to move about. But, as Captain Hartmann has said, speed is essential so we need to move as fast as possible.'

Thomas looked to see if anybody else had anything to add. He then continued:

'What I plan to do is to find a safe location, a large wood or forest on our way. I will send a runner back with the information; Sergeant-Major, you can lead the remaining men with the explosives, wire reels, detonating boxes and heavier weapons to the location. We will meet up and review the information we have gathered and brief everybody. Then we split into the two groups, get to the two targets, place the explosives and get out. We will then detonate at a pre-determined time. That is the time we make good our escape.'

'What if we get separated?' was a question asked.

'The boat will stay moored for as long as possible at the place where we go ashore. If it is not there when we return, we make our way up-river until we either find it or reach Switzerland.'

There was laughter amongst the group.

'When do we go?' asked Hall.

Hartmann answered:

'We can launch a row-boat and take the recce party across tonight. Then we move in the morning at first light and stop at the first safe place. The main party can go ashore as soon as it is safe to do so and I will wait at that location as long as possible.'

There were nods all round. Thomas picked up the meeting again.

'Oliver will stay on board to lead the defence of the boat if needs be. Clarissa will man the first aid post, should there be causalities.'

Oliver just nodded but Clarissa said that she would go ashore with one of the groups. She argued that if the group encountered trouble, any wounded men needed to be treated as quickly as possible.

'All right, Clarissa will come ashore; but you will have to carry any medical kit,' said Thomas, looking at her.

'That is what I plan to do,' replied Clarissa.

With the briefing at an end, the recce group prepared their equipment. Before departing, Thomas instructed the men. He told them of the plan and about how they would then have to get back to the boat which might have moved upstream. They were to work on the assumption that there would be German soldiers looking for them. This scale of destruction would not be put down to an accident. It would be dangerous but, unlike the trenches, they would have a fighting chance. Their skills in the field would be superior to the German guards who, it was thought, be either very young, much older or those recovered from injury.

The row-boat had been lowered into the water on the side away from the landing area. Dieter and a British sailor rowed the boat, with the others crouched inside it. The rowers skilfully manoeuvred the boat across the river to lie alongside the jetty. The men climbed up, and in darkness moved in single file to the end of the wooden jetty. They encountered no barrier and no guards. Once they had completed their task, they would come back to the row-boat, but must return to the *Schwanhild* one hour before dawn. If they did not return, they would hide up and a runner would find the boat the following evening. They quickly moved away from the landing area, avoiding houses and anywhere where they thought people and dogs might be. In doing so, they found a large wood within reasonable distance of the factories. Having entered it, they found a place that would serve as the onshore base. The plan was to split into two groups and then, having gathered the information they needed, meet back at the base to hide up during daylight hours, or return to meet the row-boat and prepare a plan of attack.

McLeod was tasked with gathering information about the armaments factory. Thomas would take the other team to explore the ammunition factory. They wasted no time and each team moved silently into the darkness. The sky was a mixture of cloud with clear moonlit spells. The men did what they were very good at, moving unseen and unheard and taking every advantage of their surroundings. The ammunition factory had a wire fence that had seen better days and which was easily breached. Moving cautiously, they did not encounter any guards, but they could see a sort of shelter a little distance away from the main factory which they understood was the place where the workers could go and have a cigarette. They did not see or hear anybody. The factory was lit up and, judging by the noise, in production. It was clear that anybody coming out of the building would not have any night vision. They discovered a rather dilapidated shed with a pile of logs in it. It would be ideal for the fire diversion. Moving round the building, they found, inside the factory and below a row of windows, large tubs of what they thought might be part of an explosive mix. Perhaps they could simply open the windows and lower explosives into them. Then, when the detonation plunger was pushed, the whole place would go up. The biggest factor would be whether the tubs would still be in place the following day; so they needed another option.

They moved silently to the back of the factory and found a door. Before they could investigate it, it opened and bright light from inside flooded the area. They quickly crouched down and, dressed in their camouflaged clothing, just blended into their surroundings. A couple emerged who, having closed the door, provided evidence that they had not come out to have a cigarette. When they had finished their close encounter, they returned inside. Thomas was pleased that it had been quick and concluded that the door must be hidden from general view, as a foreman would soon have been after them if he had known what was happening. After a few moments, he went to the door and carefully opened it. Looking inside the main part of the factory, he was hidden from general view by stacks of crates containing artillery shells. He slipped inside and quickly spotted a place where they could hide their explosive device. He slipped back outside and closed the door. He had seen all that he needed and they began to make their way back towards the wood. Their priority was to search out any defensive locations, but the Germans seemed to have no fear of serious intruders.

Whilst Thomas's group recce'd the ammunition factory, Hall's group found the arms factory equally unguarded and with inadequate security fences. The building, one of the biggest the men had ever seen, comprised an enormous steel structure with a lot of glass to make the interior lighter. Sidney Long inspected the structure and determined that the main charges would have to be set off against the central framework's legs. Destroy those, and the entire building should collapse. This was good news as it meant that the men did not have to take the risk of entering the building. The group could place the boxes of explosives on the outside, wire them up and then detonate once clear. With all the information gathered, they vacated the area as stealthily as they had arrived and returned to the wood.

Thomas was faced with the decision as to whether they should hide in the wood or return to the *Schwanhild.* Checking his watch, he knew that they had time to return to the boat; if they stayed, there was always a risk that they could be discovered. His choice was made. The return journey was as uneventful as the outward journey. The row-boat carried them back to the *Schwanhild.* Back on board the boat, Thomas was able to provide a much better briefing to the men on the subject of the targets and the surrounding area. It was going to be a long night. With the first glimmer of light announcing the arrival of a new day, the anchor was hauled up and the boat slowly moved up-river. Once they were out of sight of their overnight stopping location and the factories, Hartmann looked for a place to moor the boat.

Thomas, Oliver and Gould used binoculars to scour every inch of ground as the boat slowly moved along the river. Nobody paid them any attention. Boats plied the river all day long and theirs was just another one. Hartmann spotted a stopping-place and surveyed either side of the river. There was a landing platform which looked as if had not been used for a long time, but would serve the purpose. Hartmann skilfully brought the boat alongside the wooden jetty, which groaned under the weight of the boat as he brought it to rest. The look-outs kept a watch in every direction. There was habitation along the river banks, but few people were spotted. Hartman allowed a few men at a time to go on deck and look like they were working on the boat. If any of the passing boats became interested in them, the men were to get out of the way, leaving the German-speakers to deal with the situation. It had been a bright start to the morning with a clear sky, but it clouded over and threatened rain.

The rain held off and everybody had a good meal as daylight began to fade. Final preparations were made and everyone checked and rechecked their kit and equipment. Nothing could be left to chance. When Thomas deemed it safe enough, he and his recce group left the sanctity of the boat. They looked a rag-tag group with their ghillie suits covering most of their bodies. Heading towards the targets, they avoided houses and kept - where they could - to countryside where there was some cover in which to hide. Shortly after they had departed, they were followed by the main body, who were loaded down with explosives, weapons, ammunition, electric cable reels and rations to keep them going through the night. It was slow progress, with everybody trying to keep close to the person in front. Nobody wanted to get lost. Eventually Thomas and the recce group located the wood that they had discovered the previous night. Hamish and Dougal were sent to lead the main group into the location. Once everybody had arrived and was accounted-for, Thomas moved forward with the leaders of the two groups; at a suitable location, he pointed out the targets and routes to follow. The rain had kept off but clouds shielded the sky giving them only a few glimpses of the moon. Time was of the essence and, once the group leaders had gathered their men, the two groups moved forward to the edge of the wood. Then, in total silence, they moved towards the targets. Thomas' group was smaller, as more explosives were required at the arms manufacturing factory; that group was led by Sergeant-Major Hall. Clarissa remained in the wood with two men who were equipped with a Lewis gun and who would provide supporting fire if needed.

When Thomas reached the ammunition factory's boundary fence, his two-strong Lewis machine-gun team found a place to wait and set up, ready to provide covering machine-gun fire. The remainder passed through the fence and moved carefully towards the building. Sergeant White took two men to the shed where the log pile was located and set up a special device whereby the explosives would burn rather than explode. With the charge set, they moved away, spooling out the command wire. Thomas led the others round to the factory windows, avoiding the door. He climbed up and peered through, to see that the bins were no longer there. They had to revert to the plan where the detonating explosives were placed on the crates of shells. This opened them up to discovery, but it was their only option.

Thomas turned the handle of the door whilst two men stood close by, each of them armed with a fearsome-looking club. Shooting anybody was out of the question so they would have to be clubbed. Thomas eased open the door. He could not see anybody and was hidden from the main factory floor. He moved inside, followed by the two men who checked in either direction. As soon as it seemed safe, others carrying boxes of explosives entered and placed them where instructed. As soon as each man had delivered his box, he returned outside. A soldier brought in the end of the command wire, which was carefully attached to the detonating charge; the wire was trailed outside, carefully hidden from view in the process. There, two soldiers carried the reel and headed towards the hole in the fence, paying out the wire as they went. Thomas and the men left the building and closed the door.

They had taken only a few steps when the door was flung open, throwing a bright light over the area outside the door. They did not move but remained frozen to the spot, fully aware that their strangely - shaped and - covered bodies were exposed. The two club-carrying men were poised to spring into action. Enemy soldiers were the last thing on the minds of the man and woman who had exited the factory. The door closed and darkness covered all of them. The copulating couple could be heard hard at work as the men moved silently away. At the fence, the group departed to the wood, leaving Thomas and those responsible for the wire and the Lewis gun team on guard. Sergeant White had also spooled out detonating command wires. Finally they all retreated towards the wood, the only evidence of their presence being the trailing wires.

Sergeant-Major Hall had led his group to the arms factory. Under the direction of quarry man Sidney Long, the boxes of explosives were placed at the base of the main structure supports. The inside of the factory was lit up and the noise of machinery being operated was clearly audible. As the boxes were placed, Long added the primer and detonator and connected it to the command wire. He moved as quickly as he could, knowing that he had both sides of the factory to do. Added to that was the pressure that one mistake would render the explosives harmless.

When voices could be heard, everybody stopped and remained motionless until it was safe to continue. Following behind Long were the reel men who paid out the command wire, hiding themselves as best as possible. Eventually, all of the explosives were laid and the men moved back to the fence. In the darkness, Hall found Thomas almost by accident, but it had cost them a lot of valuable time. Long prepared the wires and the two detonating boxes. Thomas had kept Hamish and Dougal at the fence but sent everybody else back to the wood where they would form into their two groups, ready to make their way back to the boat by separate routes. Once everybody was clear, the detonating team spooled out more wire as they moved back to find a suitable spot where they lay hidden in the grass. They were now well away from the factories. Thomas gave those who had departed time to get well clear of the area and reach the sanctity of the wood before he pressed the plungers.

19

At the main entrance to the armaments factory, unseen by Thomas or his men whilst they were setting their charges, were unexpected visitors. The leader, Oberst Franze von Krupt was the officer commanding a regiment of German troops destined for the Western Front. They were on their way to take part in what was being called the final push that would ensure German victory. He was young, tall, slim and distinguished-looking, with his blond hair and a moustache that was carefully trimmed. His uniform was immaculate and bore the Knights' Cross with Oak Leaves and Swords. He was the archetypical Prussian military officer and his arrogance was displayed to the full. Rumour had it that he had shunned promotion to avoid desk jobs as he preferred an operational role, where he was as ruthless with his men as with the enemy. Krupt and some fellow officers were accompanied by a number of motorised trucks filled with his soldiers. He was a brutal leader, feared and hated by most of his men and by all those he came into contact with. This visit was no different: his men remained on the trucks, ready to do any dirty deed he commanded without question.

The factory managers met Krupt and his fellow officers and were pleased to show them round. They admired a range of heavy weapons that were in the process of being manufactured, ready for the battle-front. Krupt nodded his approval. The managers provided information about how they were key to the success of the glorious army; Krupt added to the adulation as he and his men were its personification. The flamboyant visit was short-lived: a siren sounded at the munitions factory. A man came from an office to say that he had just had a telephone call from the other factory to say that there was a fire in a log store. The workers had been evacuated to a safe distance until the fire was dealt with.

The chief manager at the arms factory had to assess the situation and make a decision. Should they stop work and evacuate as well until the fire was dealt with? If the explosives factory did blow up then it could affect them. Krupt allowed no debate and commanded that they continue working. The German fighting machine needed weapons and ammunition to win the war and to interfere with the process would be treason. The manager argued that he could not risk losing highly skilled engineers, but in the end the decision was made for them when the munitions factory erupted into one giant fire-ball. Flames shot up into the night sky; the shock wave caused some of the large glass windows in the factory to shatter. Krupt led his officers outside to mix with the arms manufacturing workers, who were already fleeing the scene. The army trucks began to move away to a safe distance. They were just in time, as the factory's main structure supports were blown apart. They watched as the building shuddered and then, as if in slow motion, it collapsed in on itself.

Thomas and his men watched as Long pushed the plunger of the detonation box. It set off the charge, causing the fire to take hold in the wood store. Flames leapt skywards and they heard the alarm being raised. They could not see the mass exodus of workers but assumed that the factory would be emptied. Then the plunger was pushed to trigger the detonation of the ammunition. They could feel the heat as they pressed their bodies into the ground. The blast sucked air from their lungs and for several moments it was very uncomfortable. The night sky was lit up and the sound of exploding shells continued unabated. The noise was incredible and deafening. It was beyond what they expected. Thomas knew that time was pressing on and that they needed to be gone by the time anybody got organised and searched the area. He told Long to bring the arms factory down. The plunger was pressed down and the charges detonated. For a moment it looked as if the building would stand, then it began to collapse. Having seen the demise of both factories, Thomas and the men pulled the remains of the command wire in, removing, as best they could, the traces of the deliberate act of destruction. He then led his men to the wood, a happy band of rag-tag soldiers who had just carried out a devastating attack on a prime German weapons provider.

In the wooded base camp there was some concern that dawn had showed a glimmer of the start of a new day. The boat was so near, yet so far away: to be exposed in daylight outside of the wood would mean compromising their means of escape. Thomas, Hall, McLeod and White had a discussion about the situation and what they should do. It was decided that with both factories down, there would be more people and traffic about than normal; so it would be safer to stay hidden in the woods during the day. They could make good their escape when night-time came. Thomas spread everybody out and formed a defensive position. It was going to be a long wait.

Everybody on the boat was on edge. They waited for the explosions which occurred later than expected. As dawn showed itself, nobody had returned and they assumed that Thomas had decided to wait and hide until nightfall. Then, in the safety of darkness, they would move out of the area and back to the boat. For Hartmann it was to be a long and very nervous wait. The explosions would draw a lot of attention and that might include curiosity about why a boat was moored so close to the scene of the devastation. Oliver prepared men and weapons for the defence of the boat, although he knew that they stood little chance against a gunboat. They had a minimum number of crew but had to maintain look-outs as well as keep the boiler stoked. Rosie fed everybody on board but did not prepare anything for the others. They would have to wait until later as she did not want any foodstuff lying about, should they get uninvited visitors and have to answer difficult questions.

Oberst Von Krupt stood with his fellow officer and watched the destruction of the two buildings. It was his engineering officer who approached him with the fact that the weapons factory must have been blown up as an act of sabotage. Krupt found it difficult to grasp that anybody could be so audacious as to blow up a factory in the heart of Germany. As soon as it was light enough, he sent his men into the two sites to search for anything untoward. He laid out a map and noted the road that ran alongside the river. He ordered men to go in either direction and set up road-blocks. They were to keep inquisitive eyes away, as well as stop anybody leaving the area until it was clear who they were and what they were doing. He was also aware that his engineers would be needed to make sure the sites were safe from further explosions. All this clashed with his orders to take his unit to the front line at best possible speed.

The look-outs on the *Schwanhild* spotted a truck, with its cargo of soldiers, arrive just along the road. Once off the truck, they set up a road-block using the vehicle itself. Hartman gave the order for all non-German speakers to go to their hiding-places. Two stokers remained in the boiler-room with Leitz, the engineer, to keep the boiler stoked so that they could quickly get up steam to make a rapid departure.

It was mid-morning before more engineers arrived and a detailed search of the sites was made. Unsafe ordinance was a priority and it took time finding and then disposing of it. In addition, more men from Krupt's unit had arrived and were waiting for orders. Everybody was impatient to do something.

There was no civilian activity on the road and the soldiers were bored just manning a block. A sergeant and two privates walked along the road until they were level with the *Schwanhild,* where they stopped. They stood looking at the boat with its small amount of wispy smoke emitting from its stack. They then walked down the short walkway to the jetty, where they walked up and down whilst looking at the boat and its cargo. Hartmann let them do their pacing for a short time, then he went down to confront them. That was preferable to them coming aboard the boat.

Hartman told the sergeant that they had stopped to do some urgent maintenance and that they would be underway as soon as possible. He said that they had heard the explosions and enquired as to what had happened. He added the question as to whether they were safe to remain where they were. The sergeant said that he did not know what had caused the explosions, but that were under orders to stop movement along the road in either direction. He thought that the worst of the destruction was over and that they were safe to stay where they were. The sergeant became bored with talking to Hartmann and so led his two soldiers back to the road-block.

Thomas and Hall returned to the edge of the wood and to a location where they could observe the damage. They spotted the soldiers. Thomas was alarmed to see that they were not older men or young boys, but young fighting men. Then they realised that there were soldiers who were obviously engineers busy checking the site, who appeared to be efficient at the job. Both men were pleased that the wires had been pulled in, as they would have immediately given the game away. A soldier joined them to relay the message that a truck filled with soldiers had been spotted going along the road in the direction of the boat.

Thomas left Hall to watch the activities at the site and went back to the main body. He ordered a recce of the part of wood that they had not been into; if everything was all right, they were to move back. It seemed that there was a front line German military presence which they had not accounted for. He found Clarissa and told her that she should expect trouble. It was imperative that she attempt to get back to the boat as soon as it was dark, as that was where the men would make for, including any wounded. She said that she would assess the situation as it evolved and take the appropriate action. In the privacy of the vegetation, he kissed her and told her to take great care going back to the boat. He left the NCOs searching out escape routes from the wood and returned to join Hall. There was certainly increased military activity and both men hoped it would be dark before they became even more active.

It was well into the afternoon when the officer in charge of the engineers reported to Oberst von Krupt. They had found was evidence that it had been a deliberate act of sabotage against the factories, which had been well planned and well executed. It was not the work of amateur saboteurs. Krupt did not delay any longer. It would soon be evening and he wanted his men out there hunting down the perpetrators. Trucks loaded with soldiers moved forward and dropped the men close to the perimeter of both buildings. The soldiers dismounted and then fanned out before moving out in a regimented order. They had orders to apprehend any suspects, but if fired on they could respond with deadly force. Krupt was going to deal with those who attacked the industrial heart of the fatherland. High command had ordered him to take his men forward to the front line where they were needed, but this act had to be dealt with as a priority and he was the person to do it. With his aggression, it would not take long.

Thomas and Hall watched for a long as they could, then withdrew as the line of German soldiers headed slowly towards the wood. Thomas was pleased to find that everybody had already moved deeper into the wood, but now he needed them to move even further. At the edge of the tree-line there was unknown and exposed ground. They scoured for any sight of the enemy. None could be seen so they had an escape route out. Hall told Thomas that he would stay with the Lewis machine-gunners and - if needs be - engage those searching. That would slow the Germans down and allow the main group a chance of escape. Thomas reluctantly agreed and, whilst Hall prepared the men and machine-guns, Thomas organised the unit into its two groups, to take different directions to evade the enemy and make good their escape.

However, because of the surrounding countryside, the two groups initially moved in the same direction, parallel with the road and the river. Then, as each leader saw an opportunity of cover, the groups went their separate ways. Darkness was covering them and their movements, but that meant that they had less opportunity to observe areas where danger may lurk and to take action to avoid them.

20

Hall could hear German voices but could not see anybody. They were ready and waited. A runner approached them from the rear to explain that, out of the woods and a short distance away, was a rather dilapidated barn which had good views towards the woods and surrounding countryside. Without hesitation, Hall ordered the gunners and their loaders to move out. The runner led the way and, once out of the wood, they followed a low hedge; moving as quickly as they could, they headed towards the barn. It was early evening and they were exposed but, at the barn, they found positions where they set up their Lewis guns and settled down to peer out onto the open ground. There was no noise, no voices, just their breathing. Then Hall could just make out German soldiers appearing at the edge of the wood. They seemed to be moving cautiously into the open and then crouching down, presumably waiting for orders.

Von Krupt had expected his men to have located the enemy by now and either captured or engaged them, but all was silent. He issued stern orders for the men to look harder and faster, as it would soon be totally dark and he knew that the enemy could slip away in the darkness. A junior officer had a message for von Krupt: they had received information from a sergeant on a road-block that a boat was moored further up-river. His soldiers had spoken to the captain, who said he was undertaking maintenance. Krupt listened to the junior officer as he explained, then cut him short. Had the soldiers inspected the boat from top to bottom? What was the boat's name? How many people were on the boat? Were guards posted to stop the boat being moved? The junior officer could only remark that both the captain and flag were German. Krupt flew into a rage and ordered the boat to be detained until it had been thoroughly inspected.

Thomas had reached the area where the boat had been moored. Leaving his group in hiding, he and Sergeant White moved forward to the road. Dressed in their special camouflage suits, they blended into their surroundings. To their right, they could see the truck forming a road-block. Ahead of them was the walkway to the jetty, but there was no boat. Clearly something had caused concern and Hartmann had decided to move. They would have to walk further along the river to find it.

The men in the barn could see the Germans begin to walk across the field, stretched out in a long line. Hall told the men to hold their fire. He would wait until they were much closer, but he also had in mind that they would not continue once it got dark. Whilst they waited, they were surprised to be joined by Sergeant McLeod and six others from the unit, who had returned to help with the rear guard. Clarissa was among them, having considered that if they got into a fire-fight, there might be casualties.

In the half-light, the figures of the Germans could be seen plodding across the fields. They were not going to stop. Hall let them get to about the half-way point, where they were exposed with little cover. He faced two choices. Pull back and find another defence location or open fire and pin them down. The problem was that he did not know anybody else's exact location. He looked out the back of the barn and one of those who had come back pointed out the direction where they had been. He could make out another barn which seemed to be quite close to a farmhouse. He made a decision to go and the group moved out as fast as they could. Keeping in single file, they made best progress across the open fields. They were thankful that the darkness would now hide them.

What Hall did not see was that the Germans had turned around and were going back towards the wood. Krupt, having studied his maps, decided that he would move his troops up and down the river in order to locate the boat: he was now convinced that it was the saboteurs' base. As men were gathered in the area of the factories, they piled onto trucks to be transported in either direction along the river. The locals, seeing and hearing the army was on the move, stayed indoors. There was something happening and it was none of their business. Krupt judged that the boat would have moved upstream and that those involved would try to make for Switzerland where they would surrender themselves. He and his staff now followed in that direction. His orders to move his unit to the Front would have to wait. He was on the hunt and ready for the kill.

One farmer was curious as to what was happening: after all, he had a family to look after. He peered out of windows from darkened rooms and was concerned when he saw a line of shadowy figures move into his barn. Had they been German soldiers, the house would have been their first place to call, looking for food and drink. Not wanting to be embroiled in any trouble, he needed to get word to either the army or the police station. He sent his eldest son, having explained the message he had to deliver. The young man made his way to the road and began to run towards the town. When he heard and saw any vehicle coming in his direction he hid. He was wise enough to know that running into the road to stop a vehicle would get him killed. It was some time before he arrived at the police station and entered. The officer on duty listened to the message and then dispatched a policeman on a motor-cycle to go and find Krupt to advise him of the situation.

The policeman passed the farm where the young man came from and continued until he found the army vehicles parked. A guard challenged him and he was taken to Krupt. The message from the farmer was passed on. Although it was dark, Krupt ordered the trucks to reverse and move back down the road, following the police officer. They stopped well clear of the farm and soldiers disgorged from the trucks.

Krupt went forward and identified where the barn was and ordered his junior officers to take their soldiers and surround the building. This was going to take time. Meantime, he and his orderly went to the farmhouse. The farmer let them in, and from a top room window, Krupt was able to obtain a vague outline of the building. Glimpses of the moon helped to light up the area, which helped. Before leaving the house he told the farmer and his family to take cover, as those they were seeking might engage in a battle. Back at his vehicles there were runners waiting, ready to take messages. Then he received word that everybody was in place.

The inside of the barn was well-kept and on two floors. Those on guard had virtually no visibility, due to the clouds and lack of moonlight. They could not see the barn they had left, nor the wood which had provided them with cover during the operation. Hall decided that they should move out under cover of darkness to catch up with the others. Hopefully they would be well away from the Germans in the morning. Of course, they might also locate the boat. One of the men who was ready to go crept outside on the opposite side of the barn and, whilst he stood urinating, looked into the distance. His brain registered that something appeared to be moving but he could not make out what. He stared in different directions and it was the same. He went back inside and found Hall who was just making sure that everybody was ready. He whispered that he had seen something moving. The impact of the situation, if he was correct, was not lost on Hall: he had not anticipated any activity on that side of the barn and had thought that they could quietly slip away. He went outside and strained to see in the darkness. Then, in a million-to-one chance, the clouds parted and the moon gave a glimmer of pale light. He could see the movement, of not one individual, but many. His brain registered the scene. Soldiers were coming towards their back. They were surrounded and their escape options closed. Back inside the barn, he ordered everybody to defensive positions. He had a visible enemy coming in on the opposite side to the one he had expected and anticipated that soldiers would be coming from the other direction as well. He directed the two Lewis guns to be moved to cover the approaching soldiers. Riflemen watched the other side.

The voice that boomed out had an accent but spoke impeccable English. It seemed to come from the direction of the farmhouse. It called on the Englanders to surrender. They were surrounded and if they did not hand themselves over, the German army would have to deal with the situation. Nobody in the barn replied. The German voice boomed out the message again. There was no reply. There several moments of almost complete silence before they heard the noise of a very pistol being fired. A green light sped up through the sky, to fall slowly to earth some distance away. It was the signal for the German soldiers to move in and begin the attack.

There was no instant epic battle of rifle and machine-gun fire; there was just quietness. The Germans struggled to keep line abreast whilst crossing the field and the British soldiers had to wait until they could see the enemy. A group of Germans could be made out crossing a drainage ditch and climbing up the other side. The first Lewis gun opened fire and cut the line of men down. The Germans returned the fire using rifles. The second Lewis gun sent a burst of bullets tearing into the enemy. The response soon came with the German machine-guns chattering, sending out their deadly hail that struck the timber of the barn.

Two men were hit in the fire-fight and Clarissa sprang into action. The wooden walls of the barn were not made to stop machine-gun bullets and some of the bullets were armour-piercing. On the other side of the barn, German machine-guns were being used to effect. This action was keeping the British heads down whilst allowing their soldiers to move closer to the barn. Two men fell from the upper floor. Clarissa checked them. Both were dead. She returned to the two wounded men. She noted that she could only hear one Lewis gun firing. Hall realised that they had limited ammunition and that it was just a matter of time. He had another difficult decision to make. Did everybody have to die or should they surrender under the overwhelming odds? He conferred with McLeod but it made little difference: he could not see them all slaughtered. A prisoner-of-war camp was a better option. He was concerned about how they would treat Clarissa and ordered her to hide. Although she objected, she did as she was told. Hall found a white cloth and waved it. There was sporadic shooting as the order to cease fire was channelled round the German troops.

Clarissa, now well hidden, knew that there were four wounded men - that she had been busy bandaging - in pain and bleeding. Von Krupt, following his soldiers, headed towards the large barn doors. Two soldiers lifted the wooden bar and swung open the doors. The soldiers entered, rifles raised and bayonets fixed. They confronted Hall and his men, hands held in the surrender position. Seeing that it was safe to do so von Krupt walked up to stand in front of his captives.

In the dimness of the light provided by oil-lamps, he then signalled to two of his men. They moved forward and bayoneted to death the wounded men. He had signalled to others to search the floor above. Two men who were unharmed were ordered below and the bodies of dead soldiers were dropped down.

Whilst soldiers made a cursory search of the barn, von Krupt confronted Hall.

'Where is your officer?'

'I don't know. We were separated.'

'How many of you were there?'

'Twelve,' said Hall.

'How did you get here?'

Hall did not answer.

He turned to a junior officer.

'Take them to the police station and guard them. I will deal with them later.'

The men were led out of the barn and down to the road. Krupt ordered his soldiers to be called back and get aboard the trucks. His business now lay further along the road, where he hoped to locate the elusive boat.

Clarissa remained hidden but knew that with daylight they would search the barn more thoroughly. She had to get away. The noise of marching men, orders being given in German and the sound of truck engines provided her with the evidence that the Hun had departed. She did not want to remain where she was for long and so, when it seemed safe to do so, she crept out of her hiding-place. Taking great care, she made her way towards the open barn doors. Finding what was left of her patients, she checked them. They were dead. They had been butchered.

She slipped out of the barn and moved away. She was not wise to the ways of military thinking but knew that she had to keep to some sort of cover where she could hide if need be. She made reasonable progress as she followed the route of the road and the river. She avoided the temptation to simply walk along the road. It all looked so easy when she was with Thomas but now, alone, with angry Hun all round, it was a different story. The hardest part would be when she had to hide as daylight came; but for now she pressed on.

Hartmann decided, after the German soldiers had taken an interest in the boat, that they would depart and move upstream. As soon as the boilers were stoked and enough steam provided to the *Schwanhild,* they quietly slipped away. It had become obvious that there were more German soldiers than anticipated and that they were front line troops, not reservists. Oliver and Gould feared for those ashore: they were tasked with waiting to collect them but they had never discussed exactly how long they should remain. The one thing that was certain was that, judging by the noise and flames from the explosion, they had attacked the targets and the ammunition factory had been destroyed. They did not know how much of the weapons factory had been demolished.

Hartmann was soon becoming desperate as he could not find a suitable place to stop. He had to move the boat further up-river than he had planned. That in turn would mean that it would take those ashore longer to reach them and they would be more exposed to discovery. He eventually saw a place alongside the river bank. It was in a poor state of repair but he thought it would suffice. The crew were only able to secure ropes with difficulty; Hartmann decided to keep a reasonable head of steam so that they could move at short notice. Oliver prepared for an attack on the boat, although they had few men to help in that task. He was thankful that during the tedious times on the journey, everybody had been trained in the use of the Lewis machine guns, rifles and Mills bombs. It was now a question of waiting.

Von Krupt sent motorcyclists ahead to search for the boat which, he reasoned, would have to stop to collect the men who were on land. Moving fast, they soon caught sight of the boat, the tell-tale smoke coming from its stack. They turned around and raced back to report their find. Von Krupt continued until he could see the boat and some of the surrounding area. It was, from his point of view, an excellent choice. There was plenty of cover for his men to move into place. The briefing he gave his officers was straightforward: attack the boat and kill everybody on board; take no prisoners. As he watched his men moving away to take up their positions, a dispatch rider arrived with a message. He was to move his troops onto the Western Front at once and with much haste. He returned a message to his second-in-command to start advancing the remaining troops and equipment towards the front line. He and the men he had with him would catch them up later; he explained that he had found the enemy and was now about to destroy them.

A look-out was on watch and hoping to see friendly faces. But only death came. He was killed by the opening shot of the battle. Two heavy machine-guns began to pour rounds into the boat. Oliver moved into a position with little cover, in order to fire a Lewis gun. One of the stokers acted as a magazine loader. He judged the sweep of the machine-gun and, using what cover he had, he fired at the enemy's gun flashes. Gould had managed to do the same thing. Hartmann wanted to cast off but, to reach the ropes, his men would be exposed to enemy fire. Those who tried to get to them were cut down. It was a battle of attrition and the Germans were winning. When a member of the crew looked from behind cover for a target, a German sniper was ready. Oliver moved his gun to different locations and emptied magazines of bullets into the area where the Germans were. It made no difference, as the returning fire was full-on and accurate.

It felt like an age, but the action was in fact short-lived. Oliver was hit in the shoulder so his loader took over firing the machine-gun. Rosie had left the relative safety of the galley and had crawled about to administer first aid where she could. She bandaged Oliver's shoulder just as Clarissa had shown her. He then ordered her to go back to the galley, and find a place to hide and stay there. She argued and Oliver got very angry. Only then did she do as she was told. As she moved away, the loader fell back, dead. The Lewis gun fell to the floor. Oliver managed to pick it up, check it and fling it into a firing position. He could not pull the trigger. He was dead. The single bullet had passed between his eyes.

Gould realised that they were not going to win this battle as he dragged the Lewis gun about, trying to find a location where he could engage the enemy. Then he saw the line of German soldiers stand and walk towards the boat, rifles pointed ahead, bayonets fixed. He stood and fired. Rounds struck the line of soldiers before the gun jammed and, as he attempted to clear it, a volley of bullets struck him. He lay with the machine-gun alongside him. Hartmann knew that when the soldiers reached the boat, he would be shot as a traitor. The Mills bombs he threw were his last challenge to those who had taken his country into a futile war. German snipers saw where he was on the bridge and when he next stood to throw, they shot him, allowing the primed bomb to stay on the bridge where it exploded.

The German soldiers made their assault on the boat and boarded it. With an air of great urgency, they searched it. Anybody alive was shot or bayoneted. There were no questions asked and no mercy shown. As soon as their job was done, the soldiers withdrew. Von Krupt was satisfied with what he had seen and with what his junior officers reported. The bodies of his own soldiers were picked up and thrown onto a truck; once all the men and weapons were loaded, the convoy sped back to the town.

The *Schwanhild* was in a sorry state. Ravaged with bullets and strewn with dead bodies, it was a tormented hulk. Thomas had led his men on a wild race, using all their skills and endurance to follow the road. They had seen the convoy of soldiers race along it and they were well hidden when it hurried back again. They had heard the battle, but were not close enough to provide any assistance. Now, crouched in a hide, Thomas could observe the boat through his binoculars. There were no Germans and no signs of any life on the boat. He feared that everybody was dead, but he would have to go aboard to see for himself. The men he had with him were allocated defensive positions, in case the Germans returned.

Thomas selected three men to go with him to the boat. Sergeant White was left in charge of the remaining men who would stay in their defensive hides. In full view of anybody on the boat, Thomas led the men across the road and down to the jetty. They saw the blood and used bullet-cases that portrayed the aftermath of a fierce battle. It was clear that the Germans had not had it all their own way: a good number had been killed or wounded. As they reached the boat, it was eerily quiet. Thomas cautiously climbed aboard and instantly saw the crumpled body of Oliver lying next to a machine-gun. He moved over to him, quietly calling his name. There was no reply and he checked to see if he was alive, but found he was not. He could now see the bodies of all those who had remained on the boat. His other men, now on board, began to search the boat. Thomas entered the mess room. There were no bodies. Where was Rosie? Had they killed her or taken her away? That was the sort of thing that happened in the fog of war. He looked in the galley and in the store-room. Nothing, nobody. One of the men joined him.

'Captain Hartmann and Lieutenant Gould are on the bridge, both dead,' he said.

Thomas realised that they had killed everybody.

'Where was Rosie?' asked Thomas, almost to himself.

There was a noise and then he was smothered. His brain raced as he could not instantly comprehend what was happening. The face of the soldier was showing a broad grin. Thomas realised that the body clinging to him was Rosie. He gently untangled himself from her until he could see the tears streaming down her face. It took several minutes for her to calm down. Speaking quickly, she then told them what had happened.

The other men joined them in the mess room and it was confirmed that there was nobody left alive on the boat. Only Rosie had survived, after being ordered to hide. She had waited in fear as the Germans stormed the boat. She knew what they were saying and that they had orders to kill everybody then get back to the unit because the regiment had been given orders to move to the front line as soon as possible. She had remained hidden in case somebody else came looking. Hearing Thomas's voice had been a miracle.

Thomas sent one of the men to tell Sergeant White to leave the two Lewis guns covering the road and to tell the rest of the men to return to the boat. Their first task was to remove the bodies to the forward hiding-place in the cargo of wood. They would have to decide what to do with them. Thomas now had to decide what to do. The group under Sergeant-Major Hall had not caught up and the other group under Sergeant McLeod was also missing. How long would it be before somebody else came to look at the boat - either military, police or civilians? What would or could they do?

Von Krupt arrived back in the town and parked his car outside the police station. He had no jurisdiction over the policemen or their activities, but none were going to challenge him. Inspector Hartmann, the local police chief, treated those held in his cells as prisoners-of-war. Von Krupt enlightened him with the information that they were in fact spies and saboteurs and were to be treated as such.

'We have added one more to the prisoners numbers',' said the Inspector. 'Your men captured her and brought her here. She is in a separate cell.'

'A woman?' thundered von Krupt. 'What woman?'

'An army nurse,' said the Inspector.

'Nurse?' shouted von Krupt. 'She is not a nurse. She must be in disguise; she is a spy and a saboteur.'

The Inspector had spoken with her and with the men who all claimed that she was indeed a nurse. She knew none of the details of the military operation, but was a member of the British Army, assigned to tend the wounded. Von Krupt had slammed the table in a rage. He would have none of it.

'The British Army do not have women on the front line

and she was behind the front line. No,' he said, 'she is a spy and a saboteur.'

The two men glared at each other.

'Show me this woman,' demanded von Krupt.

The Inspector led the way to the cell and opened the door.

Von Krupt glared at Clarissa, his arrogance reaching boiling -point.

'Who and what are you?'

'I am a nurse attached to the soldiers you have captured.'

'A nurse,' he sneered. 'Since when does a nurse wear a uniform like this?' he asked, indicating Clarissa's unusual khaki uniform displaying the red cross.

'A starched white uniform is not appropriate for working with operational soldiers,' she replied. 'In the front line we would be targets for your snipers; so we dress accordingly.'

'You are a spy and a saboteur, the same as the men we have captured,' stated von Krupt.

'She is a nurse,' interjected the Inspector. 'She should be treated as such.'

Von Krupt turned on the Inspector. 'I say she is a spy and a saboteur who was responsible for the destruction of important military locations on German soil. I will not hear otherwise and if you persist in arguing with me I shall have you shot. Do I make myself clear?'

The Inspector did not reply. Von Krupt, having had his say, pushed past to find his men. He found them waiting outside. He told them to remove the Englanders from the cells and, take them to the courtyard at the back of the police station. He ordered a sergeant to prepare a firing-squad. The soldiers were taken and lined up against a wall.

It was, for von Krupt, a simple process and he stood before the line of men to tell them of their fate:

'You are spies and saboteurs and as such do not fall under the rules of war. You are not prisoners-of-war. We have to deal with spies and saboteurs in the correct way. As such you face a firing-squad.'

He moved to one side, straightened his uniform and hat, then gave a command for the squad to bring their rifles to the aim position. The next command found them using the bolt to load a round into the rifle. The order to aim and fire followed. Inspector Hartmann and his policemen had been forced to watch. With the deed done, von Krupt marched over to the line of crumpled bodies, drew his pistol and shot each man in the head. Holstering his pistol, he walked over to the Inspector and his policemen.

'Gentlemen, that is how you deal with spies and saboteurs.'

'What are you going to do with the nurse?' enquired the Inspector.

'I will deal with her later.'

He then marched away, leaving the policemen to dispose of the bodies.

Clarissa, held in a small and dank cell, had heard the men being removed from the cells and being taken to the courtyard. Little was left to her imagination as to what fate awaited them. The sound of the rifle fire and then the individual shots left her numb. Her comrades had been murdered. She sat shivering and angry, angry that she could not escape the madness. It was quiet for some time before her cell door was unlocked and opened. Inspector Hartmann entered and stood in the doorway.

'My men are bringing you some food,' he said in broken English. He looked at the forlorn woman sitting and staring at him. 'My brother was the captain of your boat and has also been killed. Now, whilst I did not approve of my brother's actions, I consider that all of your group were prisoners-of-war and should have been treated as such. I have no power or control over von Krupt and I do not know what he will do next. He is under orders to get his men to the front line but is still here. I cannot get you out of the building because he has left soldiers on guard. I have brought you a pen, paper and envelope, and if you choose to write a letter, I will get it posted. It is the best I can do.'

She did not reply and he left her with the writing materials. A short while later, a policeman arrived with food. She did not feel hungry but penned a letter to her family and sealed it in the envelope. It was a long night and she barely slept. Her mind relived her life, indulging in the good parts. She thought of Thomas and wondered where he was and whether he was still alive.

Thomas and Sergeant White sat in deliberation.

'Sir, I think I should take a few men and go back to see if I can find the others,' said White.

'That will be my job,' said Thomas.

'With due respect, sir, you need to get this old tub ready to move. We don't have any sailors left and at least you have been on the bridge and seen how things were done. You and Rosie speak German and that will help if we get challenged. The boiler needs attending to and I know nothing of such things. I can take the best field-craft men and would be back in a few hours.'

'All right, you have a point. We have sixteen men so choose four plus yourself and leave the Lewis gunners where they are for now. We will have to defend the boat if attacked, but bear in mind that there may not be a boat to come back to. I wish you good luck.'

The remaining men prepared to stoke the boiler; they ate a meal in shifts, rotated the machine-gun teams and generally prepared the boat for sailing.

Sergeant White had reached the place where the boat had moored to drop them off for the raid. He and the team moved very carefully, looking for any signs of the remainder of the unit. There was no sound and no movement. They decided that it was futile to go any further or wait any longer so they began the task of retracing their route. They moved up a small gulley that hid them from the road and the surrounding fields. The concentrated fire of the German machine-guns cut them down before they had a chance to take any evasive action. The enemy were well hidden and had allowed them to pass through, waiting for their return, in case they had found any stragglers. The officer in charge went forward to confirm that they were dead, then ordered the soldiers and their weapons to move out. Further down the road, the driver of a truck heard the fire; when the shooting stopped and it became quiet, he drove up to meet the soldiers. Krupt thought that he had not caught all of the attackers and had left an ambush party. On the boat, the faint noise of the machine-guns being fired in the distance could be heard. Thomas knew that White did not have such weapons and concluded that they had been ambushed.

It was almost daylight when the door to Clarissa's cell opened. Two burly German soldiers entered. They hauled her to her feet and almost carried her out and along the passageway. Passing through a door, they entered the courtyard. They took her to stand in front of a high wall. Four soldiers stood facing her. Von Krupt marched in. He was clearly in a hurry.

He looked at her. His statement was short in the extreme and displayed the arrogance of the man.

'You are a spy and a saboteur and as such will be executed, as is the law in this country.'

She was not allowed any final words. He turned and gave the orders to the firing-squad. She stood proud and unyielding in her defiance towards the monster who was to end her life. Once the squad had fired they were dismissed, leaving von Krupt to fire the obligatory head-shot. He then went to join his men; on passing Inspector Hartmann, he told him to burn the body. Departing from the police station, he began a race to catch up with his unit.

Inspector Hartmann arranged for Clarissa's body to be taken to the local church where the other prisoners had been taken. He could at least ensure that they would all be buried properly. He then went with another police officer along the road towards where the army had attacked the boat. They were followed at a much slower pace by a large cart pulled by four horses. The Inspector did not question how this farmer still had his horses, when most had been taken for the war effort and had been slaughtered on the battle fields. He was grateful for the use of them and to the men who had volunteered to come along. Reaching the jetty, he saw that the boat had gone; but there was a line of bodies, each wrapped in a blanket, close to the water's edge. The Inspector checked each body before it was lifted and placed on the cart. The last body he examined was his brother's. Looking at the savage end to his life, emotion overwhelmed him. He had admired his brother for his beliefs about a wasted war, a war that was fuelled by the ruling classes of a number of countries, that had needed just a spark to ignite it and which had been provided. He had avoided the military call-up and continued his work on the river. Then their own countries drunken soldiers had visited their home-town, looking for women. When none were forthcoming, they had shot the fathers who had hid them. Their father had been one of those murdered. That had tipped the balance and his brother had taken his boat to England. He pulled the blanket back over his brother and helped the men lift him onto the wagon. With the task done, they made their way back to the town. Somebody was going to have to make a decision as to where to bury them.

21

Thomas was at the helm of the *Schwanhild* as it made its slow progress along the river. The signs of the carnage that had befallen the boat had been cleaned up as best they could. Anybody looking at it would immediately see that the boat and those on board had been involved in military action. It was now just a case of survival, and there were not many of them left. As Thomas struggled with the steering of the vessel, in his mind he struggled with the thoughts of not knowing what had happened to the others. He could not escape thoughts of Clarissa, those which caused him the most anguish. He hoped that if she had been caught, she would be treated as a prisoner-of-war and would at least survive the duration in captivity. It was the last vestige of hope he had, combined with his knowledge of the skills she had to survive.

Rosie was on the bridge beside Thomas. He had saved her and was now her guardian; that thought would never go away. Nobody admired the magnificent views; there was no inclination and certainly no time to take them in. For the eleven soldiers and Rosie, the tasks of stoking the fire, cutting wood for the boiler to help preserve the stock of coal, helping to prepare food, acting as look-outs and steering the boat were their priorities. There were no sailors or Germans on board. All of them had gone. There were no spare men and it was a rapid learning experience for all of them; but they were going full out, heading towards Switzerland.

Weapons had been prepared and located in places where the men could get to them quickly; however their use was one situation that Thomas wanted to avoid at any cost. The look-outs were on edge and fed him information constantly. Harry Cooper, one of the West End Cooper brothers, claimed to have steered a boat on the river Thames and so Thomas passed over the helm to him. After a few minutes, Cooper had showed him that he had the skill so Thomas left him to navigate the boat whilst he planned the next move.

Thomas studied the chart spread out on the small table. There were some identifiable land marks, which gave him a reasonable idea as to where they were. Sidney Long, his explosives expert, joined him.

'We are about here,' said Thomas, indicating a point on the map. 'As we get closer to the Swiss border, security will become more of a problem. I propose to stop along here,' he again pointed to the map. 'I think it will be wooded and possibly very hilly. We can make good use of the cover to move away from the river and then turn towards the border. I don't know what barriers there will be. I doubt the guards will be of a calibre to cause too much trouble; but after our experience at the factory, we will prepare for the worst. Once we cross into Switzerland, we will surrender ourselves.'

'What weapons do you propose we carry?'

'We will have to carry food as well as ammunition. Perhaps we should take a Lewis gun, there is one left. Rifles and pistols are a must. We will live off the land and avoid contact with the enemy at all costs as we cannot afford any sort of a battle with them. Our priority is to get everybody over the border. Can you speak to the men and canvass their opinions? We have come a long way and now we are close to a safe haven.'

Thomas went back to the bridge and Long went to talk to the men.

They next spoke at the meal table. 'Everybody agrees that we should abandon the boat and make our way overland. The consensus is that we do not take the Lewis gun since it is heavy as are its ammunition magazines. As the plan is to avoid trouble, it would be just a dead weight.' Thomas agreed.

'We need everybody ready to go at a moment's notice. Get some of the men to help Rosie with the food distribution. If we find a suitable place, we could get going tonight. Also get the two row-boats ready to launch.'

Long gave a puzzled look.

'I have a spare chart and have drawn a rough line of march on the opposite bank. With the boats gone, I hope the Hun will go off in that direction.'

'Will we just let the boats go?'

'No, put holes in the bottoms of them. Then they will sink when we launch them. It may keep the Hun busy for a while, searching the river for them.'

Thomas told Rosie the plan and she said that she had already sorted out most of the food. It just had to be handed out. She was ready to go. There was a call from the bridge and Thomas rushed up. Cooper had spotted a landing-place with a wood close by. This would be a test of their boat-handling skills as neither had actually moored such a craft before. Thomas rang "dead slow" on the telegraph and the boat slowed down to be barely moving. Men stood by with ropes. Cooper eased the boat towards the pontoon. Thomas rang "half-astern" and it was a few moments before the propeller dug into the water to reverse the forward motion.

The two row-boats were launched and cut loose to sink. There was a crash as the boat rammed the pontoon broadside. It stayed there long enough for the men to jump onto the pontoon and hook the ropes over the bollards. Men on board pulled the ropes as tight as they could and secured them. The boat moved away slightly, then moved back, the movement causing it to bump into the pontoon again. With the engine stopped, those down below made their way up on deck to collect their kit and a sack of food. Long counted everybody off as they jumped ashore, moved up the open ground and disappeared into the wood. When everybody was accounted for, Thomas left the boat. As he was about to be swallowed by the wood, he turned and took his last look at the *Schwanhild,* the boat that had served them so well.

Thomas moved to the front of the line and led the way through the wood. Rosie was behind him. Long brought up the rear. They were moving tactically, dressed in their ghillie suits. The first part of the journey through the wood was uphill and he could hear the laboured breath of those behind him. He set the pace of travel to suit Rosie's, as he calculated that she might be the slowest. Progress showed that that was not in fact the case. Eventually, the ground levelled; they kept going, needing to put as much distance between them and the river as possible. When they reached the edge of the wood, an expanse of open, rolling, hilly farm land spread out before them. In the distance, they could see a large pine forest. Using a compass to get his bearings, Thomas traced a line of hedgerows that would help to hide them. It was a bit of a dog-leg route however, as they could not cross open ground, they had no option but to use the cover of the hedge.

They set off and followed the zig zag division of the fields, heading towards the forest. Thomas kept up a reasonable pace, keeping an eye on Rosie to judge how she was coping. She was behind Thomas and was not going to give an inch, no matter how much endurance that required. The crossing was time-consuming but uneventful, and they were all pleased when they finally entered the forest. Thomas carried on until the light began to fade and they had found a place to set up camp. There, surrounded by trees, two men helped Rosie sort out some food but they did not light a fire. Working in shifts, they kept one man on guard throughout the night, and in the morning they prepared to press on. They walked for several hours before the forest thinned and they reached its edge. The route they had taken was up and down the contours of the land but the direction was as straight as Thomas had been able to manage. Looking at the landscape in front of them, they could see a large village off to their left but gentle rolling hills to their right. It was to the right where the Swiss border would be found. Thomas studied the area through his binoculars but could see no signs of military activity. The eagle-eyed ghillie and gamekeepers also studied the scene and could not spot anything either. It was peaceful and the war seemed a million miles away. Ahead was another forest, but there were no hedges to hide them and they would have to cross the fields to get to it. Thomas had a decision to make.

On the Rhine, the German gunboat moved cautiously towards the *Schwanhild*. The crew could not see anybody on board but they had all of their weapons trained on her. They had been warned about the last attempt to board the boat, where many of their compatriots died in the ensuing gun-battle. Moving alongside, sailors quickly jumped aboard, and using whatever cover was available, they moved through the boat. They searched everywhere and found nobody. The boat had been abandoned. They discovered the secret accommodation inside the cargo of wood and could determine that many men had been carried aboard. It took no imagination for them to understand that the destruction of the arms dump closer to Holland was no accident; and that the latest raid, which destroyed both the ammunition and arms manufacturing factories, was carried out from this boat.

The map that Thomas had drawn on and then screwed up to be purposely left behind was discovered. Officers from the gunboat studied it; having identified that the two row-boats were missing, they came to the conclusion that those on board had escaped to the opposite side of the river and would be trying to escape either to France or to Switzerland. The signaller on the gunboat transmitted a message - not in code - to the closest army Headquarters, providing them with the information.

The soldiers at the barracks were war-weary; the thought of chasing all over the countryside in search of a small group of British soldiers was not very appealing. The officer-in-charge had endured first the Eastern Front then the Western Front; he had, at long last, found a nice quiet billet away from the fighting, since he was worn out both physically and mentally. Germany was running out of steam; when the Americans entered the war with their great might, they would never be able to win: so why die trying?

That was all short-lived: when the General Staff for the area intercepted the transmission, it was plain that they had other ideas. The officer-in-charge was ordered to take his men to track down the Englanders and apprehend them.

It took considerable cajoling by the officers and NCOs to get the soldiers moving. There was an air of general reluctance but eventually they were ready to move. Trucks carried their equipment and some of the men. The rest marched. The commanding officer had gone on ahead to meet up with the gunboat. He was surprised as to how enthusiastic the sailors were about chasing after the soldiers. The crew of the gunboat had scoured the local area for signs of the enemy, but had returned with nothing.

The commanding officer studied the map which he had been given.

'Where did you find this?'

'Screwed up and discarded aboard the boat.'

'What makes you think that they crossed the river?'

'The row-boats were missing.'

'Have you found them?'

'No.'

'So we have no real evidence as to which side of the river they may be on?'

The captain of the gunboat thought before speaking.

'No,' he said, shrugging his shoulders.

'So I am expected to scour hundreds of square kilometres of countryside, yet we have not one single clue as to which way they went?'

'Well, we found the boat and it is now your responsibility. Do you want me to transport any of your men to the other side?'

'When my men arrive, we will look for traces on both sides of the river.'

They had just agreed on a plan of action when a junior officer came from the gunboat. He passed a message to the captain. Having read the contents, he pulled a face.

'I have been ordered to proceed along the river in the opposite direction, with haste. It does not say why. I will bid you good day and good luck.'

The commanding officer was not overly concerned as he watched the gunboat depart on its journey. They would concentrate the search on their side of the river.

■ ■ ■

Inspector Hartmann had stopped for coffee on his way back to the police station. As he turned a corner, he was confronted by the presence of an army staff car parked outside the building. The car displayed a pennant indicating a high-ranking officer. He hurried up the steps that took him into the building and met the front desk sergeant.

'You have a general waiting in your office, sir.'

Inspector Hartmann made no comment but went directly to his office. There he found Generalmajor Allendorf.

'Good day, Generalmajor. I am Inspector Hartmann. How can I be of assistance?'

'I have been directed by Berlin to investigate your prisoners who, it is said, are British soldiers. They will be transferred to my staff and taken for interrogation. Can you prepare the necessary documents and have them ready to travel?'

'With due respect, sir, that is not possible.'

Allendorf's eyes narrowed but before he could respond, Inspector Hartmann continued:

'They have been shot, sir.'

'Shot! Shot! What do you mean, shot?'

'They were taken into my courtyard and shot, sir.'

'Who gave you the authority to shoot them?' demanded Allendorf.

'Nobody, sir. As far as I was concerned, they were prisoners-of-war - and that included the nurse. But the senior army officer said that they were spies and saboteurs and ordered them shot. His men executed them.'

Allendorf glared. 'What nurse?'

'They had a military nurse with them.'

'Where is the nurse now?' enquired Allendorf.

'They shot her as well.'

'They shot her? Where were you whilst this was going on?'

'I was here, sir. But I was told that if I did not comply with what they were doing, I would be shot as well.'

Allendorf looked past the Inspector. He was contemplating the situation.

'They also attacked the boat that had carried the British and killed all those on board. We went and recovered all of the bodies for burial. When the soldiers left, they took their dead with them.'

'What was the name of this officer?'

'Oberst von Krupt, sir.'

'Von Krupt!' parroted Allendorf.

'Yes, sir.'

'Are you absolutely sure of the name and of what he did?'

'Yes, sir, my men will confirm what I have said.'

'Did any of this get documented?'

'Only where we had authority, sir.'

'I want every piece of paper that relates to this and I do mean every piece. Do I make myself clear?'

'Yes, sir.'

Allendorf slouched in his seat. His whole demeanour had changed.

'Are you all right, sir?'

'No, I am not,' he replied, seemingly lost in his own world.

'I have to report my findings to Berlin and I have to give them the name of von Krupt.' He paused. 'He is my nephew.'

There was a knock at the door.

'Come in,' said the Inspector.

One of his men entered.

'Sorry to interrupt you, sir, but there is a telephone call for the Generalmajor from Berlin.'

'I will take it here if I may.'

'Of course.'

The Inspector and his man left the room.

They could hear that, after Allendorf gave his report, there was no real two-way conversation, just a lot of 'yes, sir's'.

When he was finished, he came out of the office; it was noticeable that he was not as bullish as when he arrived.

'How do I get to the river? I have to find the boat and any remaining people that were on it.'

The Inspector gave Allendorf directions which were simple, and which avoided his having to send a policeman on a motorbike to guide him. Allendorf thanked the Inspector for his report and asked that the matter in question be kept private. There would be an investigation, however his priority was to draw the episode to an end. The military entourage departed.

22

Thomas made the decision to wait in the wood until dusk. Then, fully rested and with their kit such as it was, they began the journey across the fields to the next forest. With Thomas leading, they moved in single file with two guides out in front. A good pace was maintained and they were well into the cover of the trees before dawn. Having rested and eaten, they moved at a slower pace through the forest. It was a place where most of the men were quite at home. It was easy to disappear there and hide; it was also an easy place to get lost in. Thomas started to change direction and head in the general direction of the Swiss border. Progress was slow, but then the first glimpses of light appeared through the trees ahead of them, indicating that they were nearing the edge of the forest. Thomas brought the line to a halt. With one other man, and leaving the remainder in the cover of the trees, he moved cautiously forward until they could observe the countryside before them.

Thomas was aware that the river Rhine flowed through Basel and then swept round to cross in front of them, creating a natural border between Germany and Switzerland. Through the binoculars, he scanned the ground in either direction. Then it happened: a post! It stood out because it was painted red and white. He looked to the right. There was another. Back to the left and he could see one further in the distance. The undulating ground meant that he did not see all the posts, but he knew that he was looking at the Swiss border. He could just make out the barbed wire fence set back from the posts, and what looked like a trench following the line. Also on the Swiss side were observation towers, set in a way that each one could see another. Clearly the Swiss, although neutral, were on the defensive as far as their borders were concerned. That would have to be calculated into the plan for making good their escape.

Thomas spotted some ten figures in the distance, on the German side of the frontier. They were either cavalry or mounted infantry and were moving slowly along the frontier. He pointed them out to the soldier lying beside him. They were the only people that could be seen. Thomas then sent the soldier back to brief the others and to say that there was German cavalry patrolling close to the border. Long joined Thomas and experienced the view for himself. Thomas pointed out that the final part of their journey was across fairly open ground and that they would have to avoid the German mounted patrols. They then had to cross the river, pass through the barbed wire on the Swiss side, probably get across a trench and possibly get through more wire. Having done that, they had to surrender to the Swiss army without being shot in the process. Thomas was not sure if there were any defences on the German side.

Thomas left to return to the main group whilst Long remained to observe the enemy and the ground they had to cross. In the forest, amidst the dappled sunlight filtering through the trees, Thomas gathered everybody around him. He explained the situation to them:

'The border is visible, but it is going to be dangerous getting to it and across it. We have to cross the river and that means we will have to swim. I will need to know who can and who can't swim and how good you are. Once we are across, there are watch-towers that will be guarding the barbed wire fence and there might well be a trench. We have no idea what sort of an obstacle the trench would be. Then we have to move towards the Swiss defences, which I think will be trenches with soldiers on guard. We have to do all of that without them shooting us.'

One of the men, a corporal, spoke:

'Sir, I think we should take our time and observe the movement of the border patrols to get a clear picture of what to expect. We also need to see if the Swiss army carry out any patrolling.'

There was a consensus amongst them all.

'I agree,' said Thomas. 'My plan is to send the two ghillies, Hamish and Dougal, to recce the route to the river and see what is on the Swiss side. We need to find a place to cross and to have an idea of what we face on the other side. That might mean staying out overnight and getting back the following night. We must know how long it will take to move everybody to the point of surrender. We will actually cross into Switzerland at night and surrender at first light. Meantime, we will post two men on observation at the edge of the forest, to spot if there is a routine to the border patrols.'

With the light fading, the two ghillies, dressed for the occasion in full camouflaged covering, moved out of the wood and looked for a suitable route to the river. They were past masters at this type of work; the only difference was that they would normally stalk deer and stags and now they were evading the enemy. There was a full moon, which was a major advantage in terms of their having a certain amount of vision; however, that worked two ways and meant that they could be seen so they had to take care. Crossing the fields, they used what cover they could but as they approached the river, they crossed a well-worn track which was used by the cavalry on their patrols.

On the other side, they moved down towards the river and encountered a barbed wire fence. The wire was strung out and supported on large wooden "Xs". They followed the fence which ran parallel with the river, looking for a weakness that they could exploit. They continued to a place where a spit of land jutted out into the river and probably provide the shortest distance across to the other side. They found a copse of trees and a place where they could cut a hole through the wire. The noise they would make cutting in the stillness was the most riskiest part of the recce. Once through, they used the cover of the trees to prepare for the next part of the journey. Dougal decided to cross the river and recce the other side. He had stripped off most of his clothes. His boots were hung round his neck and the now rolled-up ghillie suit slung over his shoulder. He did not carry a weapon.

His opportunity came as a cloud crossed the sky to dull the light from the moon. He waded into the river and went as far as he could, then swam until he could touch the bottom and wade the rest. The crossing was cold but uneventful and on the other side he used his stalking skills to the full. He moved effortlessly up the riverbank and across open ground. He put his boots on and draped the ghillie suit over himself. Then he cautiously moved forward, to be surprised when he came to a railway line. Crossing it, he continued until he reached the barbed wire fence, which was more for show than a real deterrent. He found a place where he was able to slide underneath: having done so, he was confronted by the trench. This, again, was not going to stop a serious aggressor and certainly would not stop themselves. He could hear voices and caught sight of the occasional flicker of light. Having gone as far as he dared, he returned the way he had come. The river crossing posed no problem and once back on the German side he dressed, ready to begin the journey back to the forest.

Back in the forest, the two men found places to sleep; when they woke in the morning, Thomas was up and at the observation point at the edge of the forest. An early morning mounted patrol was spotted following what must be the course of the river. Rosie had performed miracles with what food they had, but they were running short. In the makeshift camp, the two ghillies reported to Thomas in great detail what faced them, but emphasised that it was all possible. Thomas decided that they would go that night.

Allendorf's force had arrived at the *Schwanhild* and the officers, having seen the vessel's workings, now pored over a map of the area. They reported to Allendorf; it was the senior one who spoke:

'Generalmajor, there are two options here. Either the Englanders escaped over to the other side of the river and are making headway towards either Switzerland or France. Or they could just have got off the boat and headed up into the forest and towards Switzerland. I would favour the route up here. They will know that there will be many German soldiers on the other side of the river. There will not be so many on this side. Also, there is a barracks on the other side that can undertake the search. So, if we move up through the forest we can seek them out. We believe they will attempt to cross into Switzerland; but it is a long border and they will be a small group.'

Allendorf agreed. The field officers in charge of the troops departed to brief their men. Some of their number would normally be on horseback, but horses had become a rare commodity and so they were, in effect, just infantry.

As soldiers they were a mixed bag. Some had front line service, whilst others had been too old for the Front. Then there were the young who were waiting to be sent to the trenches. The final group in the mix were those who had been wounded; whilst not fit enough for hard action, they could draw on their skills to add to what was a defence force.

Being lightly equipped, they began to move out. Although they did not know it, they were following the same route that Thomas and the survivors had done. Allendorf declined to join the march; the small Headquarters party would back-track on the road and find an alternative route to the villages that were located along the border. The one thing that Berlin had been emphatic about was that the search was to be kept low-key. They did not want to raise concerns with the Swiss and have them thinking that Germany was invading them. They were also warned that their frontier was not to be crossed under any circumstances, and that no weapons were to be fired in the direction of the border. Under those directions, Allendorf became less inclined to pursue the Englanders with any vigour. His officers were aware of the situation and so when the older soldiers found the climbs up the hills rather arduous, they did not shout and scream for them to move faster, but waited and rested until they caught up. When they reached the edge of the forest, the officers gathered together to assess the situation. They decided that one patrol would head towards the Swiss border, leaving the other two to cross open ground to another forest. However, food and rest were first on the agenda.

It was late afternoon when the two men on observation duty were startled by an unexpected noise. The horses were upon them before they had identified what it was. They did their best to blend into the undergrowth as the riders guided their beasts along the edge of the forest. They heard the voices, interspersed with laughter, as the horses were almost on top of them. If any of the riders looked down they would surely be seen and they were thankful that they had ghillie suits on. They lay motionless, with the horse and riders so close, in fact, that it surprised them that their presence did not spook the animals. If either man had stretched his arm out in front of him, he could have touched the horses' hooves. In the forest, the rest of the group had also heard the horses and men and had taken cover to hide and blend in with their surroundings. The two men who were exposed hardly dared to breathe, lest any movement was seen. Then, as quickly as they had arrived, they were gone. Thomas crept up to the men, who were in a state of shock; mostly for not spotting the enemy until they were upon them and also for not having been spotted themselves. It had been a close call.

Everybody was in a state of alert as it was evident that the enemy could pop up anywhere. The time seemed to take forever to pass before the light began to fade and they were all ready to go. Hamish and Dougal would go ahead and guide the main party which would be led by Thomas. Long would bring up the rear with instructions to keep watch behind them. They would carry weapons as far as the river and then discard them when crossing. Once on Swiss soil, Thomas wanted to surrender unarmed; they certainly would not take the chance of a gun-battle in what was to be their safe haven. As they walked, there was a gentle breeze with a partially cloudy sky and a moon that gave them some vision. As Thomas led his group out of the forest and along a track, a company of German infantry had just entered the same forest.

Their journey to the river was just a matter of each of them following the person in front. They kept to one track so as to avoid drawing attention to trails across grassland that would easily be seen by mounted riders. Thomas led and the two guides continued to move ahead, making sure it was safe. They would return to direct the group. Rosie was behind Thomas and stuck to his back like glue. A fast pace was maintained whilst crossing the open landscape, with everybody trying to keep as quiet as possible. They eventually reached the well-worn track that followed the course of the river. They doubted that there would be any military activity at night but took no chances. They quickly crossed the track and descended a slight embankment on the other side, to emerge on the wide grass river bank. Veering to the left, they followed the river and the German barbed wire fence. The moon, when it came out from behind the clouds, shimmered on the river's surface. They reached the place where a small hole had been made and they passed through one at a time. It was a slow process, leaving many exposed should they encounter any of the enemy. Once through, they moved to the safety of the trees. Long and another soldier did their best to close up the hole. They did not want to make it easy for any pursuing enemy to find their escape route.

There was to be no delay as they prepared for the most hazardous part of the escape, to cross the river. Those who could not swim were entrusted to those who could; this was Thomas's biggest nightmare. Whilst Hamish and Dougal entered the water, Thomas and Long collected the weapons and carried them out into the river, and disposing of them clear of where the main group would cross. Rosie who, from the outside looked, just like one of the men, had removed her boots, tied the laces together and slung them round her neck. She would stay beside Thomas. Once everybody was ready, they waded into the water; it was cold yet nobody made a sound. Because it was night-time, the bank on the other side could not be seen which was a distinct advantage. Thomas was very concerned about the non-swimmers. They had no proper buoyancy aids but, had adapted their capes. They tied had cord round the neck entry, then scooped air in at the open end, quickly gathering it to tie more cord round to create an air trap. Some had taken several goes before they had any semblance of a floatable device. The results were very primitive but gave a glimmer of security. They would ultimately rely on the swimmers to haul them across. When the water reached their chests, those who could not swim turned and faced away from the way they were headed. Then, drawing in a large breath, they lay back and with the aid of their improvisations, attempted to float. The swimmers had taken hold of them and once supported they kicked out, to haul the individual on their journey to the other side. Thomas did not have to hold on to Rosie as she made good progress. She was pleased to have adopted men's clothes, as swimming with a dress would have been impossible.

Thomas could not see everybody so, having ensured that Rosie had made it to the other side, he left her putting on her boots and went back into the river to help those still crossing. Thankfully, nobody panicked enough to begin shouting but there were some close moments. Then, when they could stand, it was a question of wading towards the bank. Hamish and Dougal had also walked back into the river to help the non-swimmers cover the last bit. Thomas concluded that it was because of the bond already existing amongst the men that they trusted each other implicitly. On the bank they looked like a band of desperadoes as they sat soaked and dripping water, putting on their boots. Thomas then checked everyone before they began to move forward to cross the railway line and then the last big barrier, the trench.

Soaking wet, they formed up to follow the man in front. Thomas and Rosie followed Hamish and Dougal. They waited at the railway line, listening for anything out-of-place then, careful not to make any noise, they crossed the line and moved into the longer grass. They were now moving forward to the wire fence of the Swiss border. Crouched down, it wasn't long before Dougal located the gap under it. Then, leading the group to it, they all passed underneath. A couple of men got caught on the wire but were soon freed. The next obstacle was the trench. As a group, they helped lower each other down to the bottom and were then helped to climb out on the other side. Finally they were all across and were now really in Switzerland. With great care and in silence they edged forward, soaking wet and shivering. Voices stopped them and they all went to ground. Thomas could hear them and knew that they were speaking German, but he could not determine what they were saying. He whispered the message back that they were to stay where they were until daylight.

They endured an uncomfortable remainder of the night in cold, wet clothes. Sleep evaded most of them, although there were some moments when a man would gently snore, to be kicked awake by a comrade. Dawn did not come too soon, and with the new day came the voices of Swiss soldiers as they went through their daily routines. Thomas looked ahead and could see soldiers' heads. He very slowly stood up, one hand raised, the other holding a stick with a piece of white cloth attached. The Swiss soldiers took several minutes to realise what they were looking at, then trained their rifles on the individual who had just appeared. Word spread as the alarm was raised and others took up a defensive stance. Thomas, standing and feeling very exposed, shouted out in German:

'We are English soldiers. We seek refuge in Switzerland; we surrender to you.'

There was no reply and he repeated the message. The remainder of the group remained hidden awaiting the unthinkable, Thomas' being shot.

Thomas dared not move; he was pleased when a voice, speaking very good English, asked who he was.

'We are English soldiers and have escaped from Germany. We surrender ourselves to the Swiss.'

'Come forward slowly,' said the voice.

Thomas walked forward towards what he assumed was another trench. Then he could see the person belonging to the voice. It was a young man, an officer. He was amongst seven or eight soldiers.

'Are you unarmed?' asked the officer.

'We are unarmed,' he replied.

'Who are you?'

'I am Captain Thomas Pierce of the King's Dragoons.'

'How did you get to Switzerland?'

'We were on a special mission along the river Rhine. We had to escape the Germans and did so overland.'

'Come forward,' said the officer again.

At the trench, Thomas was directed to climb down.

With rifles pointed at him, Thomas gave the officer as much detail about the venture as he thought appropriate. The Swiss officer said nothing as Thomas provided the information. When Thomas stopped speaking, the Swiss officer introduced himself as Johan Helmutt. He explained:

'We picked up German Morse code signals that reported on the destruction of the arms dump and of the two factories; also the action taken against a boat on the river Rhine. We were notified that there might be some action by the Germans close to the border but we did not really expect to see you. Please call your men forward, arms raised and without weapons.'

Thomas climbed up onto the parapet and called the others. They all stood and with arms raised, walked towards Thomas. They then climbed down into the trench and were led to where Helmutt was making a call on the field telephone. Whilst they waited, they were given mugs of strong hot coffee.

When Helmutt had replaced the telephone, he spoke to Thomas:

'Transport is being sent to collect you and take you to a military barracks. The British Ambassador is being notified of your presence. In the meantime, we shall try to provide some food for you.'

It became apparent to Thomas that the Swiss soldiers did not have a lot in the way of weapons, equipment and even provisions. As Thomas spoke to Helmutt, he was told that he had learnt English in England and was doing his tour of military duty on the front line. He explained that many of his men were not happy being in uniform because they did not get paid for defending the border. It was considered by the senior military staff to be their duty to safeguard the country. For that reason, Helmutt could not offer any change of clothing. He was really intrigued about Rosie being a member of the group but did not pursue the subject.

It was about an hour later when a truck arrived. Fortunately, the sun had come up; it was giving out some warmth and drying their now damp clothes. Under armed guard, they were transported away from the trenches. They had no idea where they were or where they were going. Helmutt had not been forthcoming on the matter, if indeed he knew himself. They had travelled some distance when the truck stopped alongside a blockhouse with a barrier across the road. Thomas was taken to speak with the officer-in-charge. The story of the groups getting to Switzerland was retold. The officer listened but when Thomas stopped, he was told that because of an agreement between Germany and Switzerland, anybody crossing the border without the correct travel documentation had to be returned to Germany.

Thomas was stunned beyond belief. Having come so far and risked so much, they would now be handed over to the Germans. He pleaded with the Swiss officer who just said that this was Swiss law and that they could not upset the Germans. Thomas said nothing to the others, who remained in the back of the truck where the cover restricted any view of the proceedings. He walked to the border barrier behind the officer and the Swiss soldiers. Then he waited whilst they went into no-mans-land, a small strip of land between the two countries' barriers, where the Swiss and German officers met. The Swiss officer explained that an English officer and his men had crossed the border into Switzerland during the night. The German officer listened and then, to the amazement of Thomas, stated that no Englanders had passed through Germany and crossed the border. He proclaimed that if they were in Switzerland, it had nothing to do with Germany.

The meeting was finished. The Swiss officer turned around and walked back to the barrier. He smiled at Thomas and they returned to the blockhouse. The Swiss officer then apologised for the procedure which had had to be respected, it being Swiss law. He then explained that the Germans never accepted that anybody could breach their border and if they admitted they had, then the officer-in-charge would be shot for allowing it to happen. It was a hideous procedure that had to be endured. Back on the truck, Thomas explained what had happened and that they were now on their way to a military barracks. They would be looked after and then be joined by somebody from the British Embassy.

In a small German village close to the border, Generalmajor Allendorf had endured a night in a tiny hotel. The following morning, he met with the officers commanding the mounted border guards and customs men. They resented the intrusion of the army into their area, especially a Generalmajor who was implying that they could not do their job properly. Allendorf, complying with the demands from Berlin, had stopped all troop movements close to the border. He was to rely on the border patrols. If there had been British escapees, and if they had managed to cross into Switzerland, then it would be their fault and not his. He had enough to worry about, what with his nephew having slaughtered prisoners of war, including a nurse.

Whilst they were engaged in a heated meeting, a border patrol had travelled along the border and not found any sign of escapees. When signs of trampled grass and an unusual repair job on the barbed wire fence were spotted, they were ignored. They would let somebody else find the potential clues and raise them if they dare. By the time the patrol arrived in the village and reported, Allendorf had told his troops to return to barracks and handed over responsibility to the border patrol and customs. He then got into his car and departed. Once he had gone and was well clear, the officers celebrated in a quiet way with a drink and a toast. On the border, things could now get back to normal; the cross-border smuggling, with its rewards for turning a blind eye, could continue.

23

It seemed like a lifetime had passed before Thomas stepped ashore in Southampton. He, along with his remaining men and Rosie, had been held in Switzerland and interviewed at length by Embassy staff. They had encountered problems with the War Office who claimed to know nothing of the secret operation, a venture for which they had provided men and equipment as well as a boat. Within the Embassy, people skilled in communications had intercepted the German Morse code messages that gave information about the raids. They had also communicated with Overbury, who confirmed the situation. It was at this point that he realized that neither Oliver nor Clarissa were among the escapees. He concluded that they were either in hiding or a prisoner-of-war camp.

The Embassy eventually provided the group with travel documents and they began their long journey home. They travelled through Switzerland, then crossed the border into France. The Germans were on the retreat, but they still took a route that was well away from the front line to reach Paris. Having spent a few days in the city, they travelled north, to eventually reach the channel ports. They now faced a wait to obtain a passage across to England. Thomas, as an officer, could have gone alone; however, he declined and waited until they could all go together. He wanted to make sure everybody that had survived made it back to England. Walking down the gangway, they stepped back onto English soil. A number of military policemen met them to form an escort as they were led away. Thomas was feeling numb; having carried out a very successful raid deep in enemy territory, he had found their homecoming was met with hostility.

Thomas was taken to a room where he was questioned first, being the person in charge of the group. He handed over each man's military documents. The questioning then began as to who they were and what they had been doing. Were they deserters? He answered the questions put to him and referred the inquisitors to Colonel Overbury and to the regimental office of the King's Dragoons. The officer leading the interrogation kept referring to a file before asking questions. When Thomas referred to Ian Boswell MP and even the meeting with the Prime Minister, there was no acknowledgement from those on the other side of the desk. The interrogation continued unabated, often returning to what had already been asked and answered. Then there came a twist in the questions. Did he know what had happened to the remainder of his group? He answered that he did not, but presumed that they had either been taken captive or killed. Did he know the name of the German officer who was in charge of the German unit who he claimed to have engaged with? He did not - he had just seen his handiwork. Then the interrogation came to an abrupt end. They would enquire into his version of events, and he would have to wait until they had their answers.

When he was returned to the others, he discovered that Rosie was missing. She had been taken away. Thomas went to discover what had happened to her. A military police sergeant and a civilian police inspector sat at a desk. When Thomas approached, dressed in a mixture of military uniform but showing no rank, he had to wait until they decided to look up at him.

'Yes?' said the sergeant.

'I am Captain Thomas Pierce and have just arrived back from a military operation; one of my unit has been taken away. I would like to know why and where they have been taken.'

There was no reaction when they learned that they might be speaking to an officer; they treated him as a nobody.

The sergeant replied in a totally disinterested manner:

'Are you talking about the woman?' He continued, without waiting for an answer, 'Well, she has no identity apart from a paper issued by the Swiss Embassy, and she's a woman. She was not wearing any sort of a proper uniform; so she's not military.'

'She is a member of my unit which has returned from Germany via Switzerland. She is my responsibility and I want her returned here until everything is sorted out,' said Thomas, straining to keep calm.

'We will tell you what to do, and not the other way round. So go and sit down or you will be arrested.'

Thomas was lost for words. He was angry, but he knew getting locked up would not help. He rejoined the others and sat down. It was about an hour and a half later when a corporal came over to Thomas.

'We cannot confirm who any of you are. You will have to wait at a holding camp until we can sort this out.'

The men became very angry but Thomas held them in check.

'All right, but we want our military identity documents handed back.'

'We have to hold on to them,' said the corporal.

Then, out of nowhere, a voice spoke:

'I say, it's Thomas Pierce, isn't it?' said a voice in a major's uniform, his hand held out.

Thomas looked at the major.

'Yes.' Then he realised who it was. 'Hello, Major Goodbody; it's good to see you, sir.'

'What are you doing here?'

'Have just got back from a secret operation and they won't accept who we are. They seem to be having trouble finding anybody to vouch for us.'

'Oh, we'll have that put right in a jiffy. I heard you were on some special job. What rank are you now?'

'Captain,' said Thomas.

Goodbody turned to the corporal.

'Take me to the officer-in-charge.'

'Yes, sir,' replied the corporal.

'See you in a moment,' said Goodbody, as the two men departed.

Within about fifteen minutes, the whole atmosphere changed. The sergeant and police inspector offered their profound apologies; but they could not have known that he was really a captain in the King's Dragoons. Moments later, they were joined by Rosie. All of the men were pleased to see her again. She explained that it had been awful, being separated and treated badly.

'What are your plans, Thomas?' asked Goodbody.

'I thought I had it all planned out, but the last operation has changed everything. It's changed me - and I may have lost my future wife. I think this lot know what has happened but are not saying anything.'

'My dear chap, what can be done?'

'I just need time to think.'

'Right-o, look, here are my contact details; get in touch if there is anything I can do to help.'

'Thanks, and thanks for sorting this mess out.'

'Not at all. Cheerio, old chap.'

Goodbody was gone, striding out of the building.

The men were provided with travel documents and directed to a mobilisation centre. Thomas was given his travel documents and directed to the King's Dragoons Headquarters. Rosie sat with the documents that would get her back to Winslade Hall. She was just bewildered by all that was going on.

'What are you going to do, Rosie?' asked Thomas.

'I shall go back to Winslade Hall and we can meet up there. I expect everything will have changed; if they have no news of Mr Oliver or Lady Clarissa, it will not be a happy place.'

'I have to go to London and report to the Dragoons to sort out my situation. I think that with the war coming to an end, my services will no longer be required,' said Thomas.

Thomas accompanied Rosie to the railway station and put her aboard a train. She waved from an open window as the train departed on its journey. Thomas held his hand up and waved until it had gone. By the time he returned to the military reception centre, his men had gone but had left a note saying which pub they would be at. Thomas was not in a celebratory mood.

He found the sergeant and police inspector, who were now most helpful. Could they help in his quest to determine if Oliver and Clarissa had returned to England? Knowing that it was an impossible task, he asked to use a telephone.

Soames answered and said he would bring Lord Overbury to the telephone.

'Thomas, is that really you?' said Overbury.

'Yes, sir.'

'Where are you?'

'Southampton, sir. We have been very badly treated since we got back.'

'Right, are you coming here?'

'I have to go to London to report to the Dragoons. Then I suppose I will have to do a debrief on the operation with yourself.'

'Look, Thomas. Stay in London - we can meet up. I have important things to tell you. I am so glad you are back.'

'Have you heard from Oliver or Clarissa?'

'I will update you in London.'

'I will call your club to arrange a meeting,' said Thomas. Then he added, 'Rosie is on her way. I just put her on a train.'

'It will be good to see her back. We will look after her,' said Overbury.

'I will see you in London, sir.'

Arriving in London, Thomas made his way to the Dragoons' depot. He reported to the guardroom. Those on duty were immaculately dressed, as befits a fine regiment. The duty sergeant eyed Thomas with great suspicion as he looked at his mixture of ill-fitting uniform. He summoned the duty officer. A lieutenant duly arrived, dressed in an equally smart uniform. Thomas gave details as to who he was and handed over the documents he had been given. The young officer, equally unsure of the scruffy individual standing before him, inspected the documents. He told Thomas to remain in the guardroom whilst he consulted with a higher authority. About twenty minutes passed before another officer appeared to accompany Thomas to the officers' mess.

Thomas felt out-of-place and embarrassed by the state of his would-be uniform. Two officers who he knew greeted him, and he felt a little more relaxed. In an effort to save his embarrassment, a uniform of a reasonable fit was found and an officer's servant was dispatched to purchase some underwear and toiletries. He was shown to a room; after having bathed and changed, he felt much better. Back in the mess, word of his exploits had got about and everyone wanted to hear all about it. He explained that he could not say anything without expression permission of the Prime Minister. The squadron commander arrived and saved him from further awkward questions. It was then that Thomas was told that he had been awarded the Military Cross for his action in trying to save the runner, even though he was wounded himself. The medal would be presented the very next day, in front of the men. Whilst fellow officers celebrated in the mess, Thomas slipped away and for the first time in a long while went into a deep sleep. He was awoken by a servant and helped to prepare for the coming day. He made it just in time for breakfast.

Following the medal's presentation, Thomas found that he was to be demobilised and should begin the process of removing himself from the army. He received a three-piece suit, shoes, shirts and two regimental ties. Then he received a large sum of money; or rather, what seemed large to Thomas, in the form of back pay. Then came the documentation of his service and commission and confirmation of his demobilisation. He was now a free man.

24

The meeting between Thomas and Lord Overbury was slightly strained to begin with, but mellowed as they began to talk. Overbury wanted to know how it had gone at the Dragoons' depot and wanted to look at the medal. Thomas asked about everybody at the Hall. He was told that Mrs Brown, because she had been married to a German prior to working at the Hall, had been arrested and interned. Before Overbury could get her released, she had been so overcome with anger and despair that she took her own life. The information had rocked the family and staff to the core.

Thomas, in desperation, asked Overbury if he knew anything about Oliver and Clarissa.

Overbury was quiet for a moment.

'We knew that you had destroyed the ammunition and stores dump, from people in Holland. That was a resounding success. The Prime Minister was thrilled at the good news, although he could not divulge how it had happened. Then we did not hear anything, until information about the destruction of the weapons and ammunition factories filtered through. Our people had a spy in the area who was alerted to discover what had happened. Well, we then knew that there had been two attacks. The first was at the ammunition factory. Our spy discovered that there had been a small fire before the explosion so everybody had left the factory and got to safety, to await the fire fighters. Then it simply blew up. Windows of houses close by were broken; some houses were damaged because of the shock wave. He found out that when the ammunition blew up, the people in the armaments factory were evacuated and that then explosives were set off. The building collapsed and weapons were damaged, resulting in the whole factory being closed. The Germans said that there had been a problem at the ammunition factory and that was the cause of the damage to the weapons factory. However, the local people knew there had been an attack. They were thankful that there was minimum loss of life amongst the workers.'

'We did plan it that way,' said Thomas.

'Yes, we know. Then you had to escape, but what neither you nor we ourselves knew was that a German infantry division was in the area on its way to France and Belgium. There was going to be a big thrust at the Front to win the war, but with two ammunition stores destroyed, morale amongst the workers was lower which would have an impact on the master plan. Sabotage was suspected, so troops were deployed - and then your troubles began. Your boat had moved further up-river and we understood that the plan was to rejoin it and make for Switzerland. We now know that the Germans found the boat and attacked it. We were told that nobody had survived. Then our spy found out that the Germans had discovered Sergeant Major Hall's party. There was a lot of shooting and they, along with Sergeant McLeod, Clarissa and others, were trapped. Those that were still alive surrendered. As prisoners-of-war, they were taken to a local police station for interrogation.'

Thomas could see that telling this story was very difficult for Overbury, but he continued:

'The German officer-in-charge, a von Krupt from a noble family, had a fearful reputation and was a million miles away from being a gentleman. The local police chief's name was Hartmann and he was the brother of the captain of your boat. Whilst he did not approve of his brother's deeds, he considered that all of your group were prisoners-of-war and should be treated as such. The problem was that he had no control over von Krupt. Clarissa stood by her story of being a nurse and knowing nothing about the operation. She told him that she was a member of the British army assigned to tend the wounded, however Krupt would have none of it. He told her that the British army did not have women on the front line, and she was behind the front line. So, he said that she must be a spy.'

Overbury, despite the stiff upper lip of the higher classes, was struggling with the story.

'Hall and the men were taken from their cells to a yard at the back of the building; under direct command of Krupt they were shot. He murdered them. He murdered prisoners-of-war. He then took great pleasure in telling Clarissa what he had done. Then, we are told, he laughed as he told her that she was next. After he left the police station, Hartmann, the policeman, took a pen, paper and envelope to Clarissa and said he would post a letter for her. He could not get her out of the building because Krupt had left soldiers on guard. He was true to his word and we eventually received the letter. The following morning, Clarissa was taken from her cell to the same yard and shot. He murdered a nurse, whose only crime was to care for others.'

Overbury could not speak. Tears rolled down his face. He was overcome. Oliver had died as a soldier, but Clarissa had been murdered.

'Do you know what happened to Krupt?' asked Thomas.

'As far as I know, he survived and has returned home a hero. He will be protected because of his family background.'

'Then our government can take up the case. He could be prosecuted for the murder of Clarissa, which was a crime even in wartime,' responded Thomas.

Overbury slumped back in his chair.

'As far as our government is concerned, she did not die in Germany: she was never in Germany. Your operation never happened. All the paperwork has been removed. You operated under the City of London Rifles and I wrote the record of the unit, apart from the actual operation, that is. The records were taken from me, and as far as I know they have been destroyed.'

Thomas sat numbed. Some thirty men, a boat's crew and a boat, on an operation that never happened. That was not right.

'How does the government explain the destruction of the military targets?'

'Accidents, I suppose.'

Thomas could not reply. He was physically unable to speak. His anger overwhelmed him.

Both men sat for about ten minutes without speaking. Each was lost in thought. It was Thomas who eventually spoke.

'What about Mr Boswell the MP? He knows what happened.'

'Members of Parliament get drawn into many things that governments get embroiled in; they can do nothing. In fact, he told me things that he should not have done. Once things have quietened down, I will go to Germany and find out what I can about what happened,' explained Overbury.

'Why will the government not do anything? Are we not the victors?'

'Our ruling class will not accept that a member of the German ruling class could ever do such a thing. After all, we are all gentlemen and gentlewomen and men of honour. The close links between Britain and Germany are even intertwined in our Royal family.'

'So it was all a waste. A total waste of millions of lives, just so the ruling classes could have a schoolboy playground fight and commit crimes without being called to account. They even shun you and your family who, from my perspective, could be considered to be part of that ruling class system.'

Overbury did not respond to his statement. He understood what Thomas was saying but was dealing with his own anger at being failed by that system.

'Thomas, we need you to come back to Winslade. Devline is set to retire and the girls have no interest in the estate. I, we, need a key man to hold it together. We can discuss the terms of an arrangement. I know Rosie will also need support at this time. She has suffered along with you.'

Thomas did not reply straight away, but considered the option.

'I will have to give it some thought. I have a lot of good, strong memories of my time at the Hall; but everything has changed. It may be too painful for me to return.'

'Of course you need time. Let me know your answer in due course. In spite of all that has been said today, it is truly wonderful that you have come back safe.'

Thomas stood and laid his MC in front of Overbury.

'Could you please hand this back to the appropriate people, sir? I am sure there must be some staff officer who did not even get his shoes dirty, who would be prouder to wear it than me.'

Thomas then walked away.

■ ■ ■

Oberst Franze von Krupt had survived the war and felt deeply humiliated. He could not understand how Germany had lost. Yes, the Americans had joined in; but the might and efficiency of the German military machine should have overrun their enemies years before. Now, as he drove through the streets of Berlin on his way to meet with members of the General Staff, he looked out of the window at a people who were not celebrating victory but suffering defeat. He considered his enemies to be pathetic as they had allowed the German army to march home complete with their weapons. If it had been the other way round, he would have wanted to crush the very life out of those he had conquered.

In the main building, he was ushered into a room. It had the trappings of history and grandeur but with an air of despair. As a mere colonel, he was in the most junior rank; although he had been offered positions of greater authority, he would never have blended in with his senior officers. He was a man of action to whom only the fatherland mattered. His uncle walked over to him and they hugged each other. Generalmajor Allendorf welcomed him back from the Front. Drinks were poured and a toast proposed.

'To a new and more powerful Germany.'

Glasses were raised and a chorus of voices endorsed the sentiments.

'Oberst von Krupt,' said a General der Infanterie, 'you are what Germany needs at this time. Good strong leaders like you are essential; we want you in the army. The question is: do you need or want the army?'

Krupt smiled as he looked at those in the room.

'I am truly honoured that you say such things but I alone cannot rebuild Germany's military fortunes. The

British and French will not allow us to do so.'

'This is true,' replied the General der Infanterie, 'Not in the short term; however in time, Germany will rise to be a power to be reckoned with. We require people like you to maintain the officer corps.'

Krupt smiled again.

'When I was returning to Germany, I came across an interesting situation. There was a bar which was full of our soldiers, of all ranks. They were listening in silence to a corporal who, standing on a box, was giving a speech. He was a funny-looking man. Rather thin, with a pale complexion and stark black hair combed to one side. A little black moustache under his nose made him look quite comical. Now, I am not known for liking speeches, but this corporal captured the very hearts of all those men. He was blaming Germany's failings on the General Staff and the officer corps. The soldiers, including junior officers, were listening and agreeing. I did not stay to hear all of what he had to say, but that corporal may be the future of Germany.'

'Did this corporal have a name?'

'He called himself Adolf Hitler.'

'Franze,' said his uncle. 'We have helped you and now we are asking you to help us.'

Von Krupt frowned. 'How havc you helped me?'

'I was sent to search for British soldiers who had attacked targets along the Rhine. Some got away and others were executed by your orders. One of them was a woman: a nurse, in fact a member of the British aristocracy. They had surrendered and were prisoners-of-war. The British raised the matter and we have gone to great lengths to keep the whole episode quiet. It has not been resolved away but we have control.'

Von Krupt looked at the faces of the men in the room.

'I captured spies and saboteurs, and following interrogation had them shot. I was on my way to the front line and could not delay. That is all there is to the matter.'

'Franze,' responded his uncle, 'you are my nephew; but Germany's need is far greater than family bonds. You will serve in the new German army and prepare it for the future.'

'Or what?' demanded an angry von Krupt.

'We will not defend you against the British in their quest for revenge over this matter,' replied the General der Infanterie.

Von Krupt sat right back in his seat. He was weighing the options: after all, what could or would the British do?

'If I were to agree, what would be my situation?'

'You will join the General Staff here in Berlin.'

'My home is at the Castle Stoltz,' he replied.

'Yes, we know it is your ancestral home and you will be able to spend time there. At present, we have to rebuild a strong Germany.'

Von Krupt considered. This was his chance to have an influence on the new Germany, which in the next war would not lose.

'Gentlemen, I accept your offer. But I need some time at home beforehand to sort out my affairs.'

The gathered group toasted their new appointee. Germany would be in good hands.

Von Krupt departed for Castle Stoltz, to savour the place where he grew up until he had to return to Berlin. Whatever happened, the von Krupt name would always be linked to the castle.

After he left Overbury, Thomas found a branch of his bank and deposited the majority of his money. The small amount left he kept. He found a hotel that was pretty run-down and entertained numerous prostitutes. It was cheap, a place where no questions would be asked. For Thomas, it was just a place to stay. The owner on the front desk told him to keep his money safe and be careful. Dressed in a suit as he was, he could become prey to the unscrupulous, of which there were many in the area. The room was better than the trenches, but only marginally so. He found a bar and got drunk. He kept himself to himself, and eventually he returned to the hotel to sleep it off. The following day he repeated the process. This lasted three days. On the fourth day, he decided that enough was enough. He telegrammed Overbury to say that he was coming to the Hall. He purchased two new shirts and some underwear before locating the local baths. He made his way to the railway station, where he purchased a ticket. He telephoned the Hall and spoke to Devline, to tell him which train he was catching. The train journey was uneventful and he used the time to improve his "day after" state.

Devline met him at the station; his reception was really warm. They chatted on the journey to the Hall. Devline updated Thomas on the latest gossip. Rosie had taken over as cook and had imparted some tales of her adventure. But the war had left a great sadness hanging over the place. Thomas listened rather than spoke. When asked if he was going to take over as estate manager, Thomas said he was thinking about it. He wanted to see how he would react to being at the Hall, with so many sad events having changed everything.

Overbury met them as they arrived with what there was left of the staff, who had congregated at the front door to welcome him back. Soames and Martha Smith were still there and had not changed. He hugged Rosie and she clung onto him. Bert Moore, the gamekeeper, was too ill to come to the house but sent a message to say Thomas was welcome to visit him. Then there was the biggest challenge. Meeting her Ladyship and Clarissa's two sisters. He was taken aback by how well he was received; they wanted to know all about their brave sister and brother. He did his best to tell the story, however it was clear that Overbury had not told them that Clarissa had been shot whilst being held as a prisoner.

The only person who Thomas could really talk to was Rosie. She had shared his experiences. He was the only one she could speak to for the very same reason. At every opportunity, they would sit and discus things. It was to be a way of unburdening themselves of the past and growing closer. Thomas had lost Clarissa and Rosie had lost her mother, on account of her marriage to a German.

Thomas took over the role of estate manager when Devline retired. With reduced staff to run the house and new agreements for tenant farmers, there were some important changes that the war had brought to society. Staff were to be treated more as employees and never as slaves. Women had a changed role in the new world and, whilst the returning fighting men opposed them, they made some important gains. After all, they had kept the country going whilst the men were away fighting.

It was some six months after his return to Winslade Hall that Overbury spoke to Thomas in private. He explained that he had received a letter from Inspector Hartmann, the German policeman. He had prepared a lengthy letter describing the events that had occurred in Germany, and had explained what had happened to those who had been executed. If Lord Overbury was inclined to visit Germany, he would be pleased to meet him and show him the burial site of the men and of his children. The letter was written in German, requiring Overbury to have it translated, which he did through contacts in London as he knew that neither Thomas nor Rosie could read or write German. He wanted to go to the town in Germany and take up the offer, but he wanted Thomas to accompany him. Thomas's first thought was that he had reservations; but he decided that he would go and do whatever he could to have the graves marked. He had no doubt that that was the intention of his Lordship.

It was a long journey by different trains to reach the town on the Rhine. Germany was still suffering from its defeat by the allies and Thomas found communication with the locals difficult. They were suspicious as to who the two Englishmen were. In the town, they found a hotel that would meet their needs; having checked in, they went to locate the police station. Reporting to the policeman on the front desk, they found that he knew who they were even before they spoke. He went to locate the inspector. A few minutes later, Inspector Hartmann came out from a back room; as he reached the men, he held out his hand. Leading them to his office, he explained that he had provided an interpreter as he did not consider his English good enough to converse about such an important matter.

Hartmann ordered coffee for everybody and then he went through the details of his very comprehensive letter. There was no doubt that he was appalled about what had happened but that there had been nothing that either he or his men could do. The German officer was ruthless. He had ensured that Clarissa was looked after whilst under arrest and, the best he had been able to do was to provide pen and paper. He was extremely pleased that the letter had arrived.

Overbury introduced Thomas as his estate manager; nothing was said about his being on the raid. When words and coffee were done, the Inspector led them to the cells and they saw where the men and Clarissa had been held.

They were then shown the courtyard where the executions had taken place. The Inspector described the inhumanity of the German officer and the men were deeply moved. The Inspector had arranged for them to be taken to a church on the outskirts of the town. It was a quiet and peaceful place. They followed him past graves of a bygone era to a quiet corner of the graveyard. A large neat mound identified the grave that was the last communal resting-place of the men. A headstone had been erected which carried the names of all those buried there. Thomas made a careful note. His one hope was that it accounted for everybody. Alongside was a grave that contained two bodies. The headstone showed that it was Oliver and Clarissa Overbury. He explained that the three Germans who had been on the operation were buried in the main cemetery according to the wishes of their families.

They spent some time at the site and the Inspector had arranged for a photographer to take photographs. He had also arranged for two bunches of flowers. Thomas laid the one for the men on the communal grave. The other was laid by Overbury for Oliver and Clarissa. Hartmann arranged for them to visit the site of the destroyed factories and then the place where the boat was attacked, where Oliver led the defence and died with the others who had remained onboard. Hartmann did not know that Thomas had been the leader of the attack, or that another woman called Rosie had survived. Thomas saw the effects of the attack on the factories. Hartmann explained that it had been done in such a way that the workforce could escape. Thomas could see the results of the operation in the total destruction of what had been a small but important part of the enemy's war production.

Back in England, Overbury notified the organisation that had been established to find the dead and have them placed in military graves in France and Belgium. He sought to enquire about having all of the bodies returned to Great Britain. That would mean that the bodies of Oliver and Clarissa would be returned to the grounds of the Hall. In the meantime, a memorial stone was to be erected. It was at this time that Thomas inspected a large cottage on the edge of the estate's land. It was in good condition, with a splendid garden and views. Probably the most important thing, though, was that the tenant, who had a large family, had moved out; it now stood empty. When Thomas raised the matter with Overbury, there was no discussion. Thomas was to be the new occupier. They kept the matter to themselves until the signing. Unbeknown to Thomas, the cottage and its grounds had been segregated from the estate; when he signed, it became his, as owner and not as tenant.

On Rosie's day off, Thomas had arranged for a picnic basket and they went out for a drive together. They drove and chatted in a very open and relaxed way. Rosie was still besotted with Thomas but made no mention of it. They sat by the river to have their picnic and then on a circular route back to the hall, they passed the cottage. Thomas stopped and said that he just had to check on something inside. She looked at the place. It was the first time she had seen it. He led the way up the path to the front door. Inside, she explored the rooms and was overwhelmed by them, concluding that it would be a wonderful house to live in. It did not escape her that nobody was living there so she enquired as to who had been in residence. He explained about the tenant. He expected the next question.

'Who is going to live here now?' she asked.

'I am,' he replied and added, 'with you.'

The answer missed Rosie altogether. 'That will be nice.'

She went out of the back door, then moments later rushed back in.

'Did you say you and me?'

'I did,' he replied.

'Well, I don't know about that, Mr Pierce.'

She bounded over and flung her arms round his neck. He proposed and she accepted.

They married in the local church. What they did not know was that, twenty years later, their three children would be of an age to be drawn into another disaster: the Second World War.

25

Now, one hundred years had passed since the start of the First World War. Mrs Pierce or, as she was referred to by all but her closest friends, Mrs P, was busy fussing over her son. It was the second time in a short period that she had seen him and was pleased that he had found the time to visit. He had been a soldier in the British army but, following the death of his brother by so-called "friendly fire", he had left; his anger had driven him to spend more than twelve years in the French Foreign Legion. He had been a senior sergeant when he left the sanctity of the Legion and became what carried the euphemism "facilitator"; more commonly known, as a mercenary. Mrs P did not know what he did for a living as, in this case, it was not really something a son told his mother.

The full English breakfast was first-class and, whilst he ate, she enjoyed talking about the good times when the boys were growing up. Then a glint came into her eyes.

'After you were here last time, I found something that you may be interested in. I'll go and get it.'

When she returned, she was holding a large, heavy-duty brown envelope. She sat down and carefully emptied the contents onto the table. It was a collection of medals.

'These are your grandfather's and your great-grandfather's medals.'

She laid them out. 'Your great-grandfather, Thomas Pierce, was in the King's Dragoons during World War One.'

Then, as if making a remarkable discovery, she announced:

'That was a hundred years ago this very year.'

She had a piece of paper with the information written down.

'He got the Nineteen Fourteen Star, the Victory Medal and the British War Medal. But he also got the Military Cross, which your father said is an important medal.'

Having finished eating, Dan took a great deal of interest in the medals.

'Your grandfather served in the Second World War, but your father never served in the military. You, of course, will have your own medals,' said Mrs P. Then she added, 'There was a letter with your great-grandfather's medals.'

She handed it to him. Whilst his mother cleared the table, he read the letter.

Dearest Papa and Mama,

I fear I am in desperate trouble and am being held prisoner. A German officer, Oberst Franze Von Krupt had some of us held in a police station. He is a very nasty and vicious man. He had our men, who are prisoners-of-war, shot yesterday. He took great pleasure in telling me that the same fate awaits me tomorrow. The police officer in charge, an Inspector Hartmann, provided this pen, paper and envelope and has promised to post this letter. I do hope with all my heart that you receive it.

Please tell my beloved Thomas, if he survives, that our future together was not to be. Of course, he may face the same end as I do; if he has not already been killed. We were separated in the action. I had to tend the wounded whilst he had to command the men; so his fate is not known to me. If he should survive and I do not, he must take care of Rosie. I know he cares for her and she for him.

I hope that this war has been worth all the sacrifice, but I doubt it. As long as people like von Krupt exist, the world will not be a safe place.

I am sorry this letter is short and I cannot say all that I would wish to; I send my love to you all. Do not despair over me as you have your own lives to live. I have known much happiness, but it seems that it must end here.

My deepest love,

Your daughter,

Clarissa.

Dan carefully laid the letter down.

'So my great-grandfather and this Clarissa were on some sort of military operation, possibly behind enemy lines. I have never heard about it. When I have time, I will delve into the records.'

'Your father never spoke about it and I don't think he knew anything. Today, there is a lot of information available which was not public a few years ago. Anyway, these are for you. It would be interesting to know what your great-grandfather Thomas and Clarissa were doing, especially if the Germans really did shoot those they caught.'

'But great-grandfather Thomas survived,' said Dan. 'I wonder what happened to him? Did he marry Rosie, whoever she was? He must have married somebody else for me to be here. I wonder who it was?'

Dan now had an interesting family history which he intended to explore further.

'More tea?' asked Mrs P.

'Yes, please, that would be good,' replied Dan, smiling as he still held his great-grandfathers Military Cross.

Mrs P came back into the room.

'My head will never save my feet. This was also left for you,' she said, handing him a long package.

He took it and undid the wrapping, to find that he was looking at a very old shotgun.

Mrs P smiled. 'I understand that it belonged to your great-grandfather; now it has been handed down to you.'

Dan left his new family mementos on the table whilst he opened his lap-top to check his e-mails. Then curiosity got the better of him: he typed the name Franze Von Krupt into the search engine. He discovered that he was a member of the German family Krupt. He had earned the Knight's Cross with Oak Leaves and Swords during World War One. There was a brief mention of his having served in the SS during World War Two. Although the family home is stated as being Castle Stoltz in Germany, he disappeared at the end of the war; it was thought that he, along with his wife and son, had fled to South America. Unconfirmed and rather complicated reports alleged that his son married an English woman who is thought to have moved back to Britain with the boy. Rather strangely, Castle Stoltz remained the family seat and was being looked after by an influential family friend who had links to the European Union. Dan decided that researching this would be a project to keep him busy.

Also published

DEATH OF A SCIENTIST
Mike Welham's thriller leads us into a world of assassination, war and politics

A Time for War

When a President and a Prime Minister want to go to war to remove a dictator and gain control of his country's vast reserves of oil, they must gain public support. A threat from the dictator President to use chemical and biological weapons gives them their reason. But the weapons inspectors just can't find the evidence that the country has such weapons. To counter this, a political dossier is created claiming the existence of weapons of mass destruction.

A Time to Die

Dr John Finch, the world-renowned British specialist in chemical and biological weapons, is a member of a UN inspection team. He discovers that no such weapons exist, that the dossier is misleading and refuses to toe the political line. His actions do not stop the war, but results in him becoming a target for a political assassination. Chuck Cornell, a member of the ultra-secret 'Black Eagles' is assigned the task, and Dr Finch is his victim. When Dr Finch is found dead in a wood it looks like suicide, but somebody has tampered with the crime scene, unidentified men are seen in the area and unusual activity at the scene is observed.

A Time for Justice?

To halt the media frenzy a formal inquiry is set up, but vital witnesses are not called and a political cover-up looks likely. The Excalibur Foundation, an organisation that seeks justice for political victims, decides to take up the case. They propose to hunt down Chuck Cornell themselves and former French Foreign Legion sniper Dan Pierce is hired for the mission. During the operation to eliminate the Black Eagle however, a political target comes into Dan's sights. Dan now holds the power to bring justice to the world, it's just a matter of squeezing the trigger.

WTC BUILDING 7

Mike Welham's thriller leads us into a world of corruption, destruction and justice?

A TIME OF CORRUPTION

Zenacon-Global Inc, a US Corporation, is one of the largest multi-national global conglomerates in the world. Both the corporation and the main board members are under investigation for serious fraud, and other irregular activities by the IRS, the Security Exchange Commission and the CIA. Building seven is where the investigation into Zenacon-Global Inc is being carried out. It is where all of the incriminating evidence is being held. The building and its contents have to be destroyed and Worldwide Executive Management mercenaries are hired to do the job.

A TIME FOR DESTRUCTION

Dr Casey Hart, an explosives expert who specialises in demolishing high-rise buildings in built-up areas, is forced to plan the destruction of building seven. The world watched as the twin towers crashed to the ground virtually in free-fall. Then seven hours later, building seven implodes into its own footprint, collapsing in just seven seconds. No fire could have caused such a failure. Only one thing could… Nano Thermate, used as part of a controlled demolition.

A TIME FOR JUSTICE

The heads of Zenacon-Global Inc instruct Worldwide Executive Management to use their *Black Eagles* mercenaries to eliminate Hart and destroy all evidence. An assassination attempt fails to kill Hart and he flees for his life. The Excalibur Foundation, an organisation that seeks justice for political victims, steps in to save Hart. Dan Pierce, a former French Foreign Legion sniper, is contracted for his second assignment: to save Hart and secure the incriminating evidence. In a dramatic twist, Federal accident investigator Grace Garcia and Katie Jackson, a reporter for the *Daily Globe,* also have damaging evidence against Zenacon. Dan has their lives in his hands, he just has to find and rescue them.

To be published Spring 2015

FALL OF THE EUROPEAN EMPIRE
A story of the Forth Reich's
quest for European domination

Following the end of the Second World War, a secret organisation in Germany continued the work begun by Adolf Hitler to dominate all of Europe and beyond. Gone are the bombs, blitzkriegs and mass slaughter. Control of the European Union will fulfill the destiny through a powerful force: money. The vast unregulated wealth generated by the EU supports the cause. Money buys power through personal greed, power and corruption, allowing the manipulation to proceed unchallenged.

Peter Mantel MEP was born in Brazil and at a very young age moved to England with his mother. In Europe he learns about his grandfather Franze Von Krupt. A ruthless officer in the First World War, he rose to become an SS

General during the Second World War. The family home is the Castle Stoltz in Germany, which is being looked after by an influential family friend who has powerful connections in the European Union. It is now time to bring Mantel "home", ready for the final act of domination.

Dan Pierce, a former French Foreign Legion sniper and now a "facilitator", discovers that his great grandparents suffered during the First World War as a consequence of actions by Franze Von Krupt . However, Dan's research draws him into the powerful and dirty world of politics where he makes the family link between Peter Mantel and the Krupt family. He discovers that Mantel is to become the head of the Forth Reich which through the European Union, has one objective leading to total domination of all member countries. What can Dan do with the knowledge? He is one man against so many. Who can he trust in a world where people sell their souls for money and power?

More details of published and forthcoming novels by Mike Welham are available at www.welhambooks.com

8666312R00175

Printed in Great Britain
by Amazon.co.uk, Ltd.,
Marston Gate.